"There's no law that says a man and woman can't share the same roof without being sexually intimate.

"After all," Ryan continued, "we're both mature adults. We should be able to handle it. At least I can." He gave Cristen a guileless look. "Of course, if you feel you just couldn't keep your hands off me..."

"Don't flatter yourself, O'Malley! You're about as much threat to my self-control as—as a three-hundred-pound eunuch."

"Then there's no reason we can't be roommates."

"None whatever," Cristen declared recklessly. "But *no* funny stuff."

A slow grin spread over his face. "I swear to you, Cristen, that whatever happens between us will be only what you want to happen."

Dear Reader,

Spellbinders! That's what we're striving for. The editors at Silhouette are determined to capture your imagination and win your heart with every single book we publish. Each month, six Special Editions are chosen with *you* in mind.

Our authors are our inspiration. Writers such as Nora Roberts, Tracy Sinclair, Kathleen Eagle, Carole Halston and Linda Howard—to name but a few—are masters at creating endearing characters and heartrending love stories. Their characters are everyday people—just like you and me—whose lives have been touched by love, whose dreams and desires suddenly come true!

So find a cozy, quiet place to read, and create your own special moment with a Silhouette Special Edition.

Sincerely,

The Editors
SILHOUETTE BOOKS

GINNA GRAY
Cristen's Choice

Silhouette Special Edition

Published by Silhouette Books New York

America's Publisher of Contemporary Romance

Dedicated to Harriett Chaney
In appreciation for her expertise,
as well as her friendship.

SILHOUETTE BOOKS
300 East 42nd St., New York, N.Y. 10017

Copyright © 1987 by Virginia Gray

ISBN: 0-373-09373-X

First Silhouette Books printing April 1987

America's Publisher of Contemporary Romance

Printed in the U.S.A.

Books by Ginna Gray

Silhouette Romance

The Gentling #285
The Perfect Match #311
Heart of the Hurricane #338
Images #352
First Love, Last Love #374
The Courtship of Dani #417

Silhouette Special Edition

Golden Illusion #171
The Heart's Yearning #265
Sweet Promise #320
Golden Promise #327
Cristen's Choice #373

GINNA GRAY,

a native Houstonian, admits that, since childhood, she
has been a compulsive reader—of everything from
soup cans to Tolstoy—as well as a head-in-the-clouds
dreamer. Long accustomed to expressing her creativ-
ity in tangible ways—Ginna also enjoys painting and
needlework—she finally decided to try putting her
fantasies and wild imaginings down on paper. The
result? The mother of two grown children now spends
eight hours a day alternately agonized and satisfied—
a full-time writer.

Chapter One

The clock on the dresser erupted, shattering the dawn silence with its strident buzz.

Sprawled beneath the tangled sheets, her head partially buried under the pillow, Cristen Moore attempted to cling to blissful sleep and ignore the rude noise. When the sound persisted, she gave a low moan and opened one eye a slit.

The small sign of life drew the attention of the gray Persian cat curled in the chair, who raised her head and stared at her mistress with an air of expectancy.

When Cristen saw the soft morning light filtering through the curtains, her eyelid dropped, and with another moan of protest, she burrowed deeper under the pillow.

For almost a full minute she didn't move, but finally it became impossible to ignore the clock's irritating, relentless blare.

Slipping a leg over the side of the bed, Cristen groped for the floor. When her foot encountered the plush carpet, she slowly struggled upright. For a moment she sat teetering on the edge of the bed, groggily tugging her wispy blue nightgown more closely about herself.

Finally, grumbling inarticulately, she hauled herself to her feet and, with her eyes still closed, staggered across the room. "All right! All right! I'm coming, for Pete's sake!" she muttered as the raucous jangle grew louder. Blindly, she slapped her hand across the dresser top until she located the clock. After several fumbling tries, she finally managed to shut off the alarm.

The cat yawned, lowered her head and curled into a tighter ball.

Zombielike, Cristen stumbled toward the bathroom.

Just inside the door she came to a halt, swaying on her feet, vaguely aware that something was not quite as it should be. Opening her slitted eyes a fraction wider, she spied a pair of big bare feet sunk into the thick nap of the blue and green bath mat.

Befuddled, she peered at them for several seconds, frowning. Big feet? Jennifer didn't have big feet.

Cristen lifted her heavy lids another fraction, and her bleary eyes tracked a slow path upward over hair-covered, muscular calves and thighs to a towel slung low around narrow hips. Above the moss-green terry cloth, her gaze followed the path of a narrow band of dark silky hair up over a board-flat abdomen to where it swirled around an "innie" navel, then up still farther to where it thickened and spread out over a brawny chest. A faint warning bell began to sound in the far regions of her sleep-fogged mind as her gaze skimmed upward to encounter vivid blue eyes twinkling down at her from a tanned, rugged face that still bore a few remaining dabs of shaving cream.

Cristen stared back. She blinked once, twice. It took a full five seconds for her brain to assimilate the information her eyes were relating. When it finally clicked she blurted out inanely, "You're a man!"

The sensuous mouth below the sable mustache curved into an audacious grin, creating deep grooves in the man's freshly shaved lean cheeks. His mischievous gaze dropped to her breasts and lingered appreciatively on the rosy crests thrusting impudently against the filmy blue silk of her next-to-nothing nightgown. Then his gaze slid downward to leisurely enjoy the scantily veiled allure of her tiny waist and the delectable womanly roundness of her hips before tracing the curving line of impossibly long legs all the way down to her feet.

"And you, sweetheart, are very definitely a woman" came the smooth reply as those startling blue eyes slowly retraced their path.

The deep, velvety voice threaded with laughter and the man's blatantly sensual inspection set the alarm in Cristen's head to shrieking, snapping her out of her stupor.

In a panic, she let out a squawk, grabbed the shower curtain and hastily wrapped it around her.

Anger and indignation seared through her. She pulled herself up to her full five feet ten inches and fixed the man with a fierce glower, her eyes shooting sparks.

"Who are you? And what the devil are you doing in my bathroom?"

Grinning, the man leaned back against the sink and crossed his arms over his massive chest. Devilish blue eyes roamed with undisguised interest over her wild tumble of auburn hair before moving on to inspect her oval face. She knew her normally full lips were set in an angry line and her green eyes were snapping, but her ferocious expression seemed only to amuse the man as his gaze dropped once again to her breasts.

"Uh, if you're trying to protect your modesty, you'd better make some adjustments to that thing," he advised, flicking a finger toward the enveloping curtain. His lip twitched suspiciously.

Distracted, Cristen looked down...and gave a stran gled cry.

A moan of distress issued from her throat as she grap pled with the shower curtain. Made of clear plastic, with only a few water lilies splattered at random over its sur face, it was almost useless as a shield.

Her face flaming, Cristen snatched frantically for three of the white flowers and, after a brief struggle, managed to maneuver them into strategic positions over her body.

Catching sight of herself in the mirror did nothing fo her composure. She looked—and felt—like a complete id iot, standing there nearly nude, clutching three painted flowers to her body with both arms. And that big jerk' enjoyment of her predicament wasn't helping matters a bit!

Giving him a killing look, she hissed, "Before I scream the house down I'll ask you just once more. Who are you and what are you doing here?"

With a casualness she found infuriating, he picked up a hand towel and calmly wiped the specks of shaving lather from his face, then cocked one brow and gave her a guile less look. "Jennifer invited me."

"Jennifer?"

Cristen stared at the man, slack jawed. Then anger surged through her, and her mouth snapped shut. If she could have gotten her hands on her roommate at that mo ment she would have gladly strangled her, even if it *did* mean she'd have to drop the stupid shower curtain. How *dare* that girl bring a man home with her to spend the night!

Rigid with anger, Cristen closed her eyes, threw her head back and screamed at the top of her lungs, "Jennifer O'Malley! Get in here this instant!"

The door at the opposite end of the bathroom connecting the condo's two bedrooms opened, and Jennifer's tousled black curls poked around its edge. "What's all the racket about? It's enough to wake—"

Jennifer's grumbled complaint halted abruptly when her gaze encountered the room's two occupants. To Cristen's utter astonishment, instead of being embarrassed or remorseful, her roommate slumped against the doorjamb and burst into peals of laughter.

"Oh, no! Oh, th-this is too... f-funny for words," Jennifer sputtered between spurts of hysterical giggling. "I t-told you... sleeping in those X-rated nighties would... g-get you into tr-trouble one of these days."

"Jennifer! This is not funny!"

"Oh, but it i-is! I-it is!" Jennifer choked.

Her boyfriend merely smiled and looked back and forth between them, his eyes dancing.

"No it is not!" Cristen insisted through clenched teeth. "I am shocked and disappointed and—and *furious* with you. How dare you bring one of your men friends home to spend the night!"

The reprimand merely set off another fit of laughter. Cristen watched in shock as her friend and roommate staggered across the room and threw her arms around the grinning, half-naked man. She collapsed against him, resting her forehead on his shoulder, and howled uproariously. Finally, still shaking with laughter, Jennifer turned, wiped the tears from her cheeks and shook her head at her friend's stiff expression.

"Cristen, you dolt! This isn't a boyfriend. This is my father!"

"That's no excuse. You—"

Cristen stopped abruptly. Horror-struck, she stared at her young roommate. Finally, realizing she was gaping, she snapped her mouth shut again and swallowed hard. "D-did you say your father?" she managed to croak in a voice not much more than a whisper.

At Jennifer's confirming nod, Cristen's heart sank. Her gaze slid helplessly to the man at Jennifer's side.

He smiled and winked.

Mortified, Cristen closed her eyes and groaned. If there is any mercy in this world, she thought hysterically, the earth will open up and swallow me.

Jennifer's father! Good grief! I'd have been better off if he *had* been one of Jennifer's boyfriends. He's probably going to insist that she pack her bags and move out today! Jennifer was of age—barely—but Cristen knew that it was Ryan O'Malley who paid his daughter's share of the rent.

Gradually, in addition to shock and humiliation, Cristen began to feel distinctly irritated. Why the devil hadn't the man identified himself, instead of ogling her like some oversexed playboy? Probably because he *is* an oversexed playboy, she decided.

Of course, she had known he would show up eventually. He had written several times, expressing doubts about his eighteen-year-old daughter rooming with a thirty-year-old divorcée. In her answering letters Jennifer had extolled Cristen's virtues and character in the most glowing terms, but even so, she had warned Cristen that he would probably descend on them to check her out for himself.

Cristen hadn't minded. On the contrary, she had approved of his protective attitude. She had been confident that she could win his approval. Of course, at the time she had naively visualized a nice, middle-aged, fatherly man— a bit overweight, perhaps, with thinning hair and a noticeable paunch. She certainly hadn't expected Ryan O'Malley to be this...this...sexy, good-looking devil!

Slowly, Cristen opened her eyes. She risked a quick look at Jennifer's father and just as quickly looked away, her mouth tightening. The beast! He wasn't even making an effort to hide his amusement! And there was nothing at all fatherly in the look he was giving her.

"Dad, as you've probably guessed, this is Cristen Moore, my roommate," Jennifer announced with a giggle. "You'll have to excuse her; she's not at her best in the mornings."

"Jennifer," Cristen warned through gritted teeth. "If you don't mind, I'm not exactly dressed for a formal introduction. So would you please take your father and get out of here?"

"See? I told you. She's an absolute crab in the morning. I've learned not to even speak to her until she's had at least two cups of coffee." Jennifer addressed the remarks to her father as she took hold of his arm and urged him toward her bedroom.

They had almost reached the door and Cristen was set to heave a sigh of relief when Ryan stopped and looked back over his shoulder at her.

"It was certainly a pleasure meeting you, Ms. Moore," he drawled in a low, insinuating voice. A slow smile curved his mouth as his gaze lowered once again to her breasts. Blatant male appreciation gleamed in the vivid blue gaze that bored through the clear plastic shower curtain. "By the way, your lilies are drooping."

Cristen gasped in outrage and clutched the crackling plastic to her. Giggling, Jennifer pulled her father out the door and slammed it shut.

"Oh! Ohhhhh, that—that—" Incoherent with rage, Cristen sputtered and fumed, groping for a word vile enough to call him. "Voyeur! Peeping Tom! That—that— overaged lecher!" The *nerve* of the man! If he had an ounce of decency about him, he'd have excused himself and left the room, or at the very least looked the other way. But oh, no! Bold as brass, he had looked his fill. And he had been amused, darn him!

Suddenly realizing that she was still clutching the shower curtain, Cristen flung the plastic sheet aside, stomped to the door and flipped the lock. The deep chuckle from the next room made her grit her teeth.

The steamy air in the bathroom was redolent with the scent of soap and masculine toiletries. The sight of Ryan O'Malley's shaving gear sitting on the counter beside her cosmetics made Cristen do a slow burn. She glared at the manly accoutrements, and with quick, jerky movements she snatched off the revealing nightgown and flung it into the hamper. Muttering under her breath, she stepped into the bathtub, pulled the curtain closed with an angry snap and turned on the water full blast.

When she emerged fifteen minutes later, her temper had cooled to a manageable level. Though still brimming with resentment, she knew full well that in this instance anger would gain her nothing and could possibly cost her a lot.

Upon drying off, Cristen hung her towel on the rack and dusted herself with lilac-scented powder, then unlocked the door that connected with Jennifer's room and made a quick dash back into her own.

After slipping into a wispy pair of white silk bikini panties and a matching bra, Cristen picked up the blow dryer and brush. She really had no choice, she acknowledged resentfully as she began to style her thick, layer-cut auburn hair into a cascade of feathery curls that billowed about her shoulders. If she had to have a roommate—which at the moment she did, Cristen admitted to herself with a resigned sigh—she certainly couldn't find a more congenial one than Jennifer.

The cat jumped down from the chair and twined herself around her mistress's legs. Bending, Cristen gave her a quick scratch behind her ears and mumbled distractedly, "Morning, Theda," then straightened and went back to work on her hair. Theda gave an indignant sniff at the desultory greeting and stalked out, her furry tail swishing.

Cristen took her time applying her makeup, stretching a ten-minute job into twenty. She then spent another fifteen deciding what to wear.

When she was finally dressed, she stood before the mirror and studied her reflection critically. The pearl-gray peasant blouse and the gathered skirt in a gray, brown and aqua paisley print were soft and feminine and accentuated her vivid coloring. Her gaze fell to where her full breasts jutted against the delicate batiste. Her nipples tingled and a prickly sensation rippled over her skin as she recalled Ryan O'Malley's brazen inspection and the warm, purely male look in those startling blue eyes.

A suit would be better, she thought, frowning. Something severe that would make her look cold and unapproachable.

The only trouble was, not a single thing in her closet could even remotely pass as severe. In the past two years she had rebelliously indulged to the fullest her penchant for feminine apparel. Because she was only an inch shorter than Bob, he had preferred her to wear simple, tailored things in neutral shades that played down her height and flamboyant coloring. During the last two years, however, she had systematically culled from her wardrobe all those plain, sensible outfits. And all those flat-heeled shoes, she thought, feeling the familiar stab of hurt and anger as she stepped into a strappy pair of ridiculously high-heeled gray leather sandals.

After giving her hair one last fluff and misting herself with a lilac cologne, she glanced into the mirror, shrugged, then squared her shoulders and headed for the door. She might not epitomize a hard-boiled career woman, but at least she looked dignified and well-groomed. And most important, she was decently covered!

Pausing just outside her door, Cristen cocked her head and listened. The heavenly smell of coffee wafted through the air to tantalize her nose, but she grimaced when she heard the low murmur of voices coming from the kitchen.

Rats. She had thought—at least hoped—that Jennifer and her father would be gone by now. She had certainly dawdled long enough. After that embarrassing first encounter, she would have given almost anything not to have to see Ryan O'Malley's mocking face again.

She sighed, knowing full well she had no choice. The man *was* Jennifer's father.

Conversation ceased when Cristen pushed through the swinging door and walked into the kitchen. Her gaze didn't even flicker toward the two people seated at the table, though she could feel their eyes following her. Her expression wooden, she marched to the counter that held the coffeepot, extracted a mug from the cabinet and filled it.

"Could I get you some breakfast, Ms. Moore?" Ryan asked politely. "I cook a mean scrambled egg. Just ask Jennifer."

Cristen shot him a slightly appalled glance and quickly looked away. "No, thank you."

Just the thought of eating an egg so early made her shudder. She could barely stand to look at their breakfast dishes stacked in the sink.

Leaning a hip against the counter, she sipped the life-giving elixir and fixed her muzzy gaze on the ladybug magnets clinging to the refrigerator door. Theda glided in, gave Cristen an offended glare and rubbed against Ryan O'Malley's boots. Fickle feline, Cristen thought sourly.

The silence was heavy and expectant, but Cristen made no effort to fill it. As far as she was concerned, verbal communication before nine in the morning bordered on the obscene.

Jennifer leaned across the table, placed her hand on her father's arm and said sotto voce, "Uh, Dad, I think I should warn you: you talk to Cristen in the mornings at your own risk."

"Really?" Ryan cocked his head, his interested gaze running over Cristen. "Is she always like this?"

"Always. For the first hour or so she's one of the walking dead."

"That bad, huh?"

"Yep."

Thoroughly annoyed, Cristen shot them a warning look.

Jennifer pretended not to notice.

Ryan smiled.

With his chair turned sideways to the table, he sat slouched low on his spine, his long denim-clad legs stretched out in front of him and crossed at the ankles. Both thumbs were hooked under the belt that circled his lean middle. He pursed his lips as though giving the matter serious thought, but his eyes danced wickedly. He looked outrageously male, and sexy as the devil. Cristen wanted to kick him.

"Hmm. Maybe it's low blood sugar."

"Could be," Jennifer concurred gravely. "As soon as she's had her ration of caffeine and a piece of toast, her disposition improves."

"Probably ought to give her a glass of orange juice when she first gets up. By the time she showers and dresses, her energy level will have risen, along with her mood."

"Good idea."

Cristen's coffee mug hit the counter with a thunk. "Do you mind?" she snarled, giving them a frosty glare. "I do not have low blood sugar, and I do *not* want a glass of orange juice in the mornings. And I'll thank you both not to talk about me as though I weren't here!"

"I see what you mean," Ryan mused. "Crabby. Definitely crabby."

"Told ya." Jennifer smirked.

Cristen made a strangled sound and shot them both a harassed look, which had no effect whatsoever on the smiling pair. Furiously she tried to think of a suitably scathing remark that would cut them down to size, but her mind went completely blank. Utterly frustrated, she mustered as much haughty dignity as possible under the circumstances and stalked out, her head held high.

Straightening in his chair, Ryan watched her over the pass-through bar, his gaze fixed on the provocative sway of her hips. She strode through the living room and disappeared into her room. A few seconds later she stormed out again, a brown clutch bag tucked under her arm, headed for the front door. She snatched it open, then, with her hand on the knob, she turned and shot them a belligerent glare.

"And for your information, I am not crabby!"

The ear-shattering slam of the door punctuated her parting shot.

Ryan stared at the door for several seconds, then whistled softly between his teeth. When he turned back to his daughter, his mustache twitched above a wide smile. "That's one helluva woman," he murmured.

He saw the teasing laughter fade from Jennifer's face, and her forehead puckered with the beginnings of a frown. She started to speak, but before she could utter a sound he said, "So tell me, how are things going with you?" He picked up his coffee mug and took a sip, then looked around the cheery yellow-and-white kitchen. "This living arrangement. Is it working out? Do you and Cristen get along?"

"Yes. It's working out just fine, and we get along quite well." She paused, a wry smile working at her lips. "Actually, Cristen's a very pleasant person to be around, once she's fully awake and functioning."

"She's a lovely woman. I suppose she has an active social life," he casually probed.

"Not so you'd notice. In the six months I've lived here she's gone out on exactly two dates. And I think she only accepted those to pacify her business partner."

Jennifer chuckled at her father's surprised expression. "Louise Fife is very happily married, and she won't rest until Cristen is, too. For the past year she's been playing matchmaker, but Cristen fights her every step of the way."

"How long has she been divorced?"

"Two years."

Ryan was quiet for a moment. Pensive, he drummed his fingers absently on the table. "Has she ever told you what caused the divorce?"

"No. She never talks about it. For that matter, she never talks about her past, period. If you mention it, she clams up. You learn very quickly that it's a forbidden subject." Jennifer shook her head sadly and shrugged. "Whatever the cause, it must have hurt her terribly, because now her whole life revolves around the shop she and Louise own."

Ryan snorted. "Somehow I have a hard time visualizing a woman as beautiful and sexy as Cristen Moore owning a toy shop."

"Actually, it's not a toy shop. It's called A Small World, and they specialize in custom-made period dollhouses and miniature furnishings, which Cristen makes. It's really fantastic."

"So is the owner," Ryan said with a grin.

Jennifer's frown returned. "Dad, look, if you're thinking what I think you're thinking . . . well . . ."

"Well, what? Come on, honey, spit it out."

The mischief in his eyes seemed to harden her resolve, and she gave him a stern look. "Look, Dad, since you and Mom split up, you've lived like a footloose bachelor, and I know the effect you have on women."

"So?"

"So I like Cristen, and I don't want to see her hurt."

Ryan drained the last of his coffee. With deceptive nonchalance he rolled to his feet and sauntered to the counter. After refilling his mug, he turned to face his daughter, took a sip of coffee, then smiled. "Hurting Cristen isn't what I have in mind," he said softly.

He stared down at the brown liquid in his cup and sloshed it around in a circular motion. Despite his teasing, he understood Jennifer's concern. Since he and Ella had split sixteen years ago, he had carefully avoided any serious romantic involvements. True, he'd had affairs—several of them—but they were always fleeting and casual.

Even so, he was far from being the heartbreaker his daughter seemed to think he was. The women in his past had been sophisticates. They hadn't expected or wanted any more from a relationship than he had; they simply enjoyed each other for a time, and when it was over they parted, with no messiness, no heartache on either side.

But Cristen didn't fall into that category. He had known that within minutes of meeting her. There was a vulnerability in her eyes, a soft fragility her sultry beauty belied. Jennifer was aware of it, too; hence, her concern.

Ryan felt a little foolish, being warned off by his own daughter. Though why he was surprised, he didn't know; nothing about this visit had gone as expected. He had pictured Jennifer's roommate as a wild, worldly divorcée, and he had come here with every intention of removing his daughter from her clutches if he didn't like what he saw. The trouble was, he *had* liked what he saw. A smile tugged at his mouth as he recalled silken-smooth, creamy skin and delectable curves glimmering through that ridiculous excuse for a nightgown. Oh, yes, he'd definitely liked it— every beautiful inch. And now, instead of his protecting Jennifer from Cristen, Jennifer was protecting Cristen from him.

"Are you saying that your interest in Cristen is more than just . . . well . . . casual?"

Ryan looked up and met his daughter's suspicious gaze with a sheepish smile. "Honey, what I'm feeling is anything but casual. If my gut instinct is right, I think I've just met the end of my carefree bachelor life."

Jennifer's jaw dropped, and she stared at her father, visibly stunned.

Chapter Two

The sharp *tap-tap* of Cristen's heels on the sidewalk exactly matched the rapid beat of her heart, and the paisley print skirt swished angrily around her legs as her long, lithe stride covered the five blocks to the mall in record time.

Normally on such a glorious morning she would have thoroughly enjoyed the walk. Spring, her favorite time of year, was working its magic on Houston.

Birds trilled their morning songs. Azaleas abounded everywhere—on lawns, in flower beds, in planters, on the formally landscaped grounds around office buildings and condos—their showy blossoms providing splashes of pink, red, magenta, purple and white against the vivid green of sprouting lawns and budding trees. The air was clean and sharp, with just a lingering hint of winter's nip. The sunshine was soft, liquid gold.

A huge oak on the corner two blocks from Cristen's condo supported a twining wisteria, and the vine's grapelike clusters of lavender flowers dripped from the tree's spreading limbs. A gentle breeze fluttered through the blossoms, causing a delicate rain of petals to drift to the ground with every sway of the oak's branches. Only the day before, Cristen had stopped to admire the lovely sight, but today she scarcely saw it. Nor did she appreciate the sweet fragrance that wafted on the breeze.

She stared straight ahead, only peripherally aware of the sights and sounds and smells of spring as her militant step ate up the distance to the mall.

The memory of Ryan O'Malley's wicked grin and the frankly sensual gleam in his eyes taunted her every inch of the way, making her temper simmer. Cristen couldn't recall ever meeting anyone who got under her skin as quickly or as thoroughly. Drat the man, she fumed. He had one heck of a nerve, coming here to check up on her when he was nothing but a...a...leering, lecherous womanizer! Every time she thought of the way he had looked his fill, her blood boiled.

Finding a nearly naked man in her bathroom had been shock enough, but discovering that he was Jennifer's father had surprised the socks off her. Or at least, Cristen amended resentfully, recalling the wispy bit of silk that had been her sole item of apparel, it would have if she'd been wearing socks.

It was ridiculous! Fathers of eighteen-year-old girls were supposed to be middle-aged. Safe and comfortable. Not Hunk of the Month material. Cristen gave a disgusted snort. The man didn't even have the decency to have a paunch. Not even a little one.

And he was no gentleman, either, she railed in silent, impotent fury. Not only had he had the unmitigated gall to take advantage of her morning muzziness—standing there looking at her like an Eastern potentate examining a slave girl he was thinking of adding to his harem—he had been laughing at her, too.

Why, for two cents she'd tell him exactly what she thought of him and what he could do with his monthly rent check.

The belligerent thought brought a wry twist to Cristen's lips. Who was she kidding? She wasn't about to tell him off. That was a luxury she couldn't afford.

And until you can, she told herself, pushing through the plate glass doors and striding into the elegant, galleried mall, like it or not, you're going to have to be civil to Jennifer's father.

Grimacing at the thought, she skirted the indoor skating rink, her leggy stride rapidly carrying her toward the stairs and the tiny shop on the third level.

Louise was talking on the phone when Cristen entered the shop. At the jingle of the bell above the door, her partner looked up and mouthed, "Good morning." Returning the silent greeting, Cristen stowed her purse in the drawer beneath the cash register.

"No, Irene. I'm afraid that won't do," Louise said after a moment.

At the mention of their realtor's name, Cristen's attention was immediately caught. She leaned against the counter and cocked her head, her brows raised in silent inquiry.

"The rent is too high for the location, and the square footage is very little more than what we have here. We need to at least double our shop space, plus Cristen needs a bigger workroom." There was a pause, during which Louise looked at Cristen and grimaced eloquently. "Yes, I know it's difficult to find anything in this area for what we're willing to pay, but I'm sure we will eventually. You'll just have to keep looking."

"I take it that was Irene Lister," Cristen said a moment later, when Louise hung up the phone.

"Yes. And as you heard, she hasn't found a new location for us." Louise sighed, scanning the cluttered shop. It was crammed almost to overflowing with dolls of every description, miniature furniture and accessories, and exquisite custom-made period dollhouses. "I just wish we didn't have to move. This location is perfect."

"Yes, well we don't have any choice. The business has grown to the point where we have to expand."

"I know," Louise replied dispiritedly. "I was just wishing out loud."

"Forget it. I checked with the mall manager yesterday, and the only empty space available is smaller than this place."

Cristen walked to the battered worktable by the bay window and picked up one of the thin sheets of wood that lay on its surface. "Is this all the mahogany veneer that came in? I ordered ten times this much. And some maple and cherry, too."

"Yes. The rest is on back order."

"Oh . . . hades!"

It was as close to cursing as Cristen ever came, and Louise's brows rose sharply at the outburst, but before she could question it, the bell over the door tinkled and a woman walked in.

While her partner helped their customer, Cristen, feeling totally out of sorts, began to lay out her tools. The day had started off badly and was going downhill. On top of the shock of meeting Jennifer's father, she certainly didn't need incompetent suppliers and bad news from their real estate agent, she thought irritably as she arranged the set of carving knives, tiny sandpaper-covered blocks, coarse emery boards, tweezers and the assortment of templates.

Why was it that everything always went wrong at once? The way things were going, before the day was over the bank would probably turn down their loan application.

Cristen sighed. Deep down, an irrational part of her even hoped the loan would be denied. The mere thought of going back into debt was depressing.

A Small World was prospering now, but it had taken her and Louise three years to pay off the original bank loan and get the business onto its feet. But if they expanded the shop and increased their mail orders as they'd been planning, they would have no choice but to borrow more funds.

Business-wise, it was a smart move, she knew, but a new loan and higher overhead would mean lean profits for a while longer. It wouldn't be easy, but she'd get by. If she was careful. The expansion would bring in more customers, and by the time the new loan was paid off the shop should be showing a healthy profit.

Then I can thumb my nose at Ryan O'Malley and his rent money, she told herself gleefully.

Irritated that her thoughts had returned to the hateful man, she scowled, just as Louise returned.

"Is anything wrong? You've been grumpy ever since you walked in, and now you look as though you'd like to throw something."

Cristen met Louise's concerned look with a grimace. "Oh, it's nothing really—just that Jennifer's father is paying us a visit. A *surprise* visit, which I knew nothing about until this morning when I stumbled out of bed."

"Ah, I see. So he's come to size up the wicked, wild divorcée, has he?"

"Apparently so."

"Well, don't fret. You don't have a thing to worry about. I'm sure you'll pass his test with flying colors. I mean, what objections could he possibly have?" Louise shot her a sour look, loaded with exasperation. "As soon as he learns of your nunlike existence, I guarantee you he'll be on a plane headed back to California."

Ignoring the gibe, Cristen murmured, "I hope you're right."

"Much as I hate to be in this instance, I assure you I'm right."

Armed with a soft flannel cloth, Louise turned away and began the daily chore of dusting the contents of the dollhouses scattered throughout the shop, starting with the sedate red brick Federal mansion.

It was perfect in every detail, both inside and out, from the white balustrade fronting the gently sloping roof to the silk-covered walls sporting richly framed paintings, a round bull's-eye mirror and a banjo clock. The polished wood floors were laid in intricate designs, and scattered over them were exquisitely detailed Oriental rugs, which set off to perfection the delicate Federal period furniture upholstered in silks and damask and Italian brocatelle. A flower-filled epergne and tiny replicas of French silverware and china were laid out in precise order on the gleaming Duncan Phyfe dining table. Gilt-edge cornices and Austrian curtains graced the windows. Scattered over the Sheraton desk and Hepplewhite occasional tables were minuscule copies of the porcelain and Sandwich glass pieces and japanned tinware that had been so popular during the late eighteenth and early nineteenth centuries.

Louise picked up a tiny sleigh bed and carefully dusted its intricately carved head- and footboards. Over her shoulder she asked, "What sort of man is Jennifer's father?"

"Arrogant, pushy and thoroughly obnoxious."

"Uh-oh. Sounds as though you and Mr. O'Malley have already clashed."

"You could say that," Cristen grumbled. "I can barely tolerate the man. Before this visit is over I'll probably end up telling him so. Then he'll insist that Jennifer move out, and I'll have to look for another roommate, and you know I'll never find anyone as easy to get along with as Jennifer."

"Well, it if happens, it happens," Louise said with her typical placid practicality. "Of course, another solution would be to sell that pricy condo of yours and move into something cheaper."

"Oh, come on, Louise. You know I'd never find anything cheaper in this area. And if I moved anywhere else, I couldn't walk to work."

"So drive. For heaven's sake, it's not as though you can't. You've got a perfectly good car parked in your garage, though I don't know how you keep the battery charged, no more use than it gets. I'm telling you, Cristen, you simply have to get over this fear of yours about driving in Houston traffic."

"It's not just the traffic," Cristen replied glumly, though she shuddered at the mere thought of trying to maneuver her huge fifteen-year-old Buick through the congested streets. "Driving is something I'm just not good at. I don't think I have the coordination for it."

"Oh, pooh. Anyone who can make these detailed miniatures has more than enough skill and coordination to guide a car down the street. All you need is practice."

"Maybe," Cristen conceded with a shrug. "But in the meantime, I'm still a lousy driver." She plucked her work smock from the peg behind her table, slipped it on and plopped down onto her chair. "Luckily though, if I keep the apartment, I won't need to risk life, limb and property by getting behind the wheel of a car. From there I can walk just about anywhere I need to go, which is the primary reason Bob and I bought the place."

"Yeah. Then he promptly walked out and left you stuck with mortgage payments you can't handle," Louise snapped. "And don't you dare clam up on me just because I criticized your precious Bob," she added in crisp warning when Cristen stiffened. "You can pull that little number on everyone else, but not on me."

Cristen stared at her friend. "You never liked Bob, did you?"

"That's not true," Louise said softly, her expression growing tender at the painful vulnerability in Cristen's face. "I liked him. I just never thought he was the right man for you."

"What's that supposed to mean?"

"Just that you weren't a well-matched pair. You're a confident, bright, vibrantly alive woman. You overshadowed Bob without even being aware of it—even when you were trying to submerge your own wants and needs in favor of his."

"You make me sound like a domineering shrew," Cristen said, unable to disguise the quaver of hurt in her voice.

"No, no. I don't mean that at all," Louise denied quickly. "It's just that Bob was...I don't know...too low-key, too malleable."

Cristen detested talking about Bob and her marriage, but she knew that once Louise got her teeth into a subject about which she felt strongly, she hung on with the tenacity of a bulldog. Her only hope of diverting her partner was to lighten the mood.

Propping an elbow on the table, Cristen rested her chin on the heel of her hand, cocked her brows and gave her friend an amused look. "I see. And just what type of man do you think would suit me?" she asked dryly.

"One whose personality and will equal yours. Someone who's strong and self-assured. Someone who's so comfortable with his masculinity that he can be tender and caring, yet still be forceful enough to stand toe-to-toe with you. And of course it wouldn't hurt if he was a big handsome devil with a sense of humor," Louise added mischievously, her brown eyes twinkling.

Much to Cristen's shock and consternation, a picture of Ryan O'Malley as he had looked that morning flashed through her mind. Leaning against the bathroom sink dressed only in a towel, he had exuded confidence and sheer male vitality, his strong face filled with amusement and sensual awareness. Instantly Cristen's spine stiffened and her expression sobered. "Sorry. That type of man doesn't appeal to me."

"How would you know? The only man you've ever been involved with in your whole life was Bob."

"I just know, that's all." Cristen picked up a sheet of mahogany veneer and studied its grain intently, letting her feigned absorption signal the end of the discussion. She was acutely aware that Louise studied her bent head sourly before turning back to her task.

"Maybe you're right," Louise muttered under her breath. "After being married to a gutless wonder, you probably wouldn't know what to do with a real man."

Cristen's head snapped up. "Bob is *not* gutless."

"Oh, no? What else do you call a man who walks out on his wife without so much as a word?" Louise glared at Cristen, her pleasant face screwed up in a ferocious scowl. Her fists were planted firmly on her ample hips, and her body quivered with righteous indignation on her friend's behalf. "And you have to admit, if Bob Patterson hadn't deserted you, you wouldn't be in the financial bind you're in. And you wouldn't have to have a roommate *or* worry about what her straitlaced, middle-aged, overprotective father thought of you.''

"I really don't want to discuss it, Louise.''

"That's just the problem. You never want to discuss it. You just keep it all locked up tight inside you.''

"What would be the point? The past is past. It happened, but it's over now and I'm fine.'' Ignoring her, Cristen picked up a template for an eighteenth-century Philadelphia highboy and positioned it carefully over the sheet of veneer. With a pencil, she began to trace the cutout shapes onto the wood's surface.

"Cristen, darn it—''

To her relief, whatever Louise had been about to say was cut off by the tinkle of the bell over the door as another customer entered the shop.

Determinedly, Cristen continued with her work. Louise was her dearest friend, and the last thing she wanted to do was quarrel with her. She even admitted to herself that, to a degree, Louise had a right to voice her opinion. She had been the one, after all, who had seen Cristen through that desolate period after Bob had walked out, when she had been almost too hurt and bewildered to function.

Cristen's hand stilled, and she gazed at the scarred surface of her worktable. Even now she could clearly recall that day when she had returned home to find the apartment empty and that awful note propped on her dressing table.

Forgive me, Cris, but I need to get away for a while. I need space, breathing room. Oh, Lord, Cris, I don't know what I need—except maybe a chance to find me, to figure out what I really want in life. Don't hate me too much, babe. I do love you. I always have. I always will. I'll be in touch.

Love,
Bob

But he hadn't kept in touch, Cristen thought, feeling the familiar bitterness well up inside her. She hadn't seen or even talked to Bob since she'd kissed him goodbye that morning and left for work, not even suspecting that he would be gone when she returned.

How many times had she read that shattering, rather incoherent message? Five? Six? A dozen? She didn't know. She could only remember feeling first shock and then a horrible, all-consuming pain, as though someone had torn out her heart and ground it beneath his heel.

But little by little the hurt had faded, and, strangely, she had even understood. She and Bob had known each other all their lives. Their families had been next-door neighbors, and, born within days of each other, the two had been constant companions since their playpen days. Their mothers had been best friends, and so had they.

From the beginning Cristen had always been the ringleader, the more adventuresome one. A reminiscent smile quirked her mouth as she recalled their youthful high jinks, the numerous times she had led an unsuspecting, always compliant Bob into some outrageous escapade, landing them both in trouble more often than not.

As children they had done everything together, gone everywhere together, and as teenagers they had dated each other exclusively. In everyone's mind, including Cristen's, they had been a pair, and when they'd graduated from college it had seemed the most natural thing in the world that they should marry.

Obviously, Bob had not agreed.

Somewhere along the way he had begun to feel stifled, had grown unhappy with being part of a pair. Cristen realized she might have been a little hurt at first, but if he had just come to her before their marriage and told her of his need to strike out on his own, to discover if he could stand on his own two feet and function as an individual, she would have understood. She might even have applauded him. But no, true to form, Bob had just docilely gone along with her plans without giving so much as a hint that he desired anything else.

For that, she didn't think she would ever be able to forgive him.

While Cristen regretted the breakup of their marriage, she had come to realize that it wasn't Bob, her husband, or even Bob, her lover, that she missed, but Bob, her friend. Deep down she supposed she'd always known that they weren't passionately in love, but they'd had something almost as important: a deep, very special bond, forged by a lifetime of shared memories. Through his actions Bob had severed that bond and cost them both something very precious.

Cristen had tried, but she hadn't been able to make Louise understand that she wasn't heartbroken over a lost love but mad as hell over a shattered friendship. Even if she had been deeply in love with Bob, Cristen knew she wouldn't still be pining for him. She simply wasn't the type to wallow in self-pity for long. She was a fighter by nature, a survivor.

And she saw absolutely no point in talking about the breakup of her marriage. Not only was it extremely personal, but a constant rehashing of the humiliating experience was like poking a newly healed wound with a sharp stick.

Why had she even bothered to defend Bob? Habit, probably, she mused. All her life she had staunchly defended him against all comers. Her feelings for him had died a slow, painful death many months ago, but some things, she supposed, were so ingrained that they were automatic.

But Louise had been right about one thing: Bob's desertion had not only inflicted emotional pain, it had also put her back to the wall financially. They had been a two-income couple when they'd purchased the condo. On her own she couldn't hang on to it and still make ends meet.

It had taken her almost a year and a half after Bob had moved out to accept that cold hard fact. Or more accurately, Cristen amended with brutal self-honesty, it had taken her that long to accept that he wasn't coming back. Even after she'd received his telegram, telling her that he'd gotten a quickie divorce in Mexico, she had not been able to believe that Bob Patterson had simply walked out of her life for good.

With a grimace of self-disgust, Cristen traced the last pattern piece and tossed the template aside. Her gaze moved to the bay window at the front of the shop and focused unseeingly on the fairy lights suspended from the huge arched skylight above the skating rink.

Bitterly, she recalled how, like a fool, she had waited and waited . . . and hoped. And every month she'd been forced to dip into her savings in order to meet expenses, until finally there had been almost no money left.

That was when she'd finally accepted that Bob wasn't coming back, that, incredible as it seemed, she had lost him, and that she was going to lose her home, too, if she didn't do something.

A roommate had seemed the only logical solution. A second job had been, and still was, out of the question, since the shop took up most of her time.

A ghost of a smile tipped Cristen's mouth when she recalled the day that Jennifer had answered her ad, how dubious she had felt about sharing her home with someone so much younger than she. She had tried to discourage Jennifer, but the girl's enthusiasm and bubbly good nature were difficult to resist, and Cristen had found herself agreeing, if somewhat reluctantly, to give the arrangement a try.

It was a decision she had never regretted. Despite the differences in their ages and all the misgivings Cristen had had in the beginning, she and Jennifer had become good friends.

With her father's help, Jennifer managed to support herself with a part-time job. Between that, drama classes three nights a week, an occasional part in an Alley Theater production and numerous dates, she was seldom home before midnight. When she was around, they got along beautifully. Jennifer was tidy, considerate, and unfailingly pleasant, and Cristen didn't want to lose her as a roommate.

Cristen had a sudden mental image of sapphire-blue eyes, eyes that glittered dangerously with masculine appreciation and blatant sexual heat. A tingling sensation raced over her skin, and a faint flush crept into her cheeks.

After that scene in the bathroom it was going to be extremely difficult to face Jennifer's father with even a modicum of dignity and poise, much less convince him that his ewe lamb was safe with her. But she would— somehow. She had to. Thank the Lord he was only going to be there for the weekend.

Still Cristen couldn't shake the horrible feeling that it was going to be a long, trying two days.

A steady stream of customers filled the shop all morning. Around ten-thirty, half an hour late, Dora Fife, their part-time helper, drifted in, wearing an outlandish secondhand-shop outfit and her perpetual vague smile. Meeting Louise's gaze, Cristen rolled her eyes, but her partner just laughed.

Cristen was quite certain that Dora could drive a saint crazy without even trying. The girl was vague, incompetent, inclined toward laziness and just plain weird. If she hadn't been Louise's niece, Cristen never would have allowed her to work in A Small World.

Not only did Dora have one oar out of the water, she was totally aimless, floating through life like a dandelion seed in the wind. She'd been attending the University of Houston for three years, but she'd changed her major so many times that she was no closer to graduating now than she had been when she'd started.

Cristen admitted to being a head-in-the-clouds dreamer herself at times, but Dora's dippyness drove her around the bend.

Except for those occasional times when the shop was really crowded, Louise and Dora took care of the customers while Cristen worked at her table.

They had learned long ago that people found it fascinating to watch Cristen fashion the perfectly scaled miniatures, which was why her worktable was situated in front of the window. The messy work, like sawing and hammering or pouring the molds for the metal pieces, was completed in the back room, but everything else she did in full view of their customers and the people passing by in the mall. Many times as she sanded and carved and fitted the small pieces of wood together or upholstered the tiny furniture or constructed and decorated a miniature mansion, a small crowd gathered around the window. Inevitably some wandered into the shop for a closer look, and once inside, few left without purchasing something.

Business was brisk most of the day. It wasn't until a lull just an hour or so before closing that they found themselves alone in the shop again.

"Whew, what a day," Louise said as she watched a gray-haired gentleman leave with his carefully wrapped package. "You'd think there was a miniaturists' convention in town, the way sales have been today." She looked down, taking a quick inventory of the glass case that held their standard period pieces. "It looks as though we're running low on camelback sofas and Queen Anne wing chairs. Oh, and Victorian hallstands. There are only two of those left."

"Hmm. I'll start on the hallstands next," Cristen replied without looking up from carving an intricate shell motif on a blockfront chest. "I already have a dozen of the sofas and chairs almost finished. As soon as the glue sets I'll put on the stain. I should be ready to upholster them by next Tuesday or Wednesday."

"Great." Louise poured two mugs of coffee and carried them over to the table. "Here. I'm sure you need this as much as I do," she said, setting one in front of Cristen.

"Thanks."

Louise perched on the corner of the table and leaned back on one hand. "Cristen, about this morning. I'm sorry I—"

The tinkle of the bell above the door cut off her apology. Cristen kept her head down as Louise slid off the table and went to greet their customer.

"Good afternoon, sir. Is there something I could help you find?" she asked politely.

"No, thank you. I've come to pick up Cristen."

Though she had only heard it for the first time that morning, the deep, rumbling baritone was unmistakable. Cristen's head snapped up just in time to see Ryan O'Malley turn his devastating smile on her partner.

"You must be Louise Fife. My daughter has told me about you. I'm Ryan O'Malley, Jennifer's father."

"*You're* Jennifer's father?" Louise stared up at him with the dazed expression of one who has just received a sharp blow to the head.

Across the room, where she had been straightening shelves, Dora simply stood and stared, her mouth agape.

Louise's incredulous gaze slid to Cristen, then back to the towering, outrageously attractive man. When she looked at her partner once again, her eyes had narrowed and held a speculative gleam that Cristen knew boded no good.

Chair legs scraped on the shop's wooden floor as Cristen shot to her feet. "What are you doing here?" she demanded rudely without thinking.

Ryan turned his devilish blue gaze on her, his mouth twitching beneath the sable mustache. He crossed to her table, and Cristen gritted her teeth. A man that large ought to be awkward and lumbering, she thought irritably. Ryan sauntered—a slow, easy, loose-limbed glide that was all supple, sinuous grace.

Low-slung faded jeans clung to his narrow hips, and a white shirt that was startling against his tanned skin molded the broad shoulders and powerful chest that Cristen remembered so well. Impressive biceps bulged beneath the short sleeves, and the mat of dark curls on his chest created a shadow beneath the loosely knitted material. Cristen ground her teeth harder as a tingling sensation feathered down her spine.

"Jennifer was worried about your being late, and since I wanted to get a look at your shop anyway, I said I'd pick you up. But don't worry, there's no need to rush. Our dinner reservations aren't until eight. You have plenty of time."

"Dinner res—" Cristen drew a deep breath against the spasm of panic that tightened her chest. "I'm sorry. I can't possibly have dinner with you and Jennifer."

"Nonsense!" Louise put in emphatically before Ryan could reply. "Of course you can."

Cristen darted her partner a quelling look, which was calmly ignored. "No, really. I...uh...I have too much to do here. I...I'm going to have to work late tonight."

Ryan crossed his arms over his chest and tilted his head to one side. His sardonic gaze seemed to bore into her, direct and unnerving. "That's too bad," he drawled. "I was hoping you and I could get acquainted over dinner."

"I'm sorry. I can't make it."

"Don't be silly, Cristen. Of course you can," Louise insisted. She was so agitated that she was practically dancing up and down. "There isn't anything here that won't wait until tomorrow. And Dora and I can close up tonight. Can't we, Dora?"

Louise sent the dumb-struck girl a sharp look. Never taking her eyes off Ryan, Dora nodded.

"You see? So you just— Oh, damn!" she swore when the phone began to ring. She darted around the counter to answer it. "Hold on just a second. I'll be right back."

Cristen looked at Ryan and shrugged. "I'm sorry, but you see—"

"Cristen, it's for you."

"Go ahead," Ryan said pleasantly, picking up the piece she had been working on. "I'll look around while you take the call."

At the counter Cristen held out her hand for the receiver, but Louise snatched it back out of reach and scowled accusingly. "Why didn't you tell me about Jennifer's father?" she demanded in an aggrieved whisper.

"I did."

"You told me he was here, but you didn't tell me he was gorgeous."

"It hardly matters, does it?"

Louise groaned. "Are you crazy? No, don't answer that. You must be or you wouldn't be trying to avoid going out with him. Well, I'm not going to let you. You're—"

"Will you give me that phone," Cristen hissed, snatching it out of her hand. Glaring daggers at her partner, she said tersely into the mouthpiece, "Hello, this is Cristen."

"Hi. It's Jennifer. Is Dad there yet?"

Cristen scowled at Ryan's broad-shouldered back. He stood on the opposite side of the shop, inspecting the Victorian dollhouse. "Yes, he is," she said through clenched teeth, straining for a pleasant tone. "But as I was telling your father, I can't possibly go out with you tonight. I'm sorry, Jennifer."

"Oh, come on, Cris!" Jennifer wailed. "You promised you'd help me entertain Dad when he came."

"I know, but—"

"Cris, please! Eric is joining us, so we'll be a foursome. If you don't come, Dad will spend the entire evening grilling the poor guy about his intentions. Besides, I've already made reservations for us at Rudi's. You can't let me down."

"Jennifer, I—"

"Please, Cris. I want you and Dad to be friends. Please say you'll come."

Friends. It seemed such a tepid word when used in connection with Ryan O'Malley. Somehow Cristen didn't think he was a man who had many woman friends. He was far too basic, too rawly male, for anything so tame. A legion of ex-lovers she could believe, but not women friends.

"Please, Cristen," Jennifer cajoled when she hesitated. "You promised."

With a sigh of defeat, Cristen rubbed the spot between her brows with the tips of two fingers. "Oh, all right. I'll come."

When she hung up the phone she avoided Louise's smug look and went to tell Ryan that she would be joining them after all. "Just give me a few minutes to put these things away," she said, gathering up tools and the dozen half-finished chests.

Cristen walked into the back room with Louise dogging her heels like a determined terrier. "Something just dawned on me," the other woman said in a voice heavy with suspicion. "You said you didn't know Jennifer's father had arrived until you got up this morning. Knowing what a deadhead you are when you first wake up, and knowing that Frenchie nightwear you're so partial to, some very interesting possibilities come to mind."

Cristen carefully put her tools away and placed the chests on a shelf with the other pieces in various stages of completion. She steadfastly ignored Louise, but her friend was not deterred.

"Just how *did* you and Mr. O'Malley meet?" Louise practically danced a jig trying to keep up with Cristen as she moved around the storeroom. When Cristen didn't reply, Louise's eyes grew round. "Oh, my. Don't tell me you walked out of your bedroom wearing one of those little nothings?"

"I wouldn't dream of telling you any such thing," Cristen replied stiffly.

"You did!" Louise crowed. "Oh, I knew it! I knew it! Oh, this is priceless. What happened? What did you do?"

"Louise, I *don't* wish to discuss it."

Chapter Three

He's flirting with me! At least... I think he is.

Cristen frowned. She wasn't sure because her experience with that sort of thing amounted to zilch. The only man in her past had been Bob, and he'd certainly never flirted with her.

Trying her best to ignore the way Ryan O'Malley's thigh was pressing against hers, Cristen stared at the after-dinner drink she was absently rotating. Since finding this aggravating, overpowering, utterly charming devil in her bathroom that morning, she'd suffered the unsettling feeling that somehow she had lost control, that her life was being turned upside down. And the feeling had been steadily growing. Just look at what had happened when they arrived at the restaurant. One minute she'd been about to take the chair the waiter held out, and the next Ryan had maneuvered her onto the banquette beside him. The man was dangerous.

And Jennifer was just as bad. The girl certainly had her father's persuasive charm, and she used it just as adroitly to get her way, Cristen thought darkly, recalling the heated discussion they'd had over what Cristen should wear. Cristen had balked at wearing the black taffeta dress, but Jennifer had insisted it was the only thing she had that was suitable.

It was also the sexiest thing Cristen owned. The ruffled neckline plunged both front and back, and the fitted bodice with its dropped waist lovingly outlined every womanly curve before leading the eye to the fantasy of deep flounces that made up the skirt. It was elegant and expensive, and it rustled enticingly when she walked. The overall effect was one of provocative, feminine allure.

It had been a rare impulse purchase after Bob's desertion. When Cristen saw the dress, she had known he would have hated it, especially on her, which had been just the spur she'd needed to buy it. It had hung in the closet ever since, unworn. Until now.

Sighing, Cristen fingered the taffeta ruffle that draped her breasts. And to think Jennifer had always seemed such a sweet, tractable little thing. Cristen wasn't used to losing arguments or being outmaneuvered, and she still hadn't figured out how it had happened, but she made a silent vow that in the future she would be on her toes around Irish charmers by the name of O'Malley—father *and* daughter.

Ryan shifted, and the sleeve of his dark dinner jacket rubbed against Cristen's bare arm, a soft abrasion that sent goose bumps racing over her skin. She inched away, but a subtle move by Ryan closed the tiny gap between them.

Cristen darted him a sharp look. Had he done that on purpose?

Ryan was talking to Eric, his expression a model of innocence. Cristen narrowed her eyes. Finally, looking away, she told herself to ignore him.

It was impossible. His slightest movement brought a tantalizing whiff of masculine cologne to tease her nose, and all along her side she could feel the heat from his body. Grinding her teeth, she stared harder at the frothy green drink.

"Well, Dad, what did you think of Cristen's shop?" Jennifer asked, cutting into the men's conversation. Catching Cristen's eye, she winked conspiratorially.

"It's fascinating. Unique. I was impressed." The smile Ryan turned on Cristen was filled with sincere admiration and a touch of speculation. "You're a talented woman."

"Thank you." Resisting the urge to squirm, Cristen wondered why she found his compliments just as unnerving as his teasing.

"She even makes replicas of people's homes on request," Jennifer added. "Or of places like Windsor Castle or the White House."

"Really?"

"Yes. Most of my houses are custom orders. They're expensive, and miniaturists are usually very definite about what they want."

"They're not the only ones," Ryan murmured, giving her an intent look that sent a frisson of alarm skittering down her spine.

"Her houses are so authentic that our set designer is duplicating the parlor of her Georgian mansion for a production of *My Fair Lady*," Eric put in.

Cristen looked at him and smiled. She liked Eric. He was a handsome young man in his early twenties, an actor Jennifer had met when they'd both had parts in a play at the Alley Theater. Earlier in the evening Ryan had subjected him to a mild fatherly inquisition, but Cristen knew that he had no need to be concerned. Eric and Jennifer made an attractive couple, and they were obviously fond of each other, but they were both too caught up in their budding careers to even consider a serious relationship.

"That's very interesting." Ryan's attention switched to his daughter. "Doesn't that open in just a few weeks?"

"Yes. And I'm understudying the lead."

The statement sparked a discussion about Jennifer's chances of filling in for the disgustingly healthy leading lady, but Cristen was too distracted by the heat and hardness of the man beside her to join in.

Did he have to sit so close?

Maybe I'm overreacting, she told herself, studying Ryan covertly as she sipped the minty drink. Maybe I'm just blowing that embarrassing first meeting out of proportion. After all, the whole thing was just a silly fiasco. Ryan is hardly to blame.

And other than those smoldering looks and a few teasing remarks, he really hasn't said or done anything objectionable. Besides sit too close and brush against you constantly, a tiny inner voice argued.

Cristen cut another sidelong glance at Ryan. Even that was probably accidental, she decided with a trace of annoyance. He hardly seemed aware that she was in the room. And that teasing, seductive tone she'd heard in his voice was probably just second nature to him. Earlier, during the short drive home from the mall, he'd even managed to imbue their mundane discussion of the weather with seductive undertones.

The band began to play a slow tune, and Jennifer looped her arm through Eric's, giving her father an impudent look. "I hate to interrupt this stimulating conversation, but I'm stealing Eric for a dance."

"Good idea." Ryan grasped Cristen's hand, meeting her startled look with a persuasive grin. "Would you like to dance? I promise not to step on your toes too often." Before she could answer he slid across the banquette and stood up, pulling her with him.

By the time they reached the tiny dance floor, her heart was thudding. It exasperated Cristen that Ryan affected her so, and when he drew her into his arms she held herself stiff and stared over his shoulder, her expression remote.

For a moment they danced in silence. Cristen could feel Ryan's gaze on her, and from the corner of her eye she saw his mustache twitch suspiciously. She tried to ignore him, but her whole being hummed with awareness. His hand engulfed her smaller one, the palm warm and dry and hard against hers. The brush of his thighs as they moved to the romantic music made her insides quiver strangely, and the heat from his encircling arm burned through her dress like a branding iron.

This is silly, she berated herself, trying to quell her twanging nerves. He's just a man, for heaven's sake. Jennifer's father. Just treat him as you would anyone else. Talk. Say something. Anything.

"You're very quiet."

The soft-voiced statement brought Cristen's head snapping up. In high heels she was nearly six feet tall, but she still had to tip her head back to meet Ryan's amused gaze. It was a distinctly new experience, one that was both pleasurable and somehow unnerving. How tall was he, for heaven's sake?

"I, uh, I was just thinking that . . . that you're not at all as I pictured you."

The mustache twitched again. "Oh? How so?"

"Well, for one thing, you don't look old enough."

Slowly, Ryan's gaze roamed over her upturned face, then scorched a path down over her arched neck and shoulders to where the tops of her breasts swelled above the low-cut gown. When he focused on her face once again his look was frankly lascivious. "Oh, believe me, darlin', I'm old enough."

Cristen's heart gave a little thump. Now *that* was definitely flirting!

"I mean to be the father of an eighteen-year-old," she said severely, giving him a quelling look that had not the least effect.

"Oh, that. Well, I guess that would depend on how you defined 'old enough.' I'm thirty-seven."

"Good heavens! You became a father at nineteen?"

"Yeah, well, that's what happens when you're young and impetuous and—" he paused, his grin widening "—hot-blooded. When your hormones are bubbling it's difficult to distinguish lust from love. Jennifer was already on the way by the time Ella and I discovered that the only thing we had going for us was sex."

"Oh. I see."

A warm flush she was powerless to prevent tinged Cristen's cheeks a faint pink. Was he always so blunt, or had he said that to test her reaction? Given his penchant for teasing, she suspected the latter.

Ryan shrugged. "At least we had enough sense to part before we ruined each other's life. We've even managed to remain friends. Two years after the divorce Ella remarried, and now she and her husband have three children of their own."

"And you opted for the single life."

"Not really. I've just been waiting for the right woman to come along." Ryan looked at her intently, his expression for once serious. "I always knew she would. It was just a matter of time."

A vague feeling of unease fluttered through Cristen. Not knowing quite what to say, she fell silent and looked away, once more staring over his shoulder. The charged silence lengthened as she searched her mind for a safer topic.

"You know, you're not at all what I expected, either," Ryan said after a moment.

"Oh, really?" Cristen slanted him a narrow-eyed look filled with irony. She could just imagine what he had envisioned: a bold, brassy swinger with the morals of an alley cat. No doubt the type he dated regularly.

The thought made her seethe. That she had been fully prepared to accept, or at least tolerate, that double-standard brand of thinking—had Ryan been the paunchy, middle-aged man she had envisioned—slipped her mind completely.

"Yes. And I must say, you were a pleasant surprise." A teasing, sexy gleam lit Ryan's blue eyes as his gaze skimmed over her from her feathery Gypsy mane to her décolletage, and Cristen knew that he was remembering the way they had met. "Very pleasant, indeed."

Jaw set, she stared over his shoulder again. She would not—absolutely would not—let him rile her. "I'm glad," she said coolly. "Jennifer has been worried that you wouldn't approve of me."

"Oh, I approve," Ryan assured her in a purring voice. He caught her eye once again, his mouth curving in a devilish grin. "From what I've seen so far, I approve very much."

Beast!

Refusing to acknowledge the innuendo, Cristen gritted her teeth and gave him a tight smile. "Thank you. I'm very glad to hear that. I would hate to lose Jennifer as a roommate. We're both very happy with our living arrangement."

"Now that I've met you, so am I. If I'd known my daughter had such an attractive roommate, I would've come for a visit sooner."

Suddenly, Ryan jerked her to him. Her breasts flattened against his chest, and their bodies molded together from shoulder to knee. Before Cristen could protest he executed a series of complicated steps, whirling her around so quickly that her head began to spin. She had no choice but to cling to him. When he resumed the slow, languorous dance and the world settled down, she threw her head back, opened her mouth and met a look of bland innocence.

"Sorry. That old couple was about to crash into us," he explained with an apologetic shrug, but his hold on her eased only fractionally.

At Cristen's skeptical look, Ryan's teasing grin grew wider. Seductive devilment sparkled in his eyes. He leaned closer and dropped his voice to a husky pitch. "By the way, I've been meaning to tell you, I like that little mole."

Cristen looked blank, then frowned. "What mole?"

"The one in the hollow just below your right hipbone." He lowered one eyelid in a wicked wink. "Terrific place for a beauty mark."

Cristen gasped. For a moment she stared at him, wide-eyed, too shocked to react. Then her body began to burn as a flush rose from her toes all the way to her hairline.

"Oh! You, O'Malley, are no gentleman, or you wouldn't have...have..."

"Noticed?" he supplied helpfully.

"Yes!" Cristen snapped. She tipped her head at a haughty angle, but when she would have pulled out of his arms Ryan tightened his hold.

"Whoa. Whoa. Don't get all bent out of shape." He chuckled, but at Cristen's affronted glare he had the good grace to look sheepish. "Okay. You're right, that wasn't nice. But you've got to admit, that episode in the bathroom *was* funny."

His grin was irresistible. Despite her best effort to keep her expression stern, Cristen's lips twitched. He'd done it to her again! With a grimace and a heavy sigh, she conceded grudgingly, "Well...okay. Maybe it was. Just a little."

"And just think what a great story it'll make for our grandchildren."

Grandchildren? The word jolted through Cristen, banishing her reluctant amusement in a flash. Just what did he mean, their grandchildren? Was he speaking collectively or...

"Anyway," Ryan continued with blithe disregard for the wary confusion in her eyes, "I couldn't resist teasing you. It's so much fun to watch you get all huffy and ruffle your feathers like a little banty hen."

"Little?" Cristen gave him a droll look. "Your analogy is a bit off, isn't it? If there's one thing I'm not, it's little."

Ryan appeared to consider her statement for a moment, a look of sheer male approval heating his gaze as it moved over her. "I guess not. But you're sure as heck one nice armful of woman."

A tiny thrill surged through Cristen. Telling herself it was foolish to feel so pleased by what was probably nothing more than practiced flattery, she tried to suppress it. "Really? You mean my height doesn't bother you?"

"Not at all. I've never cared for fragile little dolls. I'm always worried they might break. Besides, I get a crick in my neck when I kiss a short woman."

"I can imagine." Giving in to the throaty chuckle the image evoked, Cristen shook her head at the devilish look in his eyes.

"Did your height bother your husband?"

Ryan knew the moment the words left his lips that he'd blundered.

In an instant every trace of amusement vanished from Cristen's face, her expression settling into a blank mask. "I'm sorry, but my marriage is not a topic for casual conversation." Coolly, she shifted her gaze away from his.

After a moment, as though he had not even spoken and she had not answered with that terse little put-down, she said conversationally, "I understand that your company makes security systems."

"Yes. Actually, we design, manufacture and install them. Mostly for commercial users, like banks, government agencies, or large corporations—any type of business that deals in valuable goods or highly classified or sensitive information."

A sore spot. Very interesting, Ryan mused. And disturbing. Is she reluctant to discuss her ex-husband because she still loves him? Or because she's bitter? Either way, it wasn't a good sign.

The music stopped, and Cristen stepped out of Ryan's arms. "It sounds like a fascinating business," she said as they started back to the table.

"It is. With the recent advances in technology, we even have sophisticated security systems that operate on voice or fingerprint match, or a combination of both."

She murmured something appropriate, but Ryan could tell she was merely being polite. All Cristen was interested in was putting distance between them. Why?

He had barely taken his seat beside Cristen when the other couple returned. Sliding into the chair Eric held out for her, Jennifer beamed a smile across the table.

"I've got a terrific idea, Dad. Eric knows of this great little disco not far from here. What do you say we go there and really kick up our heels? This place is too sedate for dancing, anyway."

Ryan smiled indulgently. "What do you think, Cristen?"

"Thanks, but I think I'll pass," she said in a rush. "I'm tired and I, uh, I have to work at the shop tomorrow. If you don't mind, I think I'll just go home."

"You're going to work on Sunday?" Jennifer asked, her disgusted tone turning the question into a protest.

"I'm afraid so. But please, you three go ahead." The last thing Cristen wanted was to prolong the evening, especially with more dancing. For some reason she didn't really want to analyze, Ryan O'Malley made her nervous and edgy in a way no man ever had.

"I'd just as soon call it a night myself. So I'll tell you what." Ryan pulled a set of keys from his pocket and tossed them across the table to Eric. "You two take my car and go to the disco, and Cristen and I will take a taxi back to the apartment."

"Oh, no, please." Cristen turned quickly to Ryan, her eyes growing wide with the beginnings of panic. Being left alone with him would be even worse. "I don't want to spoil the evening for you. Besides, you came here to be with Jennifer. I'll feel terrible if you don't go."

"Don't be silly. It's all settled."

Protests were useless. Thirty minutes later Ryan was unlocking her apartment door, and as Cristen stepped gingerly past him her nerves were clanging like a firehouse alarm.

In the living room she fiddled nervously with her purse and shifted from one foot to the other. When she finally darted a look at Ryan she found that he was standing casually, hands in his pockets, feet braced apart, watching her with a look of faint amusement.

"Would...would you care for some coffee? Or perhaps a brandy?"

Theda, lying stretched out in her favorite spot along the back of the sofa, woke from her nap, blinked and gave them an imperious look.

"No, thanks. I had plenty at the restaurant."

"Oh...well, I, uh, I think I'll go to take a couple of aspirin. I have a bit of a headache."

Ryan removed his coat and tie and tossed both over the back of a chair. Just as casually as though he lived there, he sprawled on the sofa and slumped down on his spine in an utterly relaxed pose, legs stretched out in front of him, head resting against the back. "It's probably just tension. When you come back I'll massage your neck. That usually helps." Beneath half-closed lids, his blue eyes glittered with laughter and gentle challenge.

Not on your life, buster, Cristen vowed silently. Ignoring the fluttery sensation in her stomach, she gave him a weak smile and eased toward the kitchen. Theda was studying Ryan's ear as though it were a tasty morsel, and as Cristen pushed through the door she silently urged the cat to take a bite.

To Cristen's disgust, her hands shook as she fumbled with the cap on the aspirin bottle. She felt on edge, jittery, her nerves vibrating like a plucked string.

If only he weren't so fantastic to look at. And...so...so darned sexy.

Finally prying the cap off, Cristen took out two tablets, but when she tried to down them with a gulp of water they stuck in her throat and she coughed and sputtered and choked. "Oh, good grief! This is ridiculous." She quickly drank more water, shuddering at the bitter taste.

Godzilla's garters! Why on earth are you getting into such a dither? So the man's attractive and charming and impossibly virile. So what? It's certainly no reason to act like a love-struck teenager. Heavens! No male affected you like this even when you *were* a teenager.

Sighing, Cristen massaged her temples with her fingertips. She'd been prepared to pacify a dubious middle-aged father, allay his doubts about her suitability, not deal with a sexy male in his prime who had romance on his mind.

Cristen's head jerked up. It suddenly occurred to her that maybe she'd been right in the first place. Was Ryan testing her? Had he been flirting with her just to see how far he could get? The thought set a match to her temper, and her eyes narrowed dangerously. Why that dirty, low-down...

She took two steps toward the door before she caught herself up short. Wait a second! Wait a second! You're just guessing. It could be that he's really interested.

The thought sent a thrill zinging through her, but she quickly squelched it. Oh, sure. Great. If there's one thing you don't need, it's a man complicating your life, especially one as potent as Ryan O'Malley.

Well, whatever his reason, she told herself, heading determinedly for the living room, either way, I'll soon set him straight.

Theda was curled in Ryan's lap, the picture of smug feline bliss, turning her head this way and that to accommodate his scratching fingers, her purr a deep rumble. Both had their eyes closed. Cristen hesitated just inside the door, but then Ryan's lids lifted partway and he smiled and patted the cushion beside him. "Come join me."

Opening her eyes, Theda gave her mistress a baleful look. With an annoyed twitch of her tail, she plopped to the floor, glided haughtily to a chair and jumped up onto it. Cristen ground her teeth. There were only two chairs in the room, and with Ryan's coat in one and the cat in the other, she had no option but to join him on the sofa. To move either cat or coat would be too obvious.

As she sat down at the opposite end of the sofa, Ryan straightened and turned to face her, resting one arm along the back and bringing his bent knee up on the cushion. "So how's the headache?"

Cristen glanced at him, disturbed to find that somehow he had managed to eliminate most of the space between them. She nervously smoothed the taffeta flounces covering her thighs. "Better, thank you."

Ryan picked up her hand, and she jumped, giving him a startled look. "Are you sure?" He asked softly. "You seem tense." Examining her hand, he slowly turned it palm upward. Her nails were perfectly manicured, but the tips of her fingers were lightly callused, and there were little nicks and cuts on her palm. He grazed his thumb over them in a featherlight caress. "I think you could use that massage."

"No, that's not—"

She could have saved her breath. To her surprise, Ryan easily turned her sideways, bringing her so close to his chest that she could feel his body heat across her back.

"Now just relax. This won't hurt a bit."

"Oh, but—"

His big hands grasped her shoulders and kneaded, his thumbs digging into her back in a circular motion. "There, doesn't that feel better?"

"Yes, but...this isn't...necessary...I...ah..." Cristen's weak protest faded away in a moan as his thumbs worked up her spine. His hands were warm and strong, the pads of his fingers callused, but their abrasive rub against her smooth skin was oddly pleasurable.

"I'm not surprised you have a headache. You've been as wound up as an eight-day clock all evening." He paused a beat, and she could hear the hint of a smile in his voice when he added, "Is something bothering you?"

"No. Yes. Ryan, I'm not..." One of his hands slid up under her hair, his strong fingers flexing rhythmically over her nape, then spearing into the silken mass to move in slow, hypnotic circles against her scalp. She closed her eyes, and, like a wilting flower, her head drooped forward until her chin touched her chest.

"That's it. That's it," he crooned in her ear. "Don't fight it. Just relax."

Cristen had no choice, though she didn't so much relax as melt. His fingers were magic, soothing, arousing, warming her flesh and firing her blood until it slogged through her veins like thick, heavy syrup. She felt boneless, feverish and achy. Wonderful.

"Jennifer told me in her letters what a special lady you are. I thought she was exaggerating," he whispered in her ear as his massaging hands worked their way down her arms. "But I was wrong. You're beautiful, talented, successful, a thoroughly modern independent woman, and yet you're exquisitely feminine." As soft as the brush of a butterfly's wings, he strung a line of nibbling kisses over her shoulder and up the side of her neck, his warm breath dewing her skin and sending delightful little shudders quaking through her. Mindlessly, Cristen tilted her head to the side to give him better access.

One of Ryan's arms slid around her waist and pulled her back against him. His other hand moved in a wispy caress over her arm and shoulder; then his spread fingers feathered up her neck to curl around her jaw, and with firm but gentle pressure he turned her head.

Languorously, Cristen opened her eyes partway. Ryan's face hovered just inches from hers, flushed with desire, his blue eyes hot beneath heavy lids. Her heart thudded, and she swallowed hard. Now. Now's the time to tell him that you're...you're...

For what could have been an eternity or a split second, their gazes locked. Then, with excruciating slowness, his head moved closer and their eyes drifted shut. Ryan's moist, brandy-scented breath struck her face in soft puffs as he murmured, "I've been wanting to do this since the moment I saw you."

At the first touch of his warm lips, a delicious shudder rippled through Cristen. She quivered under the delicate caress; her breath caught. The protest she'd been struggling to recall slipped from her mind like water through a sieve. She felt strange, her body awash with new sensations, swamped with sweet pleasure.

Slowly, oh, so slowly, Ryan's open mouth rocked back and forth over hers, tempting, enticing, building her trembling response. With relentless tenderness he coaxed, claimed, conquered.

Without thought of resistance, Cristen surrendered to the soft probing of his tongue, her mouth flowering open like a blossom welcoming the sun. As he tasted her sweetness with slow, deep strokes the hand at her waist slid up over her ribcage and cupped her breast. The brush of his thumb across her nipple combined with the lazy thrusts of his tongue sent fire streaking through Cristen to gather in a hot, throbbing ache at the core of her femininity.

A low moan issued from her throat, and without conscious thought she raised her hand and clasped the back of Ryan's head, tunneling her fingers into his dark hair, her nails lightly scraping his scalp as she urged him closer.

Ryan gave an answering growl of male satisfaction. The kiss instantly changed from gentle enticement to hot, hard demand. He turned her, tightening his arms around her and holding her so close that her breasts were flattened against his chest.

"Dear Lord, you're sweet. So sweet," he murmured against her cheek as he strung a line of kisses from her mouth to her ear. "Just your taste is driving me mad." He kissed the sensitive spot behind her ear, and his tongue lapped tormentingly at her lobe.

Cristen felt the sofa cushions pressing against her bare shoulders, and she opened her eyes and found that Ryan had lowered her to her back. He was leaning over her, smiling, his expression full of sensual promise. Dazed, she blinked and stared up at him.

"Did you know that the sight of you in this dress has been driving me crazy all evening?" Slowly, he trailed his finger along the top edge of the ruffle hugging her shoulders, leaving a line of fire on her skin. His eyes followed the same path and grew steadily warmer as he traced over the rounded tops of her breasts and dipped into the shadowy cleavage. "I knew your skin would feel like warm satin." His gaze rose, and he smiled. "I've been wanting to touch you like this ever since this morning, when I saw you in that little wisp of silk."

His words cooled her passion as effectively as a bucket of ice water in the face. She jackknifed into a sitting position, taking Ryan by surprise and dumping him onto the floor.

"What the—"

Cristen scrambled to her feet and backed away, keeping a wary eye on Ryan and holding her hand out in front of her as though to ward him off, but he just lay there, propped up on his elbows, and stared at her incredulously.

"Now you—" Her voice came out in a high squeak, and she stopped to clear her throat. "Now you just stay away from me, O'Malley. Because I'm warning you right now, I have no intention of getting involved with you."

"Oh?" Ryan cocked his head to one side. "Mind telling me why?"

"Why? Because I don't indulge in affairs, that's why."

"Who said anything about an affair?"

Cristen made a sharp, dismissing gesture with her hand. "Affair. Meaningful relationship. One-night stand. Whatever you want to call it, I'm not interested. And I certainly have no intention of becoming involved with my roommate's father."

To Cristen's utter disgust, her heart was chugging like a runaway train and her chest was so tight that she could barely breathe. She waited, braced for his reaction, expecting anger or disbelief—at the very least, sardonic amusement. Ryan's shrug and calm "Okay" took her by surprise.

Feeling oddly deflated, she watched in amazement as he rolled to his feet and dusted off his trousers. He caught her staring and flashed a lopsided grin. "If you're sure that's the way you want it."

"No. I mean, yes. That's the way I want it." That's it? she marveled. No argument, no scene, no big seduction?

She backed away another step. "Now, if you don't mind, it's getting late, and since I have to get up early in the morning..." Her gaze went to the sofa and back to Ryan. "I hope you'll be comfortable on that sofa bed. If you need clean sheets—"

"I'll be fine. Jennifer showed me where they were last night."

"Oh. Well, then I'll, uh, I'll just say good-night."

"Good night, Cristen." Ryan returned her hesitant smile and watched her uneasy retreat, his expression thoughtful.

Layers. The longer he was around her, the more he discovered. Her beauty—extravagant, a bit exotic—had hit him with the force of a sledgehammer the moment he'd laid eyes on her. But beyond it was also strength, intelligence, vulnerability, that amazing talent. And temper. A smile tugged at his mouth. Oh, yes, there was temper—tightly contained, to be sure, but judging from the flashes he'd seen, it did justice to her flamboyant coloring. It pleased him as much—maybe even more—than her beauty; he appreciated spirit in a woman.

Yes, Cristen Moore was a woman of depth. Complicated. Intriguing. Alluring. He wanted to explore all the facets of her personality, peel away all the layers one by one, because he sensed—no, he knew—that hidden beneath it all lay that fascinating untapped passion, smoldering.

But there was pain also, he thought with a frown, remembering her instant withdrawal when he'd mentioned her ex-husband. With that quiet strength she had buried it deeply, but it was still there. And that bothered him.

You'd better tread carefully, O'Malley. She's a proud, strong woman. Keep it light, or she'll throw up walls you'll never tear down.

Cristen's ivory satin gown clung to her breasts and hips lovingly, then fell in generous folds that fluttered around her bare feet as she paced the floor of her darkened bedroom, too agitated to sleep.

Oh, for pity's sake! She came to a halt by the window and stared out at the scattered lights that spread all the way to the horizon. Why couldn't she just forget about that scorching kiss and put the wretched man out of her mind?

Moonlight flowed over her, turning her gown to shimmering silver. Absently, she rubbed her palm over the slick fabric covering her midriff and sighed. Come on, Cristen, you know why. It's because for the first time in your life you're attracted—really attracted—to a man.

The gentle, comfortable feelings she'd had for Bob bore no resemblance to the stomach-fluttering excitement Ryan O'Malley evoked. And that terrified her.

The last thing she wanted was to get involved with a man. Any man. Especially not like Ryan.

Closing her eyes, Cristen leaned her forehead against the cool windowpane and fought a suffocating feeling of panic. She was a normal, healthy woman, and Ryan was an attractive, virile man in his prime. That she responded to him on a purely physical level was perfectly natural, she told herself. No doubt there were hundreds—no, thousands—of men who could make her feel the same. Nothing to worry about.

Throwing up her hands, she swung around and stomped back to the bed. Lord, love a duck! What was she so frazzled about? The man was flying back to California tomorrow afternoon. With any luck, she wouldn't have to see him but maybe two or three times a year when he came to visit Jennifer. She could handle that, couldn't she? Of course she could.

Cristen slid into bed, flounced over on her side and closed her eyes determinedly. Piece of cake!

Chapter Four

Cristen had planned to leave for the shop early the next morning before either Jennifer or her father awoke, but after tossing and turning most of the night she overslept, and when she emerged from her bedroom they were already in the kitchen. Briefly she considered tiptoeing out, but after a moment's hesitation good manners won over temptation.

Cristen was not surprised to find Jennifer dressed in her comfy bathrobe, looking rumpled and sleepy-eyed. It had been sometime after two when she'd heard her come in. Stifling a yawn, her roommate looked up and murmured, "Morning, Cris. Want some coffee?"

Smiling, Ryan echoed the greeting, then fell silent, watching Cristen over the rim of his mug.

"No, thanks. I'll have some when I get to the shop." Fortunately, Jennifer was either too muzzy from lack of sleep to notice that her roommate was, for once, conversing without her obligatory coffee or too exhausted to comment on the departure from ritual. Relieved, Cristen hurried on. "Since I'll probably work all day, I thought I'd tell your father goodbye now."

Fiddling nervously with the purse strap that hung over her shoulder, Cristen fixed a polite smile on her face and turned to Ryan. "I'm glad we finally met, Mr. O'Malley. And please, feel free to visit your daughter anytime. I hope you have a pleasant trip."

Given her abhorrence for early-morning conversation and her uneasiness about Ryan, Cristen was proud of the polite, if somewhat stiff, farewell.

Ryan stood and extended his hand, his manner cordial and pleasant and equally impersonal. "Thank you, I'll do that. And I'm glad we met, too."

And that's that, Cristen thought, happily surprised. Not by so much as a look or a word did he give the slightest indication that that torrid scene on the sofa had even happened.

His obvious acceptance of her rejection encouraged Cristen, but, nevertheless, she was relieved to find him gone that afternoon when she returned.

To her surprise and utter disgust, however, it was not quite as easy to put Ryan out of her mind as she had thought it would be, especially since Jennifer couldn't seem to talk about anything else. For days after Ryan left "Dad this" and "Dad that" was all she heard out of the girl.

Louise was just as bad. She bombarded Cristen with so many questions about Ryan and dropped so many not too subtle hints about what a catch he was that Cristen finally lost all patience.

"Louise! Will you just knock it off? As far as I'm concerned Ryan O'Malley is Jennifer's father. Nothing more.

Anyway, you're wasting your time trying to matchmake. I promise you, he's definitely not the marrying kind." Her mouth set in a grim line, Cristen sanded a long piece of wood harder than was strictly necessary.

"Okay, okay, forget I mentioned him. You still ought to go out once in a while. It isn't normal or healthy for a young woman to live like a cloistered nun, for pity's sake. Why, except for that dinner the other night, you haven't had a date since I fixed you up with John's cousin Fred, and that was over three months ago."

Cristen paused in fitting a floor joist and gave Louise a dry look. "Yes, and we spent a miserable evening groping for something to talk about. No offense, but believe me, Fred is deadly dull."

"Okay, then what about Leonard DeWitt? He's always asking you to go out with him."

"Me and everyone else in skirts." Cristen grimaced and shuddered. "Cripes, Louise! The man's a scuz ball."

Leonard DeWitt managed a shoe store on the lower level of the mall. He wore his pants skintight, his shirts unbuttoned to his waist and at least five pounds of gold chains around his neck. The man was incapable of looking at any woman under forty without undressing her with his beady little eyes. Just the thought of his touching her made Cristen cringe.

"How about that salesman who's always trying to date you?"

"Harvey Metcalf? Oh, come on. Harvey's a nice man, but you know he's looking for a mother for his four kids. That's a role I have no intention of filling."

Louise pounced on the statement like a duck on a June bug. "All right. If you're not interested in marriage, then why not go out with Ryan?"

Cristen straightened abruptly, buried her fingers in her hair and clasped her head with both hands. Glaring at her partner, she said through clenched teeth, "Louise, I'm warning you. If you so much as mention Ryan's name again, I swear I'll scream."

Affronted, Louise subsided, but it didn't help. Every time Cristen looked at her friend's sulky expression she was reminded of the maddening man all over again. That night she even dreamed about him.

But in the middle of the week all thought of Ryan was pushed from Cristen's mind when, to her delight, she received a special order for a carpenter gothic Victorian mansion, complete with furnishings. It was an enormous order that would take months to complete, even putting in extra hours, and between working on it and building up their stock for the move to larger quarters, she was kept so busy she barely had time to think about anything or anyone else.

On Friday Cristen went to the shop early, hoping to work on her new commission before opening time, only to find Louise waiting for her. The moment Cristen stepped inside, her friend pounced.

"There you are! I was just about to call your apartment. I've got some great news."

Cristen stowed her purse, then bent over her table to study the scale drawings spread out on its surface. "Don't tell me. You won ten million dollars in one of those publishers' sweepstakes."

Brimming with excitement, Louise was oblivious to her teasing. "I heard a rumor that the shop next door is going out of business, and that space will be available for lease soon."

Cristen's head shot up. "Really? That far-out boutique?" At Louise's nod she grinned in delight. "Terrific!

That's great! I mean, not that they're going out of business, of course. I'm sorry about that. But if we can get that space, we could knock out a wall and double the size of our shop without moving."

Already plans were taking shape in her mind as she scanned the shop's interior. This was just the break they needed.

"My thoughts exactly," Louise said, looking pleased. "I was hoping you'd agree."

"Oh, I do. Have you checked with Henderson's office to see what could be worked out on a new lease and the cost of removing the wall?"

"Well . . . no. I thought we'd better wait until it's official. Actually, I'm not even supposed to know about it yet."

Cristen frowned. "Exactly where did you hear this rumor?"

"From Dora. She called me at home this morning to tell me because she knew we were looking for a bigger place."

"Dora? Dippy Dora? And you believed her? You're pinning your hopes on something you heard from that ding-a-ling?" Cristen groaned and rolled her eyes. "Oh, please, Louise. Give me a break."

"Dora's okay," Louise said halfheartedly.

"She's about half a bubble off, and you know it." Cristen's expression held both disgust and amazement. "Do you know that girl once asked me how boneless chickens could walk? She's a flake, Louise. I don't care if she is your husband's niece."

"I know, but she's harmless."

"I'm not too sure about that. I get an anxiety attack practically every time I even think about her working here."

"Come on, Cris. I know she drives you around the bend, but she means well. And since we have to have part-time help, it might as well be John's niece."

Cristen met her friend's gaze and sighed. She had often thought it a shame that Louise and John had never had children. The original mother hen, Louise tried to take every stray chick under her wing. And where family and friends were concerned, she was a pushover. Right now her round, pleasant face held all the pleading appeal of a puppy in a pet store window, and it was just as difficult to resist.

"All right, you win. Finish your story," Cristen said with a resigned sigh, and Louise immediately brightened.

"Well you see, Dora went out with Barney Tucker last night, and he told her about the boutique going out of business."

"Who's Barney Tucker?"

"You know, the young man who works for mall security. He got it from his cousin." At Cristen's blank look, she added, "She's a file clerk in the building manager's office."

"Ah. An unimpeachable source," Cristen drawled. Slanting Louise a scornful look, she plucked her smock from the peg, slipped it on and plopped down in her chair.

"I know it's kind of roundabout, but you just wait. I'm sure we'll find out that Barney was right."

If Cristen had been a betting woman, she would have wagered a month's profits against that likelihood... and lost. To her surprise, about an hour later the boutique owner dropped in to chat and told them that she was declaring bankruptcy.

The moment the woman left, Cristen called Joe Henderson's office. By that afternoon they'd worked out an agreement on the lease and the cost of knocking out the wall. The only thing left to do was see their banker about taking out a larger loan.

To celebrate, after closing the shop they went to dinner at an expensive French restaurant. John met them there, and when he heard their news, insisted on ordering champagne. After numerous toasts and a sumptuous meal, it was past midnight when they left, and almost one o'clock by the time John and Louise dropped Cristen off.

The apartment was dark when she let herself in. Not wanting to wake Jennifer, Cristen did not bother with a light, but tiptoed confidently across the familiar, shadowy living room. In the middle she instinctively veered around a chair, took another step and whacked her shin on something solid. With a yelp of pain, she pitched forward.

"What the—"

Cristen's breath left her lungs in a loud *whoosh* when she landed hard on something large and warm and extremely firm. It took a second—and the startling feel of hands sliding boldly over her buttocks—for her to realize that she was sprawled atop a man. And that, beneath a thin sheet, that man was lying naked on a bed!

Shock gave way to panic, and she began to struggle, but in a lightning move he flipped her onto her back and pinned her down with his body. Her instinctive scream had barely begun when he stifled it with his mouth.

Cristen fought back without thought, bucking beneath his heavy weight, twisting her head from side to side. Her hands were pinned between them, but she finally managed to wriggle one free and pound on his back with her fist. When that had no effect she grabbed a handful of his hair and yanked with all her might.

There was a moan, then, unbelievably, a chuckle.

"Aaahh, sweetheart, don't scalp me," the man murmured against her mouth, prying her hand from his hair and pinning it to the mattress beside her head.

Cristen's frantic movements faltered. There was something...something in that deep rumble that cut through her panic. Something familiar. Something tantalizing. In the brief second before his mouth had closed over hers she had glimpsed a face, and as she tried to recall it Cristen realized that the kiss, though firm, wasn't in any way brutal. As her struggles lessened it became a soft caress, a gentle enticement that plucked a responsive chord deep within her, until at last she grew utterly still.

Recognition—elusive, teasing—fluttered around the edges of her mind, but even as she grasped at it her body responded to his with a knowledge of its own. Their legs were entwined, tangled in the sheet that draped his lower body, their torsos pressed together as though they were one. Cristen was acutely aware of his strength, his heat, his potent masculinity, the shocking intimacy of their position. A tingle ran over her skin, making her first hot, then cold, then hot again.

His lips were warm and wet, his tongue a gentle marauder. Cristen's mouth quivered and softened. A low growl issued from the man's throat, and for a moment the kiss changed from a slow, rocking, tender torment to sheer hunger.

Then it ended. The man lifted his head, and Cristen's eyes drifted open, blinked and slowly grew round.

Propped up on his elbows, his face illuminated by the small square of moonlight spilling through the window, Ryan grinned down at her. Cristen sucked in her breath, but before she could make a coherent sound he winked and murmured outrageously, "You know, we really have to stop meeting like this."

His unmitigated gall took her breath away. "What! You...you...Ohhhh!"

Ryan's grin widened.

"Get off me, you lout!" Cristen shoved his chest with her free hand and bucked her hips, but the intimate contact brought a dangerous gleam to his eyes, and she quickly subsided. She scowled up at him, so furious that she could barely breathe. "You...you big buffoon! You scared me half to death, do you know that!"

"Sorry," he replied, but there was nothing in the least repentant about his look.

"What are you doing here, anyway? You're supposed to be in California." She shoved his chest again and scowled more darkly. "And will you *please* get *off* me?"

Ryan didn't budge. He released her hand and shifted his fingers through the feathery auburn curls spread out against the sheet. Through half-closed eyes he studied their silky sheen in the moonlight as though it were the most fascinating thing he'd ever seen. "You said I should feel free to visit Jennifer anytime I wanted." He looked up, and his amused gaze collided with her stormy one. "So here I am."

Cristen clamped her teeth together, barely stifling a groan. Trust him to take that polite platitude literally. "But you were here just last week," she pointed out irritably.

"I missed her."

"I see. Well, would you mind telling me just what the devil you thought you were doing, grabbing me and kissing me like that? I thought we had that matter settled."

"We did. We do." He gave her a guileless look and lifted one bare bronze shoulder. "But I couldn't let you wake up the whole building screaming, now could I?"

His reasonable tone made her want to give him a swift kick. Or better yet, considering their positions, a sharp jab with her knee.

"I hardly think it was necessary for you to—"

"Shh, you're going to wake Jennifer."

"I don't care if I wake the governor!" she shrieked, infuriated by his audacity. "You've got one heck of a nerve—"

"What's all the yelling about?"

Light suddenly filled the room. Cristen and Ryan both looked around to see Jennifer standing just inside the hall door with her hand still on the light switch. Her dark curls were mussed and she was rumpled and half asleep, but as she took in the intimate position of the two people on the bed her eyes grew comically round. "Oops. Sorry, I, uh, I didn't mean to...that is..." She fluttered her hands nervously and stumbled backward. "I'll, uh, I'll just go back—"

"Jennifer, wait! You don't understand! Come back here!" Cristen yelled.

Ryan's chest began to vibrate with silent laughter. Cristen gave him a hard shove and hissed, "Will you get *off*!"

Obliging, he rolled to the side and collapsed on his back, letting his stifled chuckles blossom into rich, full-bodied laughter as Cristen scrambled from the bed.

She fumbled to straighten her clothing and swiped impatiently at her disheveled hair. She was torn between her anger and embarrassment, and her flustered gaze bounced from Jennifer to Ryan, then quickly darted away again when she saw that the sheet had slid so low on his hips that he was barely decent.

"I, uh, didn't know your father was here, you see," she began anxiously, darting Jennifer a self-conscious look. "And I...I stumbled into the sofa bed in the dark and fell over him. When you came in he was, uh, he was just checking to see if I'd hurt myself."

Ryan let loose with another burst of guffaws and doubled up, clutching his sides.

If looks could kill, the one Cristen shot the convulsed man would have annihilated him on the spot. At that moment the urge to fold up the sofa bed with him in it was almost irresistible.

Determined to ignore him, she gritted her teeth and turned back to Jennifer. The smug little smile that had replaced her roommate's shocked expression sent Cristen's temper up another notch. "Now look. It's not what you think—"

"Whatever you say, Cris," Jennifer assured her with such blatant tongue-in-cheek insincerity that Cristen wanted to chunk something. Hard.

In control of himself again, Ryan lay back, fingers laced behind his head, and watched Cristen with a look of unholy amusement.

Exasperated, she turned to him and snapped, "Granny's garters! Don't just lie there grinning like the village idiot. Help a little, can't you?"

"Certainly." Ryan raised himself up on his elbows and assumed a pious expression. "Jennifer, regardless of what you saw, absolutely nothing happened. Do you think I'd indulge in hanky-panky just because a beautiful woman fell into bed with me?"

Cristen closed her eyes and groaned.

"You? Never."

"Good. It's nice to know a daughter has faith in her father." He dropped his severe pose, and one corner of his mouth kicked upward. "Actually, though, I really thought she was a cat burglar."

"Uh-huh. So you were frisking her, right?"

"Right."

"Find any concealed weapons?"

Ryan's heavy-lidded gaze slid lazily over Cristen. Its touch sizzled along her nerve endings and sent a tingle racing over her back and shoulders and down her arms. Slowly a smile grew on his lips and he emitted a low, wicked "Hmm."

At the sound Cristen sucked in her breath and bristled like a cat whose fur has been stroked the wrong way.

"Now look here," she huffed. "I won't stand for—"

She stopped abruptly and glanced from father to daughter. Ryan's mustache was twitching, and Jennifer was biting the insides of her cheeks. Both pairs of blue eyes danced with mischief and lighthearted laughter.

Cristen's blistering put-down dissolved on her tongue. Her arrested expression changed from indignation to faint chagrin, and slowly, a reluctant smile tugged at her mouth. "Very funny, you two."

"Oh, Cris, if only you could have seen your face. It was priceless. I know we probably shouldn't tease you, but you do ask for it, you know," Jennifer reproved with a chuckle and a warm look. "You're always so intense."

"Jennifer's right," Ryan put in. "You really should loosen up, learn to go with the flow. Life's more fun that way."

He was propped up in the bed, leaning against the sofa back, watching her in that sexy, devilish way of his. The sheet was pulled up to a semimodest level just below his waist. Above it, his chest was bare and broad and furred with a mat of silky black hair. As she stared at its enticing swirling patterns, Cristen was reminded of the morning they met, and she felt the same fluttering sensation in the pit of her stomach. His hair stuck up in places where she had yanked it, and a faint beard stubble shadowed his jaw, yet he looked absurdly attractive: rakish and bold and thoroughly male, lying there supremely unconcerned about his nearly naked state.

Cristen wondered if he knew what it was doing to her. The gleam in his eyes told her that he did, and she glanced away.

"You're probably right," she agreed. "I guess I've just been working too hard lately. You know what they say about 'all work and no play.'" She managed a lame smile and edged toward her bedroom. "Since it's late, and I'm sure you're both as tired as I am, I'll say good-night. I, uh, I'm sorry I disturbed your sleep."

"Cristen." Ryan's voice stopped her just as she reached the hall door, and she paused and looked back at him. Warmth and gentleness had replaced the teasing laughter in his eyes. "I'm sorry if I frightened you. I didn't mean to. I just acted on impulse."

The simple, sincere apology plucked an emotional chord deep inside Cristen, and she reacted to it every bit as sharply as she had to his physical appeal. It made her even more uneasy. She looked at him for a moment, gave an uncertain smile and nodded and without another word stepped through the doorway.

In her room she leaned back against the closed door and stared off into space, a slight frown drawing her brows together. What was she going to do about that man? He was a flirt and a tease, definitely not a man to be taken seriously, so why did she react to him like a prickly hedgehog?

Was it because of this stupid physical attraction she felt for him?

Cristen pressed four fingers over her lips and closed her eyes as the memory of his kiss came stealing back. Since high school she'd heard and read about the explosive passion that could erupt between a man and woman when the chemistry was right, but she had never really believed it. Certainly she'd never experienced it before.

And I could have darned well done without it, she thought resentfully. She didn't care for that heart-pounding, weak-kneed, woozy feeling that came over her at Ryan's touch. The loss of control was both frightening and irritating.

But then again, maybe her testiness with Ryan simply meant that she'd lost her sense of humor, as Jennifer had implied.

With slow steps, she crossed to the bed and sank down on its edge. In one of her rare displays of compassion, Theda jumped onto Cristen's lap and purred her sympathy. Obeying the head-butting command, Cristen scratched behind the cat's ears. "Do you think that's the problem, Theda? Have I become a humorless dullard?"

What had happened to the reckless, lighthearted girl who had led Bob into one scrape after another as they were growing up? The young woman who had met life head-on with laughter and buoyant optimism and a slightly irreverent sense of humor? Had she let a wrecked marriage destroy her?

Cristen had always been goal oriented. Ambitious. Determined. She knew that. But since Bob's departure she had used work as a panacea, letting it fill her life until there wasn't room for anything else. Not pain, not heartache, not bittersweet memories.

Not joy. Not laughter. And certainly not love.

Cristen gave a mirthless chuckle and stroked her hand absently down Theda's back. "Leaping lizards! I must be going soft in the head, Theda. It's ridiculous to even think of love in connection with Ryan O'Malley."

Narrowing her eyes, Theda gazed at Cristen and meowed.

"Oh, he's a charming devil, I'll grant you that. But you have to admit he's hardly a man for forever after."

She looked away, her wry smile fading. In any case, a man in her life was the last thing she wanted. Or needed.

A gentle nudge sent Theda plopping to the floor, and Cristen went to the dresser and withdrew a pink silk nightgown that was slit up both sides to the tops of her thighs. She draped it over her arm, stepped out of her shoes and headed for the bathroom.

"Cristen, you're not going to work today, are you?"

Cristen had barely set foot in the kitchen the next morning when Jennifer hit her with the question. With only the slightest hesitation, she continued toward the counter, casting the girl a bleary look that would have silenced a horde of crazed fans at a rock concert.

But not Jennifer.

"It's Louise's weekend to man the store, so you don't really have to go in, right?"

Taking her time, Cristen poured coffee into a large mug. She took a sip, closed her eyes and took two more. Finally, cradling the mug in both hands, she turned, leaned back against the counter and looked at Jennifer through the wisps of rising steam. "No."

Her shuttered gaze slid to Ryan, who was leaning back at ease in his chair, following the exchange. She'd been tempted to lie and say she needed to go in to the shop, anyway, but the night before she'd vowed that she was through hiding. She would be pleasant and polite, but distant. When he realized she wasn't interested, Ryan would soon tire of whatever game he was playing.

"Oh, good! Then you can take Dad apartment hunting."

Cristen blinked groggily and frowned. "What?"

"Apartment hunting," Ryan interjected. "You know, as in 'a place to live.' Or at worst, to sleep and eat and hang your clothes."

As Cristen's foggy brain grappled with the statement, her eyes slowly widened. "Here? You mean you're going to move here to Houston?"

"Sort of. I'm going to open a branch of my company here. I'll probably alternate between Houston and the San Francisco plant every other week for the next year or so, or at least until I get everything running smoothly." Ryan grinned at Cristen's appalled expression. "So you can see, since I'll be spending at least half my time here, I'll need a place of my own."

The staggering news brought Cristen wide awake. Heaven above! He was going to live there!

"Isn't that great?" Jennifer chirped. "Now I can see Dad often."

Too stunned to reply, Cristen just stared.

"Of course, he's going to be terribly busy for a while, locating a site for his plant and getting it built and all, so he's going to need help finding the right apartment," she continued, oblivious to Cristen's shell-shocked look. "I told him you wouldn't mind helping."

"Me? You want *me* to find him an apartment?"

"Sure. You know Houston a lot better than I do."

"But—"

"Don't worry about it, Cristen." Ryan gave his daughter a mildly reproving look. "I told you it was too much of an imposition to expect Cristen to spend her free time helping me. I'm sure I'll manage to find something on my own. It'll just take me a little longer, that's all."

"No problem. Take as long as you need," Jennifer declared airily. "Cristen and I don't mind, do we?"

"Mind?"

Jennifer stood and retrieved the coffeepot, tossing Cristen a confident glance. "I told Dad he was welcome to stay here with us until he found a place."

She dropped that bombshell as she turned to refill her father's mug, and thus missed Cristen's aghast stare.

Stay with us? Here? Indefinitely! Sheer panic welled up inside Cristen at the thought of sharing her home with Ryan, of his occupying her sofa bed every night, of being on the receiving end of those warm looks and that teasing, sexy smile every morning and every evening. Of growing used to having him around, of possibly becoming more attracted to him, of...

No. Oh, no. Not on your life. A visit was one thing, but having him living there, God only knew how long... No, she couldn't risk that.

But what choice did she have? An outright refusal was out of the question. He *was* Jennifer's father, and, manners aside, technically she supposed he had a perfect right to stay there, since he paid Jennifer's rent.

Jennifer was looking at her expectantly. Ryan's face remained impassive, but Cristen thought she saw amusement dancing in his blue eyes.

She clenched her jaw and forced her lips into a stiff smile. "Of course you must stay with us, Ryan. And I'll be happy to help you find an apartment."

Even if I have to beat feet all over town every waking moment of this entire weekend.

Chapter Five

What do you mean, it's too high tech?" Cristen looked around in confusion at the modern high-rise apartment. It had every gadget and convenience she had ever heard of, and a lot she hadn't. "I thought that would appeal to you. After all, you're in a high-tech business yourself."

"True. But when I get home I like something a little...homier." Ryan shrugged. "This place seems more like a laboratory. Or something out of *Star Wars*."

He stuck his hands into the trouser pockets of his dark three-piece suit and strolled across the pearl-gray carpet to the wall of tinted glass.

Thoroughly frustrated, Cristen watched him through narrowed eyes as he jingled the change in his pocket and gazed out at the terrace and the sprawling city below. She felt like reminding him that only the day before she had shown him a charming town house with an old-world ambience, done completely in antiques, but she bit back the words.

For the past five weeks she had been running herself ragged searching for an apartment. She'd located several she thought were exceptional, but he'd found something wrong with every one; it was either too large, too small, too remote, too closed in, too fancy, too stark—the list was endless.

And in the meantime, every other week, Ryan was happily ensconced in Cristen's condo.

"I take it, then, that you're not interested."

Ryan looked at her over his shoulder and smiled. "It's really very nice, Cristen, but it's just not me. Have you any others you can show me?"

Irritated, she shoved her envelope purse under her arm, turned on her heel and stalked toward the door. "No, I do not," she tossed back in a tight, clipped voice. "This was the fifth one we've looked at today."

Still jingling his change, Ryan trailed after her. "Hey, Cristen, I'm sorry to put you to so much trouble. Look, why don't I just do my own hunting from now on? It'll probably take me longer, but I'm sure I could manage to squeeze out a couple of hours a week to scout around for an apartment."

And at that rate you'll still be camping out at my place when you start drawing Social Security, she moaned silently. "Oh, no. No, I wouldn't hear of it. I said I'd find you an apartment, and I will. I'll just have to keep searching, that's all. Come on. Let's get home and go through the want ads."

Ryan grinned at her retreating back. "Okay. If you insist."

Cristen fumed all the way home, but Ryan either didn't notice or chose to ignore her bad humor. He chatted amiably as he drove through the heavy Saturday afternoon traffic, sublimely unruffled by either it or his companion's curt, monosyllabic replies.

Cristen didn't know whom she was ticked off with more: Ryan for—she suspected—deliberately dragging his feet, or herself for allowing it.

They heard the phone shrilling when they reached the door of the condo. Cristen tapped her foot impatiently while Ryan fitted his key into the lock. Eager to vent her ire on something, she stalked past him, snatched up the offending instrument and snapped out a stinging "Hello."

"Cristen? I . . . did I catch you at a bad time?"

After years of close friendship it took only those few words from Louise for Cristen to know that something was wrong. In an instant her annoyance evaporated. "What is it, Louise? What's the matter?"

Drawn by her worried look and the note of concern in her voice, Ryan stepped nearer, frowning. The frown deepened as he watched her grow pale, her expression changing to shocked disbelief.

"They turned us down? But . . . why?"

There was a pause, and anger tightened Cristen's face as she listened to her partner. "I see. Didn't you explain about—"

Another pause, longer this time, and then Cristen sighed. "I see. Well, I guess that's that."

The murmur of Louise's voice drifted to Ryan, but he couldn't make out her words. He watched, his concern growing, as Cristen listened intently, her teeth worrying her lower lip.

"I don't know where we go from here, Louise," Cristen said in a dispirited voice. "Let me give it some thought."

When she hung up the phone she just stood there with her hand still on the receiver, deep in thought.

"What's wrong?"

She gave Ryan a distracted look and raked a hand through her hair. "Oh, uh, just a business problem."

"Want to tell me about it? Maybe I could help."

"I doubt it." Cristen attempted a smile, but it came out a grimace. She wandered to the window and stared out, absently fingering the edge of the drapery. "You see, after keeping us waiting for weeks, and despite the fact that we paid off our original loan promptly, the bank has turned down our application for a new loan. We need that money to expand our shop."

"Did they give you a reason?"

"Several. Money's tight. They don't feel our collateral is adequate. But apparently the main reason is that they're concerned about the business being so heavily dependent on me. About my ability to keep up with the increase in demand. Louise explained that we've worked out a student training program with the university art department. The students who participate will earn credit for learning the craft and receive a small salary, and I'll have a steady stream of apprentice helpers." Cristen let out her breath in a long, defeated sigh. "But the loan officer still wasn't convinced."

"So what are you going to do?"

"I don't know. Try other banks, I guess. Though we'll probably run into the same problem."

Ryan studied her back, the tense set of her shoulders, and after a moment came to a decision. "Look, instead of going through that hassle, why don't you borrow the money from me?"

Cristen swung around, her eyes wide. "From you? But ... you don't even know how much we need. And besides, you have your own business expansion to worry about."

"I have a fair idea. And don't worry, I may not be in the Rockefeller class yet, but I can afford to lend you what you need."

At a loss for words, Cristen just stared. From things Jennifer had said and the scope of his business, she had known that Ryan was doing well, but until now—until that casual offer of what to her seemed a staggering amount of money—it hadn't really hit her that he was actually wealthy. Now that she thought about it, though, compared to the cost of building a whole new factory in Houston, their needs probably seemed piddling.

It was a tempting offer, but pride wouldn't let her accept. "Thank you, Ryan. It's very generous of you to offer, but . . . no. I'm afraid we can't accept."

Ryan sighed, a look of mild exasperation on his face. "All right. If you won't take money from me, how about if I cosign a bank loan? They won't turn you down if I stand good for it."

"I . . . you'd do that?" Cristen was stunned. It was the perfect solution. Unless they defaulted on the loan, which she had no intention of doing, Ryan wouldn't be out a penny.

"Sure. It's the least I can do, after you've put up with having me constantly underfoot for weeks. So what do you say?"

Cristen couldn't control the smile that spread across her face, or the relief and elation that swelled within her. After only the briefest hesitation she blurted out, "I say yes! Yes!"

She stuck out her hand, and Ryan took it between both of his. "Oh, Ryan, I don't know how to thank you."

"Well..." With a gentle tug, he pulled her closer, the familiar teasing glint sparking in his eyes. Cristen's chest tightened. "...I could probably think of—"

Before he could finish, the front door burst open and Jennifer tore into the room like a whirlwind.

"You're never going to guess what happened today!" she squealed. "Never in a million years!" Breathless, her face flushed and deliriously happy, she twirled around the room with her arms outstretched, almost crackling with excitement.

Bemused, Cristen and Ryan exchanged a questioning look and shrugged.

"What? What?" they demanded in unison, laughing as Jennifer's freewheeling pirouettes carried her around them like a demented dervish.

At last she stopped and looked from one to the other, her eyes shining and wide. Looking as though she would burst at any second, she pressed her clasped hands to her breast and gasped. "I got a part in a Broadway play!"

"What!"

"Jennifer! That's wonderful!"

Everyone started talking at once, and between hugs and congratulations Jennifer managed to explain that a producer had come to the Alley Theater looking for an unknown to play the ingenue in a new play.

"You wouldn't believe how fast the word got out," she said, still flushed with excitement. "I bet every actress in town under twenty-five showed up within twenty minutes after our director made the announcement."

"But you got the part." Grinning from ear to ear, Ryan radiated fatherly pride.

"Yes! Isn't it wonderful? We start rehearsals in three weeks. And in the meantime, I've got a million things to do. Such as pack and make travel arrangements and find a place to live and...and...Oh, all kinds of things!"

"Don't worry about a place to live," Ryan said. "Some friends of mine, Arnold and Sue Jordan, live in Manhattan. I'm sure they'll be glad to have you stay with them, at least until you can find another roommate like Cristen to share with."

Cristen sobered, her high spirits taking a nosedive at the casual statement. For the first time since Jennifer had made her announcement it hit Cristen that she would be losing her roommate. She pulled away from the other two, who were still talking jubilantly, and sank down on a chair.

"What's the matter, Cristen?" Ryan asked when he noticed her dazed dejection. "Aren't you happy for Jennifer?"

"Yes. Yes, of course I am. I'm delighted. Really." Seeing the doubt in their eyes, she made a face and flapped her hand. "Oh, don't mind me. I'm just down because I suddenly realized that now I'll have to look for a new roommate myself."

"Oh, Cris. I didn't think about—" Jennifer turned to her father with an agonized look.

Frowning, Ryan pursed his lips thoughtfully. "Actually, that's no problem. That is...it doesn't have to be."

"What do you mean?"

His brows hiked upward, and he spread his hands wide, palms out. "I could be your roommate."

"You!"

"Dad! That's a great idea!"

"I thought so."

"You *must* be joking!"

"No, I'm not."

"No, he's not," Jennifer echoed.

"But...but you can't! It just wouldn't...we couldn't—"

"Why not?" Ryan asked, cutting into Cristen's incoherent sputtering.

She stared at him, shocked right down to her toes.

"Well, for one thing, you're a man."

"So?"

"Oh, for heaven's sake, Cris. Dad's just suggesting that you be roommates, not that you...you know...*live* together."

"But that's what it will look like. What everyone will think."

"So? Let them. Besides, who's going to care? Louise? She'll probably be delighted. And your folks are out in Arizona in that retirement community. You told me yourself they never come to Houston."

"I don't see what the big fuss is about." Leaning back against a chair, Ryan folded his arms across his chest. "After all, I've been living here for weeks now, and a lot of that time Jennifer wasn't even around. If anyone was going to notice, or care, they already have by now."

"Well...yes, I suppose that's true, but..."

"The arrangement would benefit both of us," he pointed out. "I won't have to rent an apartment and leave it vacant half the time, while you, on the other hand, will be receiving full rent from a roommate who's only here every other week. And," he added with a devilish, immodest grin, "I'm handy to have around the house, even if I do say so myself."

Cristen couldn't argue with that. Since moving in, Ryan had taken care of innumerable odd jobs and minor emergencies around the apartment, such as repairing the disposal, replacing leaky faucet washers and unsticking her bedroom window, all without being asked. Just the night before, when the water heater had gone on the fritz, he had somehow gotten it working again. Last Sunday when she had gone to drive her car around the block, as she did every few days to keep the battery charged, it had been dead as a doornail, and Ryan had hooked up cables to his rental car and jump-started it.

Gnawing on her inner lip, Cristen looked at him doubtfully. She'd be a fool to agree to the arrangement. And yet ... there *were* advantages to it.

But there are risks, too, she reminded herself. And she didn't entirely trust Ryan. Or yourself, a little voice prodded.

"If I agree—" Cristen raised her hand to quell Jennifer's cry of delight and fixed Ryan with a stern look. "Mind you, I said *if* I agree ... do you promise to behave yourself? No heavy passes or seduction scenes?"

Ryan managed a look of affronted innocence. "Have I stepped out of line, even once, since I've been staying here?"

"Well ... no."

He hadn't. She'd been braced for it, but he had thrown her for a loop by acting the perfect gentleman. It had been unnerving, like waiting for the other shoe to drop. It had also made her feel like a fool. And worse, his sterling behavior hadn't in the least stopped her from being aware of him, from feeling all prickly and tense—and yes, excited—whenever he was near.

"And we've gotten along well, haven't we?"

"Yes." She looked at him askance, her narrowed gaze suspicious and a bit surly. If anything, too well. Ryan, blast his hide, had been the perfect houseguest: amiable, considerate, helpful, maddeningly neat. He hadn't said or done a single thing she could complain about.

"Then there's really no reason why we shouldn't share this apartment, is there?"

"Well . . ." Cristen nibbled on her thumbnail, her forehead furrowed. Put that way, it did make a lot of sense. It was tempting. Very temp—

Lordy, Cristen! Are you nuts? she demanded, giving herself a mental shake. I can't believe you're even considering this crazy plan. Not an hour ago you were bustin' your buns to get him out of here. And you know why too.

She hated to admit it, even to herself, but she had actually begun to enjoy having Ryan around. Even worse, she missed him during those times when he was in California, and she looked forward to Friday evenings when he returned. It was fear of that growing attachment that had spurred her frantic efforts to find him an apartment of his own.

If you've got a lick of sense, you'll give him an emphatic, irrevocable, unconditional no, she told herself firmly. "Look, Ryan, it just won't work."

"Why not? There's no law that says a man and woman can't share the same roof without being sexually intimate. After all, we're both mature adults. We should be able to handle it. At least I can." He gave her a guileless look. "Of course, if you feel you just couldn't keep your hands off me . . ."

"What? Don't flatter yourself, O'Malley! You're about as much threat to my self-control as . . . as a three-hundred-pound eunuch."

"Then there's no reason we can't be roommates."

"None whatever," Cristen declared recklessly. It was a good arrangement for both of them, she told herself, ignoring the sudden tightness in her chest. And as Ryan had pointed out, they were adults. She was perfectly capable of curbing her wayward reactions. It was all a matter of adjustment. And attitude.

"Great." Ryan rubbed his palms together. "So we've got a deal, right?"

"As long as you understand the ground rules."

"Which are?"

"We share the work, don't interfere in each other's life, and..."

His brows bobbed up at her stern expression. "And?"

"And *no* funny stuff."

A slow grin spread over his face. "I swear to you, Cristen, that whatever happens between us will be only what you want to happen."

Cristen frowned. It wasn't exactly the assurance she was looking for, but there didn't seem to be any way to complain without appearing foolish.

Before Jennifer's squeals of delight had died away Cristen was having second thoughts, but Ryan didn't give her a chance to voice them. With the speed and command of a general mustering his troops, he took charge, turning his attention and their energies to getting his daughter moved.

Within an hour he had contacted his friends in New York and arranged for Jennifer to stay with them. By that evening he and Jennifer had paid off her bills at the various stores in town, sold her car, picked up her clothes from the cleaners and closed her bank account. The next day Cristen helped her pack her things, and at eight that evening she and Ryan put the excited girl on a plane bound for Kennedy Airport, where the Jordans would be waiting.

It wasn't until then, when Cristen found herself standing beside Ryan at the observation window of the terminal, watching the plane grow steadily smaller against the

dusky eastern sky, that she began to fully comprehend just
what she had agreed to.

Before, there had always been Jennifer's ebullient presence to defray the tension between them. Even when she
had not been around, it had been felt.

But now—now there's just the two of us, Cristen
thought in growing panic as she walked back through the
terminal beside Ryan. All the way to the parking garage he
talked about Jennifer, happy for her one minute and voic-
ing typical parental concern the next. Cristen barely heard
him. She was too acutely conscious of his hand resting on
the small of her back, the occasional brush of his body as
he guided her through the throng of people. The merest
touch seemed to burn right through her clothing.

When they were both seated in the car, Ryan turned to
her before starting the engine. "Is there anyplace you'd
like to go, anything you need to do before we go home?"

Home. The word started a fluttering in Cristen's stomach. Why did it sound so much more intimate now? "No,
thank you."

Nodding, Ryan flicked the ignition key and drove out of
the garage.

Dusk deepened into night, and the lights along the freeway flickered on. Unconsciously digging her fingers into
her soft leather purse, Cristen stared out the side window
as Ryan guided the rented Continental through the speed-
ing traffic. With every monotonous *thump-thump* of the
tires on the sectioned paving her nerves wound tighter.

She glanced at Ryan out of the corner of her eye. His
shadowy profile was lit by the glow from the dash, his
expression serious and intent. Since leaving the airport
behind he had fallen silent. She wondered if he was thinking about Jennifer.

Or about what would happen when they got home.

Oh, stop it, you ninny! she told herself severely. Nothing's going to happen. Absolutely nothing. You have an agreement. And it's not as though the man hasn't slept under your roof before. The only difference is that now he'll be occupying Jennifer's old room.

Despite the bracing lecture, which lasted all the way home, Cristen's nerves were stretched tight as a drum when they stepped inside the apartment.

From her customary place on the back of the sofa, Theda looked up and meowed expectantly, but Cristen walked by without even looking at her. Huffily, the cat leaped to the floor and wound herself around Ryan's ankles.

"I think it's time for some loving, don't you?" Ryan murmured throatily, and Cristen jumped as if a firecracker had suddenly exploded under her feet.

"What!" She spun around, bristling with outrage, but her furious expression froze, then grew slack with mortification at the sight of Ryan, squatted down on his haunches, stroking the sinuously twining cat. "Oh. I, uh, I thought..."

Ryan looked up and cocked one brow. Blue eyes twinkling, he watched the scalding color rise up her neck and flood her face. The sable mustache twitched. "You thought what?"

Cristen wanted to hit him. He knew exactly what she had thought, darn him. And he was enjoying her discomfort.

She lifted her chin. "I thought I'd make some coffee," she said in a crisp voice that dared him to so much as hint otherwise. "Would you like some?"

Ryan gave Theda one last scratch behind the ears and rose to his feet. "No, thanks. I have some papers I need to go over, and then I think I'll have an early night." He moved past her, and as he reached the hall door he turned and winked. "See you in the morning. And don't forget to lock up."

Cristen's jaw sagged. Standing in the middle of the floor as though turned to stone, she stared after him.

It took even longer than usual for the discordant din of the alarm to drag Cristen awake the next morning, mainly because of the hours she'd spent tossing and turning. Sprawled on her stomach, her body as limp as a wet rag, her hair a wild tangle, her white shorty nightgown bunched up around her shoulders, she instinctively tried to shut out the raucous clanging by burrowing under the pillow. The maneuver failed, as it did every morning. Groaning, she flung the pillow aside and hauled herself out of bed.

Following her usual semicomatose routine, she stumbled to the dresser with her eyes closed and patted her hand along its surface in search of the shrilling clock. On the third slap her fingers splashed into something cold and wet.

Cristen started, and her heavy lids fluttered open. A squat glass filled with orange juice sat beside the clock, and four fingers of her right hand were immersed up to the second knuckle in the sticky liquid.

For a second she stared dumbly at the absurd sight. Then her face scrunched up in a disgusted grimace. "Oh, yeeeck!" She jerked her fingers out of the juice and slung her hand, which only succeeded in dotting the bureau with a spray of drops. Growling, she snatched a wad of tissues from the box on the dresser and dabbed at the mess.

The alarm clock continued its relentless shrill.

"Oh, will you *shut up*!" Cristen snarled, giving it a whack with her free hand. Miraculously, her aim was good, and the cacophony ended with startling suddenness.

She tossed the damp tissues into the wastebasket and wiped her sticky fingers with a fresh one. It was then that the sounds coming from the bathroom registered. Running water and... Cristen's head whipped around, her eyes growing steadily wider. And *whistling*!

Her suspicious gaze slid from the bathroom door to the squat glass, then back. "Why, that—"

With another frustrated growl, she snatched up the glass and marched toward the closed door. She stormed into the bathroom without knocking, flinging the door open with such force that it banged against the wall.

In the mirror above the sink, Ryan's calm gaze met her fiery one. The hand holding the razor paused only momentarily before raking another swath through the lather that coated his cheek. "Good morning." The dark mustache kicked up at the corners. Below it his teeth were a white slash.

"Just what is this?" Cristen demanded, slamming the glass down on the counter.

Ryan glanced at it, then tipped his head back and drew the razor up the underside of his jaw in long, smooth strokes, expertly removing lather and whiskers. "Looks like orange juice."

"And how did it get onto my dresser?"

"I put it there." He grinned as he held the safety razor under the running water. "But you don't have to thank me. It was no trouble."

"Thank—" Cristen sputtered, her mouth opening and closing like a banked fish's. "Listen, you," she finally managed, "I'll thank you to stay out of my room. And you can take your orange juice and—"

"Ah-ah-ah, watch your mouth," Ryan admonished, his eyes dancing wickedly.

"—stick it in your ear," she continued pugnaciously. "I don't need it, and I don't want it."

She was the picture of outraged femininity, face flushed, eyes snapping, her tousled auburn hair almost crackling with temper. Taking it in, Ryan grinned.

"Oh, but you do. I'll admit you're gorgeous when you're angry, but a glass of juice first thing in the morning would perk you up, and you wouldn't be such a grouch." Turning back to the mirror, he whistled softly through his teeth while he wielded the razor over the other side of his face.

"I am *not* a grouch," Cristen insisted with cool hauteur. She immediately spoiled the effect by screeching, "And if you don't knock off that whistling, I swear I'm going to punch you right in the mouth!"

Ryan rinsed the remaining dabs of shaving cream from his face and blotted it with a towel. Over its damp folds, his amused gaze speared Cristen. "I'll make you a deal. I'll stop whistling if you'll drink the juice every morning. How's that?"

"What! No way! If you—"

"Come on, Cris. If we're going to live together, we've got to compromise. And what's a little glass of juice, after all?"

She eyed him sulkily, knowing he was right but loath to admit it. Finally, her mouth twisting, she muttered, "Oh, all right. But you leave it in here. No more traipsing in and out of my room. You got that?"

"Sure. Whatever you say. But you will drink it, won't you?"

"Yes, I'll drink the darned stuff."

"That's my girl." Holding an end of the damp towel in each hand, he looped it around her neck and pulled her close.

Alarm bells began to clang in Cristen's mind. She stared at his furry chest and felt her whole body flush as it hit her that, except for the towel draped dangerously low around his hips, Ryan was naked, and that she had carried on the entire argument dressed in nothing but a shorty see-through nightgown.

Cristen made an agonized little sound, but before she could move Ryan tipped up her chin and placed his mouth on hers.

The kiss was incredibly soft and tender and filled with a searing heat that shimmered through her and made her toes curl against the cool floor tiles.

It was over before she could summon the slightest protest. Ryan lifted his head slightly and smiled down into her bemused face. "That was just to seal our pact, you understand."

He dropped another quick peck on her mouth and gave her cheek a pat. "The bathroom's all yours. I'll have breakfast ready in twenty minutes, so shake a leg." He winked at her and headed for the door at the opposite end of the bathroom.

Chapter Six

Wait! Darn it, O'Malley! I don't even eat breakfast!"

But it was too late. By the time she had recovered her senses enough to protest, the door had clicked shut behind him.

For several minutes Cristen stood rooted to the spot, torn between fury and laughter. That devil! How did he always manage to charm her? She had stormed in here with every intention of tearing a strip off his hide, so angry she'd been about to burst. She touched her lips gently with her fingertips and shook her head in wonder. Instead, she'd ended up agreeing to do exactly what he wanted, and getting kissed senseless in the bargain.

Embarrassed color flooded her cheeks when she turned and caught sight of her reflection in the bathroom mirror. The short nightie left almost nothing to the imagination. The embroidered ruffle hem barely reached the tops of her thighs. Beneath the silky white material, her breasts jutted impudently, her nipples' areolae dusty rose. Cristen's gaze slid downward, a distressed groan escaping her as she followed the veiled curves of midriff, waist and hips to the minuscule bikini panties. Above the opaque triangle, her navel was a provocative shadowed indentation.

Dear heaven! She couldn't believe she'd barged in on Ryan looking like an escapee from an X-rated movie.

Not that he hadn't already seen her in the scandalous nightie. Cristen's gaze lit on the glass of juice, and her color deepened. A shiver raced through her, and her insides fluttered wildly at the thought of Ryan entering her room while she slept. Given the way she practically went into a coma when sleep claimed her, there was no telling what position she'd been in. Or what had been exposed.

"Well, there's no point in worrying about it now." Cristen pushed the embarrassing image aside and reached for the glass of juice, then hesitated. She looked at it sourly and shuddered. The thought of putting anything but coffee into her stomach before ten o'clock in the morning was revolting. Slyly, her glance went from the glass to Ryan's door, then back. She could just pour it down the sink. Her fingers moved closer to the glass, then jerked back.

"No, you can't, Cristen," she told herself in utter disgust. "A bargain is a bargain." Though the idea rankled, Cristen knew that Ryan was right. If the crazy living arrangement was going to work, they would both have to compromise.

Scowling at her reflection, she snatched up the juice and chugged it down. If she were smart, though, she thought, shuddering again, no matter how much she enjoyed frilly, naughty lingerie, she would make a drastic change in her style of nightwear, at least during the weeks when Ryan was in residence.

* * *

The delicious smell of freshly brewed coffee and frying bacon assailed Cristen the moment she stepped from her room. It had been her intention to skip even her usual morning coffee, but the tantalizing aromas drew her toward the kitchen as though she were in a hypnotic trance.

She pushed through the door, took two steps and stopped abruptly, her mouth going dry at the sight of Ryan.

Barefoot, his hair still tousled, he was standing at the stove, turning bacon with a fork. His sole article of clothing was a pair of frayed, faded cutoffs that rode low on his narrow hips. The soft denim molded his buttocks and manhood with indecent familiarity, the faded material worn almost white at revealing stress points.

He flashed a grin when he looked up and saw her. "Hi. This will be ready in about a minute."

Cristen forced her legs to carry her across the kitchen. "Don't bother cooking any for me. I never eat breakfast." She filled a mug with coffee and took two scalding sips before turning to lean back against the counter.

"Nonsense. Breakfast is the most important meal of the day."

"Fine. Then you eat it. I don't like breakfast, I don't want breakfast and I'm not going to eat breakfast." Actually, the slug of juice had whetted her appetite. Not only was her stomach growling—the delicious cooking aromas were driving her crazy—but Cristen figured she had done enough compromising for one morning. It was Ryan's turn. Besides, he had to learn that he could push her just so far.

Ryan studied her determined expression and after a moment shrugged, his crooked smile kicking his mustache up at one corner. "Suit yourself."

He turned back to the stove and lifted the bacon onto a platter lined with paper towels. Deftly, using only one hand, he picked up two eggs, cracked them open on the edge of a skillet and dropped them in. They sizzled and popped in the bubbling butter while he jiggled the pan expertly. The broad, flat muscles in his back stirred with the slight movements.

Cristen tried not to look at him, but his nearly bare body drew her fascinated gaze like the relentless pull of the moon on the tides. Her yellow linen dress was light and casual, but his brief attire made her feel conspicuously overdressed . . . and uncomfortably hot.

Swallowing hard, Cristen tracked his spine downward. His back was smooth and bronze to a point several inches below his waist, where a line of white showed above the low-slung waistband. Below it, the tight rounded flesh flexed with every shift of his feet. A long ravel dangling from the frayed bottom of his cutoffs swung constantly, drawing her attention to his legs. They were long and heavily muscled, the skin tanned beneath the dusting of short dark hair. As she stared at him Cristen felt her body grow warmer, her nipples tighten against their lacy confinement.

Oh, Lord, he's a beautifully made man, she thought a bit desperately. Big and lean and powerful. And sexy as all get-out.

Dragging her gaze away from Ryan's body, Cristen gulped another swallow of coffee. Her heart thudded so hard that her chest hurt.

Ryan lifted the eggs onto a plate and set it and the platter of bacon on the table. "Sure you don't want any? There's plenty."

"No, thank you."

He shrugged and went back for the toast, making a detour by the refrigerator for the jam. His bare feet made faint slapping noises on the tile floor.

Just when she thought he would settle down and eat his breakfast, he stepped closer. "Excuse me. I need another cup of coffee." Smiling apologetically, he reached around her.

Cristen found herself staring at his hairy chest, which was only inches from her nose. Trying not to look at the tiny brown nipples nestled in the shiny thatch, she lowered her gaze, but then it settled on his navel and the enticing whorl of silky black hair that surrounded it and arrowed downward toward . . .

Groaning silently, Cristen jerked her gaze upward and pressed back against the counter. Her heart pounded, and her thighs seem to liquefy. With every shallow breath her senses were assaulted by the seductive scents of soap and after-shave and male flesh. His body heat seemed to surround her, scorching right through her clothes, and when his leg brushed against her she jumped as if she'd been scalded.

"*Must* you run around like that?" she snapped.

He stepped back and gave her a blank look. "Like what?"

"Like *what*? Great gobs of goose grease! You're practically naked, that's what!"

He glanced down as though surprised. "Oh. Does it bother you?"

"Of course it bothers me. How would you like it if I ran around in next to noth—" She broke off at the lecherous delight on Ryan's face, appalled by her blunder. "Never mind. Don't answer that." She gave him a withering look. "You know what I mean."

Ryan chuckled. "Yeah, I know. Look, I'm sorry. I'm used to being casual when I'm at home. I'll just go slip on a shirt."

At the door he stopped and looked back at her, a quizzical half smile on his face. "Goose grease?" He shook his head. "Did anyone ever tell you that you have a very, uh, *quaint* way of cussing? Not to mention colorful."

A faint blush tinted Cristen's face, and she sent him an abashed look. "My mother always abhorred bad language. As a kid, whenever I swore she washed my mouth out with soap." She shrugged, and her mouth twisted in a wry grimace. "So I invented substitutes. To this day, whenever I even think of a genuine curse word I can taste soap."

"I see. Well, that explains it." Chuckling, he disappeared through the doorway.

Cristen stared after him, his willingness to cooperate taking her by surprise. After her complaint about his attire, she had expected him to come back with some sexual innuendo, or at the very least tease her about being prudish.

A pleased smile curved her lips as she turned and reached for the coffeepot. Maybe, just maybe, this arrangement might work out, after all.

The slap of bare feet on the floor announced Ryan's return. Lifting her mug from the counter, Cristen turned back. "Well, you were certainly quick, I must say. I—" She stopped abruptly at the sight of him, her smile wilting and her eyes growing steadily wider.

Ryan was wearing a cropped black T-shirt that barely reached his midriff. It was faded and full of holes, and the bottom edge was so jagged that it looked as if it had been whacked off with a pair of hedge trimmers. If that weren't bad enough, emblazoned across his chest in big red letters were the words, SEX IS A MISDEMEANOR: DE MORE I MISS, DE MEANOR I GET.

"Well? How's this?" Ryan tugged on the tattered lower edge of the disreputable shirt and grinned at her like a small boy who fully expected a pat on the head.

Cristen deposited her cup on the counter with a thud and stomped toward the door. "Don't ask. Believe me, you don't want to know."

Louise was pleased over Ryan's offer of help, but as Jennifer had predicted, she was ecstatic to learn that he was Cristen's new roommate.

"That's terrific! He's perfect for you. Absolutely perfect!"

"Louise! I'm sharing my apartment with the man, not my bed."

"But you *are* living with him."

"Yes, but it's strictly platonic. A business arrangement. And even at that, he'll only be here every other week."

A Cheshire cat grin spread over Louise's plump face. "Well, at least that's a start," she said complacently.

Cristen threw her hands into the air and gave up. She knew it was useless to try to convince Louise that there was nothing going on between her and Ryan. Louise was going to believe what she wanted to believe. Besides . . . Cristen wasn't entirely convinced herself.

She wanted to believe that nothing was going on— needed to believe it for her own peace of mind—but Ryan was such a virile, sensual hunk that there was no way she could be indifferent to him. And she knew, deep down, that for their arrangement to work she would have to maintain a distance, develop a certain amount of detachment. She could not afford to think of Ryan as a man. An attractive... sexy... fascinating... interesting... eligible man.

It isn't fair, she lamented silently as she labored over the parquet floors in the miniature Victorian mansion. Why couldn't he have been old and fat and bald? Or at the very least, nondescript and dull? Why did he have to be such a teasing, tormenting, thoroughly appealing rascal?

Cristen tried to put Ryan out of her mind, but it was impossible. All day long, whenever she thought of their encounter that morning, she was torn between anger and arousal. Both reactions worried her.

Blaming her fretting on the strangeness of the situation, she told herself that once they adjusted, once the newness of it wore off, things would settle down. Nevertheless, she entered the apartment warily that evening. She wasn't sure what kind of greeting to expect, but certainly not the exuberant one she received from Ryan.

He came bounding out of the kitchen the moment she opened the door, a glass of milk in one hand and a cookie in the other. "Cristen! Great, you're home! I thought you'd never get here."

"What is it? What's wrong?"

"Nothing. Everything's terrific. But, man, have I got something to show you." He polished off the cookie in two bites and chugalugged the milk, then put the glass down on the end table and grabbed her hand. "C'mon, let's go."

"What? Go where?" Cristen hung back as he dragged her toward the door. "Wait a minute. Where are you taking me?"

"You'll see," he said mysteriously.

His grin was white and wide, and his eyes sparkled with anticipation. Cristen eyed him dubiously, especially when he led her into the elevator and pushed the button for the underground garage. She tried to recall all the bracing lectures she had given herself about keeping a distance between them, but his enthusiasm was difficult to resist. She had never seen him quite like this before. He was about to burst with eagerness and excitement.

Though she tried to tug her hand free, Ryan maintained his hold all during the elevator ride, and when the door slid open he hauled her along with him.

"It's right over here," he announced as he blazed a path through the rows of cars in the parking garage. Several times Cristen had to break into a trot to keep up with his rapid, ground-eating stride. Finally he came to a halt and turned to her, beaming like a kid on Christmas morning. He flung his arm wide with a flourish. "Well, there she is. What do you think?"

"She" was a low-slung, wicked-looking sports car. Cristen stared at it, not quite sure what to say. Cars, to her, were akin to alien creatures: strange and mysterious and a bit scary. She knew very little about them and cared less. She couldn't even tell one make from another unless she was close enough to read the manufacturer's emblem. But it didn't take a car buff to recognize that this was a mean machine, the kind every male dreamed of owning.

It was a metallic green, so dark that it was almost black, its lines long and sleek and slightly menacing. Just sitting there, it gave the impression of leashed power, a crouched jungle beast poised to pounce.

Cristen gave Ryan a vague smile. "It's, uh, very nice."

"Nice!" He looked mortally wounded. "Good Lord, woman! How can you say that? A two-week vacation is 'nice.' A warm fire is 'nice.' An ice cream sundae is 'nice,' for heaven's sake! What this car is, is great! Fabulous! One in a million!"

"Uh, yes. I'm sure it is," Cristen mumbled. His affronted tone struck her as comical, but she didn't dare laugh, or even smile, because she knew that for once Ryan was perfectly serious. Trying her best to appear interested, she asked, "What is it?"

"What *is it*?" He looked as though a puff of wind could knock him over, he was so stunned. "Geez, Cristen, I can't believe you don't know. This is a vintage 1975 Jaguar, for the love of Mike!"

How fitting, she thought, eyeing its sleek lines. "I didn't know they rented those."

"It's not rented. I bought it this morning. I figured, since I'm going to be here so much of the time, it would be better to have my own transportation. Anyway, I've always wanted a Jag."

He ran a caressing hand along the car's roof. "This baby'll go from zero to one hundred in just a fraction over fifteen seconds."

"That's ni—uh, wonderful."

Ryan climbed in behind the wheel and proceeded to point out dials and gauges and rattle off names that made Cristen go glassy eyed. Then he rushed around to the front of the car, threw up a hood that looked about half a block long and started tossing out words like *rpm* and *gear ratio* and *synchromesh transmission*.

Cristen smiled and nodded her way through the discourse, but for all she understood he might as well have been speaking Swahili.

Finally he slammed the hood shut, and she watched, dazed, as he took a clean handkerchief from the back pocket of his trousers and lovingly buffed off his smudged fingerprints. Then, circling the car, he launched into a lengthy dissertation on aerodynamics and wind resistance.

Cristen tuned out his words but, watching him, her amazement grew steadily. She had never been able to understand men's fascination with what was, essentially, a pile of metal and rubber. It was ridiculous the way they carried on. Heavens! She'd seen new fathers show less pride in their offspring.

Still, she admitted reluctantly, an indulgent smile tugging at her mouth as she watched Ryan's lips move, there was something endearing about his enthusiasm.

"...but of course, to fully appreciate what it can do, you have to experience it firsthand." His grin was boyish and eager, and Cristen blinked as his words slowly sank in. "So what do you say? Wanta go for a quick spin?"

"I...sure. As long as I don't have to drive."

"Are you kidding? Honey, don't you know that a man's car is his second most prized possession?"

He wasted no time hustling her into the passenger seat, then hurried around to the other side and slid in behind the wheel. As they fastened their seat belts Cristen slanted him a curious look.

"Second, huh? What's number one?"

With a flick of the ignition key the powerful engine roared to life, then settled down to a deep-throated purr. Ryan fixed Cristen with an intent look. His teeth gleamed white in the shadowy interior as a slow, sensual grin curved his mouth, and she felt her stomach give a little lurch. "Why, his woman, of course. And he guards both jealously."

His choice of words and the husky pitch of his voice sent a sharp little thrill through Cristen, and she looked away in confusion.

Ryan put the car into gear and stepped on the accelerator, sending the crouched vehicle leaping forward like the dangerous, snarling jungle cat for which it was named.

The minute they hit the streets Ryan let out a whoop of sheer joy and headed for the freeway, his mood as effervescent as fine champagne. The moment of intense sexual tension in the garage might never have happened.

The rush hour was over, and they zipped easily through the traffic. Once on the Southwest Freeway they were out of the city in a matter of minutes, and Ryan poured on the gas. Though he drove fast, he handled the powerful car with a sureness and control that inspired confidence. Wrapped in the sheer luxury of the opulent interior, Cristen settled back on the cream-colored, buttery soft leather seat to enjoy the exhilarating ride. Before long, caught up in Ryan's infectious mood, she added her laughter to his.

"Boy, this baby can go!" Ryan pronounced gleefully, flashing Cristen a broad grin as they approached Sugar Land. "And she handles like a dream."

His high spirits drew another indulgent chuckle from his passenger. "Yes, I'm sure. But unless you want to pay a bodacious fine, you'd better turn around before we get to Richmond," she advised. "The police there take a dim view of going even so much as a mile over the speed limit."

"Spoilsport," Ryan grumbled, shooting her a look of mock annoyance, but at the next exit he made a U-turn under the freeway and headed back. In a disappointingly short time they were pulling back into the condo's parking garage.

Before Cristen could unbuckle her seat belt, Ryan bounded out of the car and around to her side. He opened the passenger door and reached for her. Cristen swung her legs out and grasped his hands, and he practically lifted her from the ground-hugging vehicle.

"Well, what did you think?" Still holding her hands, his brows cocked expectantly, he waited for her reply.

His eagerness and sheer delight were both amusing and, somehow, strangely touching. Cristen smiled back at him. "I think it's a great car. Absolutely wonderful."

The grin that lit Ryan's face was incandescent. "Hot damn! It is, isn't it!" he hooted. In a burst of enthusiasm, he grasped Cristen's waist, lifted her high against his chest and whirled her around and around.

"Ryaaannnnn!" Laughing and squealing his name at the same time, Cristen clutched his shoulders and held on for dear life.

It was a wild, exuberant dance that made Cristen feel giddy, her head spinning as the world dipped and twirled around her. Ryan's baritone laughter mingled with her higher-pitched giggles and bounced loudly through the cavernous garage.

As the mad whirl ended and Ryan loosened his hold, letting Cristen slide to the floor, it seemed the most natural thing in the world for him to kiss her.

The action cut off Cristen's laughter in midgiggle and stunned her rigid. Her eyes went wide. Her hands jerked from his shoulders and hovered above them in midair, fingers spread.

"Mmmmmmm." The sound of sheer delight rumbled from Ryan as his lips rocked over hers. The kiss, like the impulsive spin, was enthusiastic and wholehearted. Hard and hungry and joyous.

It was also warm and wonderful. Cristen strained to resist its drugging allure, but after a moment her hovering hands balled into tight fists, then flexed open. Giving a moan of surrender, she relaxed within Ryan's embrace, wound her arms around his neck and clasped his head, burying her spread fingers in his dark hair.

His mouth was firm and persuasive, his mustache a tickling enticement. With gentle strokes his tongue probed and coaxed at the fragile barrier of her lips. They flowered open, and Cristen's shuddering sigh drifted into his mouth as he deepened the kiss.

You've got to stop this, she told herself even as she gloried in the feel and the scent and the taste of him. This is foolish. Insane. If you've got an ounce of sense, you'll get a grip on yourself and step away.

But she couldn't. Not yet. The sharply sweet sensations held her spellbound.

She felt on fire, burning, consumed by a delicious ache. A hunger she couldn't control drove her on, and for that brief, mindless moment she let herself go, giving in to the demands of her yearning flesh. She kissed him back fervently, eagerly, delighting in the thud of his heart against her breast, the low growl of pleasure that vibrated from him. His scent was a heady delight, musky and male, his taste intoxicating. She felt as though she were drowning in endless pleasure.

A car zoomed down the ramp into the parking garage, the low purr of its engine shattering the tomblike quiet and jerking them out of their sensual haze.

Cristen stiffened and pulled back, but Ryan merely pressed his face into her neck. "R-Ryan, stop." She hunched her shoulder against his marauding kisses and turned her head aside, biting her lower lip.

Heaving a sigh, Ryan released her and took a half step back. He glanced around and gave her a rueful grin. "Sorry. I guess I got carried away."

She frowned. "You promised no seduction scenes. Remember?"

"Hey! That wasn't a seduction scene. That was just a friendly kiss." He draped his arm around her shoulders and turned her toward the elevator. "No reason to make a big deal out of it. After all, what's a little kiss between friends?"

"But—"

"Especially roomies. Now c'mon. I put a chicken in the oven before you got home. It should be ready just about now."

Surprised and confused, Cristen looked up at him as he nudged her into the elevator. "You cooked dinner?"

"Sure. You said we'd share the work. Besides, I enjoy cooking. I also picked up some groceries."

Cristen stared straight ahead, her thoughts in a jumble. She felt strange, disoriented, reeling like someone who has just stepped off an out-of-control merry-go-round. How could he be so ardent one minute and so blasé the next? Out of the corner of her eye she glanced suspiciously at his too innocent face. Had that kiss really been just a casual buss between friends to him? If so, she was in deep trouble, because *her* knees still felt like mush, for heaven's sake. If that was all it was, she'd hate to see him when he was on the make.

Chapter Seven

Little men with hobnail boots were stomping around inside her head, chipping away with pickaxes. Fiends, every one.

Elbows propped on her worktable, eyes closed, Cristen massaged her forehead and temples with her fingertips. If they didn't stop soon, they were going to excavate right through.

The carpenters hammering away next door didn't help any. Even so, Cristen was glad that the alterations were under way at last. If everything went as planned, they would knock out the wall in a few days.

"Do you have another headache?"

"Uh-uh." Cristen looked up at Louise with pain-glazed eyes. "Same one. The aspirin I took earlier is wearing off."

"Maybe you ought to see a doctor."

"It's just a headache. It'll go away."

Besides, Cristen didn't need a doctor to tell her what was causing her headache. She had the answer to that in one word: Ryan.

"Well, if you won't see a doctor, you at least ought to go home and go to bed. All this racket can't be helping any."

"I'll be fine, Louise. Don't fuss."

Louise gave a disgusted snort. "Mule stubborn, that's what you are," she muttered, stomping off.

Cristen sighed and lowered her head once more, her fingertips resuming their rotating movements. She had been a fool to think she would become inured to Ryan with time. Whoever said that familiarity breeds contempt was full of sheep dip. Either that, or he'd never met an Irish charmer by the name of O'Malley.

Cristen sighed again. It was all so confusing. On the surface, everything seemed to be working out just great. Certainly Ryan was sticking to his part of the bargain. Since that impulsive kiss in the garage, over a month before, he had not stepped out of line in any way.

Except for teasing you whenever he gets a chance, she amended. And there's no use kidding yourself, you even like that. Cristen groaned and rubbed her temples harder. Which just goes to show how far gone you are, you silly twit.

In truth, Ryan had not done anything objectionable. If anything, he was as close as you could get to a perfect roommate: friendly and casual, pleasant to be around, helpful, amusing. He was neat and clean and had no disgusting habits, unless one counted whistling before seven in the morning, and, true to his word, he'd stopped that, thank the Lord.

The problem was the direction their relationship was taking, the feeling of closeness, of intimacy, that was developing between them.

And she suspected that Ryan was deliberately promoting it.

Cristen had tried to remain aloof, but it was difficult. How could she be cool to a man who had a hot, delicious meal ready when she came home from work? Who left a steaming mug of coffee and a glass of juice for her in the bathroom every morning? Who did the dishes when it wasn't even his turn, just because he knew she was dead tired? Who went out to pick up a newspaper and returned with a bouquet of fresh daisies?

And then there were the little things, the subtle things: his toothbrush next to hers, his shaving cream and razor and cologne sitting on the cabinet shelf beside her body lotion and talc, his terry-cloth robe hanging on the back of the bathroom door, his favorite brand of beer in the refrigerator, those sports magazines on the coffee table . . . his name beneath her own on the mailbox.

Intimacy without intimacy.

But most disturbing of all was that mixture of contentment and excitement she felt whenever he was around. Cristen found Ryan wildly attractive and sexy, but she also enjoyed his company, their moments of quiet conversation, their companionable silences, even their occasional sparring.

She had thought she would be grateful for those times when he was in California, but instead she was lonely and at loose ends and found herself working longer hours just to avoid going home to an empty apartment. Yet when he was there she was torn between the pleasure she took in his company and fear that he was becoming too important to her. Too necessary.

Living with Ryan was making her crazy!

From next door came the high-pitched whine of a power saw, then the clatter of a piece of lumber hitting the floor. The hammering started up again, but an instant later all other noise was drowned out by the shuddering grind of an electric sander.

An open can of soda sat on the corner of the worktable, its lower half beaded with condensation. Cristen picked it up and rolled it over her forehead.

And worrying about living with Ryan was giving her headaches.

Ryan was due to fly in from California that evening. As the hours passed, anxiety and anticipation drew Cristen's nerves tighter and tighter. The pounding in her head became excruciating. By midafternoon Louise put her foot down.

"That's it. I'm tired of watching you suffer. You're going home," her partner pronounced in a tone that dared Cristen to argue. Though a good eight inches shorter than Cristen, Louise grasped her arm, lifted her out of the chair and all but frog-marched her toward the door. "Right this minute. And I'm taking you."

"Louise! You can't! The store—"

"Dora can take care of the store until I get back. It won't take but fifteen minutes, at most. Now don't argue. You're going home and going to bed, and that's final!"

"Dora?" Cristen wailed, horrified.

But there was no arguing with Louise when her mothering instincts were aroused. Within minutes she'd brought her car to a stop at the entrance to Cristen's condo.

"Are you sure you don't want me to come up with you?"

"No, no. I'll be fine." Opening her eyes to mere slits, Cristen raised her head off the back of the seat and groped for the door handle. "You just hurry back to the store before Dora pulls one of her crazy stunts."

Louise chuckled. "Come on, Cris. What could she do in fifteen minutes?"

"Who knows? Last week she suggested that I spray paint a Queen Anne dining table pink. She'd seen one in a Barbie dollhouse that she thought was cute."

"Oh, Lord. I'm surprised you didn't attack her." Louise heaved a despairing sigh and shook her head. "I swear, sometimes I think the only taste that girl has is in her mouth."

Cristen grunted and climbed from the car with exaggerated care, shielding her eyes against the bright afternoon sun with her cupped palm.

"Now you go straight to bed," Louise called after her.

The admonition was unnecessary. At that moment two aspirin, a dark room and a cool cloth for her forehead sounded like heaven.

Theda glanced up from her perch on the back of the sofa and gave Cristen a curious look when she let herself into the apartment. Paying her no mind, Cristen tossed her purse onto the first horizontal surface she came to and made a beeline for her bedroom.

She was barely halfway across the living room when all hell broke loose.

Without warning the world seemed to explode in a cacophony of earsplitting noise, a raucous clangor overlaid with the blaring, scale-climbing *whoop-whoop-whoop* of a siren.

"Oh! Oh!" In mindless panic, Cristen clapped her hands over her ears and danced around, wild-eyed. She jumped up on the sofa, did a high-stepping romp over the cushions, jumped down again and turned in agitated little circles, shrieking with every breath.

At the same time, Theda shot three feet straight up into the air, yowling like a banshee. Her eyes were wild, all four legs extended, and every hair on her body was standing on end. The cat hit the sofa like a spring, and before you could blink twice, bounded to a chair, onto the floor and clawed her way up to the top of the draperies. When the racket didn't stop, she leaped to the floor again and streaked around the room, bouncing from wall to floor to wall in a furry blur.

It was pure bedlam. Between Theda's caterwauling, Cristen's hysterical screeching and the clanging, whooping alarm, the decibel level was torturous.

In the middle of the furor Cristen whacked her shin against the coffee table. Her shrieks turned to yelps of pain. She grabbed her leg, but the racket was more than she could bear. Torn between protecting her throbbing head and her throbbing shin, she alternately hopped on one foot clutching her leg and limped in circles holding her ears.

At that moment, Ryan came charging in from the hall like an attacking warrior, his bloodcurdling battle cry adding to the pandemonium. He was barefoot and bare chested, his expression wild and fierce, and in his upraised hand he wielded a bathroom plunger like a weapon.

Hysteria had Cristen by the throat, and all she saw was a half-naked man coming at her with a club. Her panic and the volume of her shrieks doubled.

Ryan skidded to a halt in the middle of the floor. His fierce expression dissolved, and his jaw dropped. He stared, dumfounded, at the sight of Cristen, running around squawking like a demented chicken, and the puffed-up, yowling ball of fur racing around the walls.

"Cristen, what the devil—" He broke off, unable to hear himself think, much less make himself heard, in the hullabaloo. He was still holding the toilet plunger aloft, and it suddenly struck him that he must resemble a comic imitation of the Statue of Liberty. Muttering a curse, he flung it aside and made a lunge for Cristen, catching her by the shoulders before she could scamper out of reach again. "Cristen, for God's sake, calm down!" he shouted, giving her a shake.

The glazed look of panic cleared from her eyes, and they widened as recognition struck her. "Ryan? Oh, Ryan!"

He saw her mouth form his name, but he couldn't hear her. "What? *What?*"

For a moment Cristen clutched him, but then she grimaced and covered her ears again.

"Oh, hell!" Ryan stalked across the room and jabbed at the panel of buttons set into the wall by the front door.

The sudden cessation of noise was as startling as the alarm had been.

Theda let out one more indignant yowl, hissed and spat and streaked out of the room, leaving the two humans staring at each other in the magnified silence.

Cristen kept her hands clapped over her ears, not at all convinced that her pounding head wouldn't roll off onto the floor if she let go. Her heart was thudding ninety to nothing, and she was breathing like a marathon runner at the finish line. She was too addled to think, but slowly, as her eyes went from Ryan to the small panel of buttons that hadn't been there that morning, it began to dawn on her that he was somehow to blame for that god-awful racket. She glared at him, her lips thinning.

"What—" She broke off, wincing at the sound of her own voice, then continued in a precise tone that was barely one notch above a whisper. "What, may I ask, was all that about?"

A sheepish look crossed Ryan's face. "That was supposed to be a surprise."

"Oh, you surprised me all right. You idiot! You darn near scared me out of ten years of my life! What *was* that?"

"A burglar alarm. The security in this building is lousy, and I was worried about your being here all alone while I'm in California. I took an early flight today so I could have it installed and working by the time you got home." He darted a sheepish look at the toilet plunger. "When you tripped it, I had just finished and was cleaning up in the bathroom, and I grabbed the closest thing at hand to use as a weapon." Ryan frowned. "What are you doing here this early, anyway? I thought someone had broken in."

"I came home because I have a headache," she said through clenched teeth. "A pounding, painful headache that now, thanks to you, has reached an excruciating level."

She bared her teeth in a saccharine smile of pure irony and limped toward the hall door. Still clutching her head, she moved with exaggerated caution, as though she were made of glass that might shatter at any moment.

"Oh, hell, sweetheart, I'm sorry. I didn't know." Ryan trotted along behind her, hovering worriedly. "Is there anything I can do? Anything I can get for you?"

"Just leave me alone, O'Malley. You've done enough."

Paying no heed, Ryan darted around her into the bedroom, threw back the bedspread and plumped her pillow, then rushed back to her side. "Here, let me help you." Slipping an arm around her, he cupped both her elbows and led her to the bed as though she were a ninety-year-old invalid.

"Ryan—"

"There now, love. Don't fret," he murmured as he eased her down onto the side of the bed. "I'll take care of you. First we'll get you out of these clothes..."

He reached around her, lowered the zipper on her dress and pushed it off her shoulders.

"Wait! Don't—" Cristen grabbed at the dress, but the silky material fell about her waist, revealing the bodice of her pink satin and ecru lace slip. Crossing her arms over her breasts, she glared at him impotently. "Now, look! I don't need—"

"... and into something comfortable," he continued, heedless of her protests. He dropped down on one knee and slipped off her shoes.

"Ryan, will you... Hey! Stop that!" She slapped at his hands as they slid up under her skirt, but Ryan deftly unfastened her garters and peeled the silky stockings down her legs.

"Okay, lift up and we'll get you out of this," he commanded gently, and she obeyed without thinking, then watched, thoroughly muddled, as he removed the dress and went to hang it in the closet. But when he returned with her lavender lace nightgown and reached for her slip straps, Cristen clapped her hands over her shoulders and glared.

"If you don't mind, I'm perfectly capable of undressing myself. I have a headache, not two broken arms." She held out her hand imperiously. "Just give me the nightgown and get out of here."

Ryan frowned dubiously, then nodded and dropped the scrap of lavender silk into her lap. "Okay, you take care of that while I get something for your headache."

Ignoring her sputtering, he marched into the bathroom. When he returned a few minutes later the pink satin slip and matching garter belt and bra were draped over a chair and Cristen was lying in bed with the sheet pulled up to her chin.

She tried to glower at him, but her head was pounding so hard that she couldn't quite manage it, and after he had doused her with aspirin she lay back and closed her eyes, sighing gratefully when he placed a cool damp cloth over her brow.

"Now you just rest," Ryan said, closing the draperies over the windows. "Take it easy and let those tablets do their job. You'll feel better in no time."

He came back to the bedside and stared down at Cristen, his eyes full of tenderness and concern. She was lying still and quiet, drifting somewhere between sleep and wakefulness, her lovely face etched with pain. Despite the shadowy dimness of the room, Ryan could see how pale she was, the fragile look about her eyes that not even the sweep of her lashes could hide. Emotion clogged his throat and swelled his chest with painful intensity. He was filled with the need to protect, to cherish, to possess.

Reaching out, he smoothed his fingertips over the silky hair at her temple and smiled, a crooked, bemused smile. The feelings were new and strange, and a little daunting. Over the years he had known and enjoyed many women. Some he'd cared for more than a little. But it had never been like this. Not anything like this.

Oh, he'd known right from the beginning that Cristen was something special, even that in her he had probably met his fate. What he hadn't known, hadn't expected, was that that first thrill of excitement and attraction would grow into something so strong, so powerful, so all-consuming—so exquisitely, painfully urgent that all else faded in importance. His business, the life he had in California—heaven help him, even his own daughter—took second place to Cristen. When he was asleep, she haunted his dreams. Awake, she occupied his thoughts, filled his heart, his very soul, with a sweet, yearning ache.

Living with her, getting to know her, had been a pure joy; not touching her, sheer torment. When he was gone he counted the days until he could return, lived for the time when he would see her again. She was his present, his future . . . his life. Lord, how he loved her.

Ryan drew in a deep breath and let it out slowly. She loved him, too—or at least she would if she'd let herself. He knew damned well she wasn't indifferent to him. But she kept fighting it.

Why? Why was she so determined to keep a distance between them? He had a hunch it was because of that ex-husband of hers, but he couldn't be sure. The times he'd tried to get her to talk about him she had very bluntly closed the door in his face. Was she still carrying a torch? Or had the marriage simply turned sour, the split-up so hurtful that she was still bitter? Though he and Ella had parted amicably, he knew that for some couples marriage was little more than open warfare, with divorce being the final battle.

Ryan sighed. Whatever the reason, her determination not to become involved was a formidable obstacle. But he'd overcome it. Eventually. If this slow courtship didn't kill him first.

He had made a little progress, but sometimes it seemed that for every step forward, he took two back. Ryan thought about the fright he'd given her with the burglar alarm and grimaced. Great going, O'Malley, he chided himself. That little number probably set things back two months.

Cristen's breathing was slow and even, but she made a little moaning sound and rocked her head back and forth on the pillow. Ryan bent and turned the damp cloth over to the cool side, and she sighed. Smiling, he let his finger-tips linger on her cheek and dropped a soft kiss on her mouth.

Fight it, my love, if you must. Sooner or later, I'll win you over. You'll find that I can be a very patient man. Especially when the stakes are this high.

"He's driving me crazy!"

"How? By being thoughtful? Come on, Cris. Putting in a burglar alarm was a very nice thing to do."

"I know. It's not that. It's ... it's ... oh, I don't know. Things just seem to be getting out of hand. Our living arrangement was supposed to be strictly business."

Louise looked up from straightening a display case of Louis XIV furniture. "You mean it's not?" she asked hopefully.

"No. I mean, yes, of course it is." Cristen grimaced, her brow furrowing. "It's just that this whole arrangement is becoming much too ... too ... cozy."

"Oh? How so?"

Since it was Saturday, the carpenters were not working. Cristen had hoped to take advantage of the quiet to get some of the more tedious work done, but she gave up trying to fit the elaborate fretwork above the arched doorway in the Victorian mansion. Sighing, she leaned back against the corner of her worktable and folded her arms across her midriff. "It's hard to explain. There's no one thing, really. It's just that there seems to be a feeling of ... closeness, intimacy almost, developing between us. And there doesn't seem to be anything I can do to prevent it."

"Ah, I see." Louise closed the glass case and moved to the next one. Over its top she gave Cristen a wicked grin.

"I knew that living with that gorgeous hunk would stir up your libido."

"Louise! That's not the problem at all," she lied. At her friend's look of patent disbelief, Cristen felt her face grow warm. "Well...not entirely," she added reluctantly, shooting her resentful glare. "What really disturbs me is, we're beginning to act like a couple instead of two people who happen to share the same roof."

Cristen thought about the way Ryan had coddled her the night before, letting her sleep off her headache, then bringing her a bowl of hot soup on a tray and insisting that she remain in bed. The way he had watched her to make sure she ate it all. It had made her feel cherished and warm. And vaguely threatened.

"Hmm. Maybe there's hope for you yet."

"Louise! Will you behave? I'm talking serious problems here."

"Okay, okay. But I think you're blowing this all out of proportion. I mean, how intimate can you get without actually becoming lovers?"

"Plenty. One day last week I hand washed all my lingerie and hung it in the bathroom. When I got home I found that Ryan had folded it and put it away. Do you have any idea how unsettling that was?"

"Probably not nearly as unsettling as it was for Ryan," Louise hooted. "Considering your penchant for sexy unmentionables. Anyway, you can't blame a guy for not wanting to fight his way through a forest of stockings and teddies every time he goes into the bathroom. And you told me yourself that he's a very neat person."

Cristen released her breath in a long sigh. "Yes, he's neat," she agreed in a soft, reflective voice. "And considerate. And helpful." Pensive, she plucked absently at a loose thread hanging from a button on her work smock.

"Fun to be with." She wound the thread around her finger and tugged, and the button hit the floor and rolled way. Paying it no mind, Cristen stared across the shop. "Did you know that whenever Ryan is in town and I work late, he's always waiting outside to walk me home?"

Louise's face softened at the wistful note in Cristen's voice. "No, I didn't. Does that bother you?"

"Yes."

"Why? Because you're attracted to him?"

"Yes. No!" Cristen glared, but Louise merely cocked her head and waited. "All right. Yes, I am attracted," she snapped after a moment. "But I don't want to be!"

Louise fought back a grin at her belligerent tone. "Why not?"

"Oh, Louise. There are all kinds of reasons why not."

"Name one."

"All right." Giving her friend an exasperated look, Cristen raised her hand and ticked off on her fingers: "One, he's light-years ahead of me in experience; two, we're totally different; three, the man's a footloose bachelor. He's probably left a string of broken hearts from here to California, and I have no intention of becoming his latest conquest."

"And suppose he's serious?" Louise asked gently. "Suppose this time he wants love and marriage? Commitment?"

Stark vulnerability etched Cristen's features. Longing and despair mingled in her eyes, creating a sheen of moisture that she hastily blinked away. Her lower lip quivered ever so slightly, and she clamped her teeth over it and looked away, holding her head high. "I . . . it wouldn't matter. I've already tried marriage. It's not for me."

"I see. Well then, you'd better do something to shake up that cozy little routine you two have going."

"Like what?"

Louise pursed her lips thoughtfully. "Does Ryan ever go out with other women?"

The question sent a wave of something very like pain through Cristen, but she squashed it at once. "No. Occasionally he gets calls from a woman, but he says she's his secretary." More than once Cristen had wondered about the owner of that sexy voice and what kind of relationship she had with Ryan.

"Then maybe you ought to introduce him to someone."

"Me! I don't know any single women. Except Dora, and I wouldn't wish that nitwit on anyone."

"Okay then, you go out with another man. That should put a damper on things."

Cristen's mouth twisted wryly. "And just whom do you suggest I go out with?"

Louise gave her an innocent look and spread her hands wide. "There's always Leonard DeWitt."

"Oh, pul-leeze. I'd rather kiss a camel on the lips."

Giving her friend one last disgusted glare, Cristen turned back to the worktable and picked up the intricate piece of fretwork. "If that's the best suggestion you can come up with, forget it. I'll just have to think of something else."

"Suit yourself."

Two hours later Cristen was carrying out the painstaking task of installing three flights of ornate stair rails when Louise tapped her on the back.

"Cris, there's someone here who'd like to see you."

Cristen stood with one knee braced in the seat of her chair. She was bent over, almost the entire upper half of her body inside the dollhouse. "Tell them I'm busy," came her muffled reply.

"Will you get out of there!" her partner hissed.

Frowning, Cristen looked back over her shoulder to see Louise frantically rolling her eyes. She started to refuse again but gave up when she felt a hard yank on her skirt.

"Oh, all right." With a disgruntled sigh, Cristen backed out of the dollhouse and straightened just as Louise said brightly, "Look who's here."

Cristen was not a great believer in coincidence, and when she turned and saw Harvey Metcalf standing by the cash register, she darted her partner a sharp look.

Unfazed, Louise put her hand in the small of Cristen's back and prodded her toward the pleasant-looking, middle-aged man, smiling brilliantly all the while. "Thank you, Harvey, for coming by so quickly," she gushed as they reached the counter. "We're running low on simply everything: shipping cartons, bubble pack, sacks—you name it."

At the blatant lie, Cristen narrowed her eyes once more, sure now that she'd been set up. Harvey worked for the company that supplied them with packaging products. Relatively speaking, their account was small and easily could have been handled over the phone, but Harvey dropped in regularly to take their order. He had been by only two weeks before, and their stock was more than adequate.

"No trouble. I had to call on another customer in the mall, anyway," he assured her. Then his gaze sought Cristen, and she fidgeted at the disturbing warmth in his hazel eyes. "Hello, Cristen. You're looking as pretty as ever."

"Thank you, Harvey," she said politely, shooting her partner a look that promised retribution.

While Louise gave him a hefty order for all the things they didn't need, Cristen braced herself for what she knew was coming. Every time Harvey came into the shop he asked her out, and though she always refused, it didn't stop him from asking. Despite Louise's advice, Cristen was not sure she could bring herself to accept a date with Harvey. He was a nice man, but she had the uneasy feeling that an evening spent in his company would be about as exciting as watching paint dry on a wall. Besides, she told herself, she didn't want to encourage the man when there was no hope of her ever returning his feelings.

Harvey was nothing if not predictable. As soon as his business with Louise was finished he turned to Cristen with that hopeful-spaniel look in his eyes. "I was wondering if maybe you'd like to have dinner with me this evening," he said diffidently.

"Actually, I, uh..." Cristen chewed on the inside of her lip and glanced at Louise, who was standing behind Harvey giving her frantic signals. "I really don't think—"

When the phone rang Cristen reacted to it like a drowning man reaching for a lifeline, snatching it up before the first peal was complete. "Hello," she said in a rush, sending Harvey an apologetic smile and ignoring Louise's scowl.

"Hi, Cris." Ryan's deep baritone rumbled through the receiver, and Cristen swallowed hard, the sense of reprieve she'd felt fleeing. "We knocked off early at the site today because of the rain, so I thought I'd do the grocery shopping. Is there anything special you'd like for dinner tonight?"

The question was a timely reminder of just how cozy their relationship had become. "I..." Cristen hesitated. She glanced at Harvey and chewed her lip again. Finally she drew in a deep breath and tilted her chin. "Don't bother cooking anything for me. I won't be home for dinner." She smiled across the counter at Harvey and winked. "I have a date tonight."

Harvey's face lit up. He looked as though he'd just won a million-dollar lottery. Louise nodded approvingly.

The silence coming through the phone line was so thick that you could cut it.

"A date, huh?" When Ryan finally spoke his voice was soft and controlled, and inexplicably, Cristen's throat became painfully tight.

"Yes."

"I see. Well...I guess I'll see you in the morning then."

"Yes," Cristen said softly.

Chapter Eight

Would you like to come in for coffee?" The last thing Cristen wanted was to prolong the evening, but, perversely, lingering anger drove her to extend the invitation.

"Thanks. I'd like that."

Surprised and obviously pleased, Harvey looked at her as though she were the most wonderful woman on earth, and Cristen sighed.

Guilt. It was such an insidious, nagging, depressing, totally irrational emotion—and it had tormented her all evening.

Guilt for not returning Harvey's feelings, guilt for using him so shamefully, guilt for thinking he would be a crashing bore, when he was really an interesting, well-informed, sensitive man—it all twisted together to form a tight knot in Cristen's stomach.

Worse, her conscience had pricked her constantly over Ryan, too. It was absurd, and she knew it, but she felt as though she were being, somehow...unfaithful.

That she felt any guilt at all about Ryan made her furious. It's my apartment, Cristen told herself angrily, unlocking the door and ushering Harvey in. I can invite whomever I want. For that matter, I can go out with whomever I want. Ryan O'Malley doesn't have any claim on me. He's just my roommate.

Even so, when they stepped into the living room Cristen was relieved to see that Ryan wasn't around.

He had left only one small lamp burning, and she moved quickly around the room, turning more on. "Have a seat, Harvey. I'll be back with our coffee in just a minute."

As far as Cristen was concerned, instant coffee was a sacrilege, an abomination. Normally, she would not have violated her taste buds with the vile stuff, much less served it to a guest, but the minute she hit the kitchen she put the kettle on and began to forage through the cabinets for the sample jar she had received in the mail. Now that the defiant gesture had been made, she was anxious for Harvey to leave.

She slung sugar bowl, creamer and cups onto a tray, spooned in the noxious granules, splashed the barely steaming water over them and hurried back into the living room with a smile pasted on her face. "Well, here we are. How do you like yours?"

"Black with one sugar." Harvey rose politely to take the tray from her and set it on the coffee table. He looked disappointed when, after handing him his cup, Cristen settled into a chair with hers instead of joining him on the sofa, but he smiled and took a sip. "You have a lovely place," he said, glancing around.

"Thank you. We—uh—I like it. And it's very convenient to the shop."

"Yes. And it's a great neighborhood."

"Yes." Cristen smiled and sipped the revolting brew. Surreptitiously, she glanced at the mantel clock and wondered how long it would be before he left. Much more of this and she was going to fall asleep.

"You know, Cristen, I—" Harvey stopped abruptly, staring past her, an arrested expression on his face.

With a puzzled frown, Cristen followed the direction of his gaze and nearly fell out of her chair.

Ryan stood framed in the hall doorway, stretching hugely, back arched, arms bent, elbows up, his clenched fists pressing against his neck. His eyes were closed, and his mouth was open in a jaw-popping yawn. The only thing he wore was a pair of pale blue pajama bottoms, which rode indecently low. They were made of a thin, soft cotton that clung to his hips in a way that made Cristen's eyes bulge and her throat go dry. Speechless, she stared at his concave belly, the sharp points of his hipbones, the brawny, furred chest, the little tufts of black hair beneath his arms.

His contortions came to an end, and he ambled across the living room, scratching his chest, but stopped short at the sight of them.

"Oh! Hi, Cris. I didn't know you were home." Ryan sent her a warm, welcoming smile, and then he seemed to notice Harvey. A look of surprise crossed his face. "I'm sorry. I didn't know you had company." Altering his course, he crossed to the sofa and held out his hand. Dazed, Harvey took it. "You must be Mr. Metcow."

"Metcalf," Harvey corrected, looking askance at Ryan's pajamas.

"Yes, of course." With an aplomb that left Cristen speechless, Ryan perched on the arm of her chair. He rested an arm along the back and played idly with the feathery curls that lay on her shoulder. Aghast, Cristen stared at his muscular thigh beneath the taut cotton, her heart thudding like a wild thing. Heat from his bare, brawny chest and encircling arm scorched her cheek, neck and shoulders. With every shallow breath she drew came dizzying scents of soap and healthy male.

Do something. Don't just sit here! Cristen's common sense prodded. But Ryan's nearness had her so flustered that she couldn't think, and the best she could do was give him a warning glare.

Jauntily swinging one bare foot, Ryan smiled and turned back to Harvey. "Did you get your business settled?"

"Business?" Harvey blinked like a startled barn owl.

"Yes. I talked to Louise earlier this evening, and she told me you're a salesman for one of their suppliers." Ryan tipped his head back and gave Harvey a piercing look. "It was a business dinner you had, wasn't it?"

"No, it wasn't. It— Who *are* you?"

"Oh, sorry." His grin was wide and guileless. "I'm Ryan O'Malley. I live here with Cristen."

"You *what*?"

Oh, no. Now you've done it, Cristen thought. Beneath the cover of her arm, she reached with her other hand, pinched a piece of flesh at Ryan's side and gave it a vicious twist. He jumped, but the smile remained fixed on his face.

"What Ryan means, Harvey, is we're roommates," Cristen explained quickly. "We share this apartment."

"Oh, I, uh, I see." Harvey's uncertain gaze went back and forth between them before finally coming to rest on the masculine hand sifting through Cristen's hair.

"Yes, Cris and I share a lot of things," Ryan said, looking down at her warmly. His hand left her hair and stroked in a gentle circle over her upper arm. "We're quite...comfortable together, aren't we, love?"

"Ryan—"

"Which reminds me. Did you use my razor this morning?"

"Your— No! Certainly not!" Cristen sputtered.

"Oh. Well the blade was as dull as an old maid's love life, and you're in such a stupor when you wake up, I thought maybe you'd picked it up by mistake."

He turned to Harvey, shaking his head with amused tolerance. "You wouldn't believe how hard it is to get this woman out of bed in the morning. Even when she's up and moving, she's practically comatose until she has something in her stomach. And a regular grouch if you so much as speak to her. I have to coddle her something awful."

Smiling, Ryan looked down at Cristen, his voice dropping to a low caress. "But I have to confess, it's no hardship. Not when she's so darned beautiful. All warm and rosy with sleep and her hair all mussed, and wearing almost nothing."

"Ryan!"

Harvey set his cup down with a clatter and shot to his feet. "I...uh...I'd better be going."

"No, Harvey, let me explain. You see...that is..."

"It was nice meeting you, Harvey," Ryan said. "Feel free to drop by anytime. We'd be happy to have you. Wouldn't we, Cristen?"

"Yes. No! I mean—"

"Uh, yeah. Same here," Harvey mumbled over his shoulder, scuttling toward the door like a fleeing crab. "I enjoyed the dinner, Cristen. I'll be seeing you."

"Harvey, wait—"

But he had already bolted out the door.

For a full ten seconds Cristen stood staring at it in befuddled disbelief. Then, like a thermometer plunged into
boiling water, her anger began to rise, and she turned
slowly to face Ryan.

He met her smoldering gaze with a bland, open look that
made her want to slap him. "Seems like a nice guy."

"Oh, he is. He's a very nice guy." She began in a slow,
deceptive, sugary tone, but with every word it rose in heat
and intensity, until she ended on a shouted "Whom I will
probably never lay eyes on again, thanks to you!"

"Me! What did I do?"

"I don't know how you can even ask. Not after saun-
tering out here the way you did in those indecent pajamas."

"Indecent?" Ryan glanced down at the garment in
question and sent her a puzzled look. "I thought they were
kind of conservative." Then his wicked grin flashed. "Just
be glad I had them on. Before I moved in here I slept in the
raw."

"Oh, wonderful," she said with thick sarcasm, rolling
her eyes. The comment inspired erotic images that sent
both her temperature and her anger soaring, but Cristen
got a grip on herself and pressed on doggedly. "And if that
weren't bad enough, you plopped yourself on the arm of
my chair as though you had every right to be there and
dropped all those outrageous innuendos."

"I was just trying to be friendly," he claimed with a
wounded air.

"Friendly, ha! You deliberately gave Harvey the
impression that you and I are lovers. Now he thinks I'm
the kind of woman who would go out with one man while
sleeping with another."

"Oh, come on, Cris. You know you don't care what Harvey thinks. Louise told me he bores you silly. That you weren't the least bit interested in him."

Cristen threw her hands in the air. "Oh, great! Now my partner is siding against me." She snatched up the cups and stalked toward the kitchen, so furious that steam was practically coming out of her ears. Ryan followed right on her heels.

"Now you just listen to me, you lop-eared son of a cross-eyed mule. No matter how I feel about a man, I will not have you trying to scare him off. Is that clear?"

Ryan grinned. "Gee, I love it when you talk dirty."

Cristen made a low sound and plopped the cups into the sink. "Now, Ryan, I'm warning you—"

"Ah, come on, babe. You're getting all worked up over nothing." Standing behind her, he grasped her upper arms and massaged gently. "Loosen up."

"Nothing?" She shrugged off his hands and whipped around. Scowling fiercely, she poked his bare chest with her forefinger. "I do not call interfering in my personal life 'nothing.' You embarrassed me and made Harvey look like a fool, and I will not have it."

As she spoke she advanced on him, head thrust forward, eyes squinting, punctuating her words with several more jabs, backing him up a step with each one. Ryan looked suitably chastised, and, riding the crest of her anger, Cristen didn't notice the telltale twitch of his mustache.

"Sharing this apartment does not give you the right to poke your nose into my affairs," she informed him just as Ryan bumped against the table and sent it screeching back several inches. A chair teetered on two legs, but he snatched it upright before it could topple over.

"Affair! You mean you wanted to have an affair with that jerk?"

"No! Of course n—" She stopped and shot him an exasperated glare. "That is not the point, and you know it, you pea-brained, boneheaded jackass! You— And just what are you grinning about?"

Ryan's eyes twinkled. "You're talking dirty again."

"Dir— Why, you...you...". She couldn't think of anything vile enough to call him except several colorful epithets that she knew would merely delight him more. Finally she contented herself with giving him another hard poke. "Very funny. But you'd better wipe that smirk off your face, O'Malley, because you're just about a hair away from getting a fat lip."

She pivoted on her heel and stomped out, muttering under her breath with every step. Ryan hurried after her.

"Come on, Cristen. Don't be mad. Where's your sense of humor?"

"It moved out when you moved in."

She stalked across the living room and down the hall, her high heels hitting the floor like hammer blows, with Ryan a half step behind.

"But you have to admit, the whole thing was kinda funny, especially when your friend turned that apoplectic purple."

"I'll admit nothing of the kind."

"Okay, okay. I tell you what. How about if I explain things to ol' Harv tomorrow? Huh? Will that help?"

"Absolutely not. You stay away from Harvey."

At her door Cristen whirled around and held up her hand, and Ryan almost plowed right into her. "And I'm warning you, from now on you mind your own business."

She slammed the door in his face so hard that it rattled the hinges and made his ears ring.

Ryan winced and looked at it ruefully. Had he gone too far? He ran a hand through his hair and heaved a sigh. He shouldn't have done it, of course. And he really hadn't meant to. Though the thought of Cristen out with another man had eaten at his gut all evening, he'd told himself that he'd be adult about it.

But dammit! He hadn't counted on her actually bringing the guy into the apartment. When he'd heard them talking, all his good intentions had gone flying.

In the morning, he supposed he'd have to apologize and see what he could do about making amends.

After checking the front door and turning out all the lights, Ryan returned to his room and stretched out on his bed. With his hands laced beneath his head, he stared through the darkness at the ceiling. Perhaps it was time he pushed a bit harder. Cristen was a strong woman, and for some reason he didn't understand, she was determined to keep him at arm's length. He was almost positive that her actions tonight had been purely defensive. Which meant that she was aware of the feelings growing between them and was running scared.

That was a good sign. Wasn't it?

Closing his eyes, he gritted his teeth and tried to will away the hot, yearning ache in his loins...and the even greater one in his heart.

God, he hoped so.

It was almost eleven before Cristen emerged from her room the next morning. She entered the kitchen and found Ryan sitting at the table, drinking coffee and reading the Sunday paper. He looked up warily, his expression sheepish and questioning.

Cristen glanced at him, lifted her chin and made for the coffeepot. In addition to his outrageous behavior, she now had another reason to be annoyed with him: he had interfered with her sleep.

And sleep was something Cristen took seriously. She usually abandoned herself to it with childlike gusto, dropping off quickly and enjoying deep, untroubled slumber, but the night before she had tossed and turned for hours, fuming over Ryan's outrageous behavior. She always enjoyed the luxury of sleeping in on her days off, of awakening naturally without the rude blare of the alarm clock, but this morning, thanks to Ryan, she'd overdone it and awakened feeling groggy and irritable.

As usual, he had left coffee and orange juice in the bathroom for her, but both had been room temperature by the time she finally stumbled in to take her shower. She had dumped the former down the drain and drunk the latter, though she'd been sorely tempted not to.

Cristen poured her coffee and took a sip. She turned to find Ryan watching her over the top of the newspaper.

"Still mad?"

Leaning back against the counter, she took another sip and turned her head to stare out the window, presenting him with her profile. She let several more seconds tick by, then replied coolly, "Shouldn't I be?"

"Yep."

The unexpected answer took the wind out of her sails. Cristen looked at him in faint surprise, then firmed her mouth, suspecting he had done it on purpose.

"I was out of line, and I'm sorry. I had no business interfering in your life any more than you have in mine. My only excuse is, I was jealous. You see, I'd been looking forward to having dinner with you last night. I guess, living together like this, I've gotten kind of possessive."

Flummoxed by his honesty, Cristen could only stare. Oh, great. How was she supposed to respond to that? After all, given their situation, a certain amount of possessiveness was understandable. She'd felt a few pangs herself on those occasions when his sexy-voiced secretary had called, so she could hardly object. Yet she couldn't help feeling vaguely threatened. She had a nasty suspicion that with that disarming apology, Ryan had somehow advanced a step closer.

"I'm really sorry for embarrassing you, Cristen. Will you forgive me?"

"Well..." She pursed her lips and looked at him, but after a moment she gave an exasperated sigh. "Oh, I guess so."

"Great! And to make it up to you, why don't I take you out someplace? We can spend the day just having fun. Do something wild and crazy."

"Ryan, I don't think that's—"

"Come on, Cristen, don't say no. You'll enjoy yourself, I promise. And it'll be good for you. When was the last time you just relaxed and let yourself go? I've known you almost three months, and in all that time your whole life has been work, work, work. On your days off you either go into the shop or bring a project home to work on. The trouble with you is, you take things too seriously. You've been working so hard for so long, I don't think you remember how to have fun."

It was true. Hadn't she admitted much the same thing to herself not long ago? Work had been her salvation in the early days after Bob had walked out, but she was over all that. Now she worked from dawn till dark out of habit. Even in the evenings while watching TV she hemmed small tablecloths and napkins or made tiny Oriental rugs, using a turkey-tufting stitch on petit-point canvas. It was obsessive and stupid to work so much, she knew. And it was turning her into a dull, one-dimensional person.

Cristen looked at Ryan uncertainly. He was right. She needed to relax and have fun. It had been ages since she'd even tried. But still, spending the day with Ryan would be foolhardy and reckless. She really shouldn't. . . .

"Come on, Cris. Come with me." He gave her an ingenuous look, his smile coaxing. "That way I'll know you really do forgive me."

It was blatant emotional blackmail, but Cristen wasn't immune to it, despite the scowl she aimed at him. "Where would we go?"

Though her voice still held a note of doubt, Ryan sensed he had won, and he grinned his delight. "Well, let's see. We could take in a movie. Or go to the beach or the park. Or..." He snapped his fingers. "I know. Why don't we go ice skating?"

"Ice skating?"

"Sure. Why not?"

"Because I don't know how. I've never been ice skating."

He looked first shocked, then disapproving. "Do you mean you've worked for years within sight of that beautiful rink and you've never once put on a pair of skates and tried it?" When she shook her head, his expression grew determined. "Well, that settles it. We're going. It's high time you discovered what you've been missing."

"No, Ryan. I don't want to go skating. I'm not the athletic type."

"Don't worry about it. There's nothing to it. You'll have a great time. You'll see."

"No. Absolutely not. You are not getting me on that ice, and that's final."

* * *

"Are you sure it's easy?"

"Positive."

"It doesn't look easy."

Cristen clutched Ryan's arm and eyed the skaters. They glided by so fast that it made her dizzy to watch them, an elongated circle of color and motion, constantly shifting and changing. Some skated smoothly, their style graceful and sure, others lurched around mechanically, and a few plucky souls fought a constant battle with gravity, not always winning. There were racers, gliders, plodders and fancy figure skaters; fat ones, skinny ones, old and young and everything in between.

"Just hold on to me," Ryan said, edging Cristen toward the ice. "We'll take it nice and slow, and you'll have the hang of it in no time."

The sidelong look she gave him expressed her doubt, but she clumped along gamely on the thin blades. "How does anyone walk in these things?" she complained. "I feel like Frankenstein's monster. They must weigh ten pounds each."

Ryan laughed and patted her arm. "It'll be easier once we're on the ice."

They paused to step onto the rink, but before they could, a small child bumped into Cristen and darted around them. She held on to Ryan with a death grip, her free arm flailing as she teetered precariously on wobbly ankles. When she regained her balance she grimaced up at him dryly. "I certainly hope so."

The constant scrape of blades over ice blended with the canned music and the dull roar of voices. The pervasive odors of sweat socks and leather and human bodies hung heavily in the air, and every now and then Cristen caught a whiff of mustard and grilling meat from the concession stand. Poised on the edge of the ice, she glanced up at Ryan and wrinkled her nose. "This place smells like a cross between a frozen locker room and a cheap carnival."

Ryan grinned. "Complaining won't do any good. You're still going out there. So come on, let's move it." He looped his left arm around her waist, took her right hand in his and urged her forward.

The instant their skates touched the ice they began to glide, and Cristen gave a distressed little moan. Her torso seesawed back and forth for a moment, fighting the motion, but Ryan steadied her.

"Easy. Easy. Just relax. I won't let you fall. Just do what I do. Right. Left. Right. Left. That's it," he encouraged when she managed a few jerky steps forward.

Cristen held on to Ryan so tightly that the tips of his fingers were bloodless. She felt as awkward and unsure as a child just learning to walk.

A petite blonde in a short-skirted red costume skated by, eyeing Ryan. In a clear spot just ahead of them she went into a fancy backward maneuver and topped it off with a spin that made her skirt stand straight out, revealing her pert, leotard-covered derriere.

Cristen's mouth turned down sourly. God, how she detested petite blondes.

The woman made five laps around the rink to their one, giving Ryan a flirtatious look every time she went by. Once, she even had the gall to skate around them in a circle and wink before moving on.

Her behavior incensed Cristen so, she forgot to be nervous. Gritting her teeth, she concentrated fiercely on Ryan's instructions and maintaining her balance. By the time they had completed their second circuit, she had the rhythm and was doing much better.

"You ready to try solo?" Ryan asked.

She started to refuse, but at that moment the blonde went by again in a flash of red. Cristen narrowed her eyes. "Yes. As a matter of fact, I think I am," she said, watching the woman execute a spinning leap and land like a feather.

Show-off! she fumed.

Ryan took his arms from around Cristen's waist, skated with her a short way and released her hand. She wavered a bit, then caught the rhythm again. On the third forward glide she shot him a triumphant grin... and the next instant her feet and bottom changed places.

Cristen hit the ice with a solid *whomp* that clacked her teeth together. Stunned, she sat there for a moment with her palms braced on either side of her hips, staring at the tips of her skates.

"Are you okay?" Ryan asked, coming to a halt beside her.

"Yes," she muttered through clenched teeth. "I'm fine."

Ryan suppressed a grin. With his hands clasped behind his back, his expression grave, he skated around her several times, his gaze sweeping over the ice. Cristen narrowed her eyes and watched him suspiciously.

"What are you looking for?"

Ryan glanced at her and said, straight-faced, "Cracks. There're sure to be some."

"Very funny, O'Malley. You're just a barrel of laughs."

She would have said more, but the cute little blonde arrived at that moment, coming to a halt with a flourish that sent ice shavings spraying—most of them right into Cristen's face.

"Can I be of any help?" she asked sweetly, batting her false eyelashes at Ryan.

Cripes, Cristen thought, they look like spiders perched on her eyelids.

Ryan gave her his sexiest smile, his blue eyes glinting with approval and wicked awareness. Cristen had to resist a strong urge to grab his ankles and jerk him off his feet.

"Thank you, but no, I don't think so."

Cristen scrambled to stand up, but every time the blades of her skates touched the ice her feet shot out from under her and she went sprawling again. Ryan offered her his hand, but she just scowled at him and struggled harder. Finally he moved behind her, hooked his hands beneath her armpits and hauled her up.

She tried to shake off his hold, but the action almost landed her on her backside again, and she was forced to grab on to his arm, though the need to do so galled her.

"Are you sure?" the blonde persisted. "I'd be happy to help you teach your friend the basics." She struck a graceful pose and smiled beguilingly at Ryan. Cristen didn't even warrant a glance.

"That's very nice of you, but I think we can manage. Cristen's a fast learner. She just needs a little practice."

Gritting her teeth, Cristen brushed the ice shavings off the seat of her jeans and glared daggers at the pair. They were both talking about her as though she weren't there. And if body language and the looks that passed between them counted, there was a lot being said without benefit of words.

What was it about cutesy, pint-sized women that men found so fascinating? Cristen wondered sourly. This one was definitely starting to get on her nerves. Did she have to stand there swaying her hips like that?

Of course, Cristen. Don't be an idiot. How else is she supposed to draw attention to her slender thighs and that itty-bitty costume, for mercy's sake?

Cristen drummed her fingers against Ryan's arm. Next to the almost life-size Barbie Doll, she felt like an Amazonian bag lady in her old jeans and cotton blouse.

"Oh. Well, okay," the blonde said with obvious disappointment. "But if you change your mind, I'll be around all afternoon." She gave Ryan one last regretful look and skated away.

With a tiny knowing smile tugging at his mouth, he watched her for a moment before turning back to Cristen. "Well, are you game for more?"

Cristen jutted out her chin and returned his teasing look with an icy stare. "Certainly. Did you think I'd quit just because of one little fall?" Or one man-hungry blonde? she added silently.

The fall was far from the last one Cristen took. After circling the rink once more with Ryan, she insisted on skating unaided and spent the next several hours doggedly striving to stay upright. It was not an easy task. But once committed to a course of action, Cristen could seldom be diverted. Her mother called it bullheadedness. Cristen preferred to think of it as perseverance.

With gritty determination, she picked herself up over and over again and plodded on, stubbornly refusing Ryan's help.

"Good Lord, Cristen," he said after she'd taken a particularly jarring fall. "This isn't some sort of test, you know. There's no law that says you have to learn to skate. Why don't you call it quits and let's go somewhere else? Or at least let me help you."

"No. No, I'm not going to quit until I've skated all the way around this rink without falling," she declared tightly. "Even if it takes me all night."

It almost did. By the time she finally achieved her goal it was late afternoon. Cristen crossed her starting point and made for the exit, not even slowing down to accept Ryan's congratulations. She was bone tired and bruised and ready to get the heck out of there.

It was bliss to shed the heavy skates, and after Cristen had turned them in she headed for the ladies' room, eyeing the rink balefully as she went. After today, she doubted that she would ever again enjoy the view from her shop window.

All her extremities were cold, especially her rear end, and in the ladies' room Cristen discovered why. She had spent so much time flat on her bottom on the ice that the seat of her jeans was soaked. Screwing up her face in disgust, she mimicked in a sarcastic singsong, "You'll have fun, Cristen. I promise.

"Darn you, O'Malley. I'll get you for this. It'd serve you right if I rode home in your precious Jaguar this way," she muttered angrily.

Tight-lipped, she stomped to the wall hand dryer and whacked the flat knob with the side of her fist, then turned, braced her palms on her knees and stuck her rump up under the stream of hot air. As warmth seeped through the heavy material and into her chilled flesh, Cristen's mouth twisted.

Who are you kidding? Ryan risk damaging his upholstery? He'd probably make you ride on your knees facing backward. Or maybe even run along beside.

A teenage girl came in and goggled openly. By the time she emerged from one of the stalls, her startled expression had changed to a smirk, which, as she took her time washing and drying her hands, grew increasingly irksome to Cristen. At the door, the girl looked back and, with a giggle, called out, "Bye, hot pants."

Cristen made a face at the swinging door. "Smart-mouthed kid."

For the most part she had the ladies' room to herself after that, and of the few other females who wandered in, none felt compelled to make cute remarks.

It took twenty minutes and about fifty jabs on the blower button before her jeans were in any condition to come into contact with the Jaguar's leather bucket seats. Thawed and dry, Cristen emerged more charitably disposed toward Ryan, but the feeling lasted only as long as it took her to spot him.

Leaning against a post to one side of the rink, a silly smile on his face he stood talking to the little blonde.

Chapter Nine

Cristen stopped dead in her tracks and watched them, her mouth thinning. Even from where she stood it was easy to see that the woman was flirting for all she was worth. She was batting those ridiculous fake lashes so hard that it was a wonder Ryan didn't have windburn. Not even a blind man could miss the signals she was sending out.

And Ryan was eating it all up with a spoon.

When he threw back his head and laughed at something the woman said, Cristen saw red. She didn't stop to ask herself why she was so furious, but simply put her nose in the air and headed for the exit. She marched right past them without so much as a glance.

"Cristen? Cristen, where are you going?" Ryan called after her. "Cristen!"

She ignored him. Her leggy stride carried her quickly through the crowd around the rink and down the almost deserted passageway.

"Cristen, will you stop?"

Ryan's voice was coming closer. Cristen could hear the soft thud and squeak of tennis shoes on the mall's marble floor, but she fought the undignified urge to break into a run. As she reached the exit doors Ryan caught up with her. Ignoring him, she shoved them open and marched on.

"Cris, for God's sake—"

She started down the four steps that led into the parking garage, but Ryan took them in one leap, then turned and blocked her way before she reached the bottom.

"All right. Now I want to know just what the devil is going on. Why did you stomp off that way?"

"Get out of my way, Ryan."

"Uh-uh. Not until we talk."

"You want to talk? Then go back to blondie. You seemed to find her fascinating."

Ryan looked astounded. "That's what this is all about? You're jealous?"

"I most certainly am not!" she flared hotly.

Surprise turned to delight, and Ryan's grin spread wide. "You're *jealous*!"

"Will you stop saying that! I told you, I'm n—"

Ryan's whoop of joy cut her off, and she let out a shriek when he snatched her off the steps.

She clutched his shoulder as he held her high against his chest and whirled around. "Ryan! Stop it!"

Laughing, he obeyed but continued to hold her aloft. Cristen looked around in a panic, afraid that someone would see them, but there wasn't another soul in the garage. She scowled down at him and shoved at his shoulders, but the strong arms looped beneath her bottom clamped her tightly to him.

"What is the matter with you?" she hissed. "Do you have a fetish about parking garages? Do they turn you on or something?"

"No. But you do." At her swiftly indrawn breath the foolish grin on Ryan's face melted into tenderness. "Only you."

Cristen's eyes grew round, and Ryan looked at her with a hint of reproach. "Ah, love, surely by now you've guessed how I feel. You knocked me for a loop the moment we met. I've thought about you constantly and gone to great lengths to be with you. I don't want any other woman. Especially not that obvious little flirt back at the rink."

Pleasure shot through her at his words and made her heart pound with unbearable excitement. Calling herself a fool, Cristen struggled to subdue it. She frowned, trying to look severe, but she was so flustered that she couldn't quite pull it off. "Ryan, stop this. We have an agreement."

"Agreement be damned," he said cheerfully, his grin returning. "Anyway, that was before I knew you cared. And don't you dare deny it," he warned, chuckling at her indignant expression. "Not after stomping off in a jealous huff like that. But now that I do know, I think it's time we renegotiated our agreement."

"Ryan, I—"

But he had already loosened his hold. As Cristen slid down his body their gazes remained locked. His eyes glittered with exhilaration and sheer masculine pleasure, hers with mingled desire and apprehension as sensual awareness swelled between them.

The moment stretched out, taut with anticipation. It was as though all the oxygen had been removed from the air. Neither breathed. Neither spoke. Neither looked away. For those few seconds the world was reduced to just the two of them. Nothing existed but the throbbing tension, the erotic friction between their bodies, the unspoken promise of pleasures yet to be tasted.

With a hint of a smile playing about his lips, Ryan watched Cristen slide lower. Her pointed toes reached for the floor, and when they touched the concrete his head swooped, his mouth closing over hers with a swift sureness that allowed no protest.

There wasn't a woman alive who could have resisted that kiss; Cristen was sure of it.

His lips were warm and firm, his mustache a whispery brush of sable. The twin tactile pleasures electrified Cristen. Her heart seemed to stop beating for a millisecond, then took off at a gallop. Every nerve ending, every pulse point sprang into frenzied life.

You're such a fool, Cristen, for ever thinking you could escape this, she thought. But even as she berated herself she pressed closer, melting in Ryan's embrace. It was madness. Sheer madness. And it was irresistible.

He didn't release her until he had kissed her thoroughly and she was limp and shaking with need.

Feeling her tremble, Ryan pulled back and gazed into her upturned face. Her slightly puffy lips, the slumberous look in her eyes, brought a satisfied, purely masculine smile to his mouth.

He curved his big hands around either side of her neck and stroked his thumbs back and forth along her jaw. "All I'm asking is that you give it a try," he said persuasively. "Relax and go with your feelings and see what happens. I think we can have something very special together, Cristen, if you'll just give it a chance."

"I..." She caught her bottom lip between her teeth and looked at him, her eyes filled with indecision.

Ryan waited a moment, then tipped his head forward, giving her a beguiling look. "Will you, Cristen?"

Before she could reply, a group of rowdy teenage boys pushed through the mall doors and came loping down the steps. "Whoooie! Way to go, man!" one called when he spotted them. Instantly the others joined in with catcalls and whistles.

Cristen turned red to the roots of her hair, but the razzing didn't faze Ryan. Flashing them an arrogant grin, he tucked Cristen against his side and urged her toward the car. "Come on. Let's get out of here."

She went willingly, too unstrung to think about what she would do, what would happen, when she and Ryan got home.

But, typically, Ryan did not do the expected.

After giving her a long, searching look, he backed the car out of the parking slot and headed for the exit. "There's a new place over on Richmond that serves great ribs. I don't know about you, but after all that skating, I'm starved." He guided the purring Jaguar down the ramp and eased into the flow of traffic on Westheimer. When he stopped at the light he shot Cristen a quizzical smile. "How about it? You game?"

The suggestion took her so by surprise that she answered without thinking. "Yes. That sounds fine."

But a moment later Cristen was not sure if she was grateful for the delay or disappointed. That it was only temporary, she never doubted for a second. Ryan was going to demand an answer, some sort of decision from her. Even if she wanted to, she couldn't avoid giving one. Those few moments in the parking garage had changed everything. There was no going back to the polite pretense they had been living. Either she stopped fighting the attraction and let the relationship develop, or Ryan would have to move out. Cristen closed her eyes, panicked at the thought of either happening. Darn it! Why did he have to bring everything out into the open? she fretted.

The restaurant was a small, unpretentious place called Adam's Rib, which served cafeteria style. The decor was standard for a barbecue joint—red vinyl booths, laminated tables, brick floor, light fixtures made of wagon wheels, lots of branding irons, spurs, singletrees, bridles and horseshoes hanging on silvered, natural cedar walls— but it was neat and clean, and the aroma coming out of the kitchen more than made up for the phony quaintness.

Since it was only a little before six, the restaurant wasn't crowded, and when Cristen and Ryan had gone through the line they carried their trays to a secluded booth in the corner.

Ryan dug right in, but Cristen dawdled. She looked at the plate of food and wondered why she had ordered it. How could she eat when her insides were tying themselves into knots? Taking her time, she spread her napkin in her lap and dumped sugar into her iced tea. Ice cubes clattered and her spoon clanked noisily against the inside of the glass as she stirred it. And stirred it. And stirred it.

Ryan looked up from gnawing on a sparerib. His amused gaze went from Cristen to the swirling liquid, then back, and she stopped abruptly, jerking the spoon out so fast that tea splattered over the table.

Pretending not to notice, Ryan discarded the bare bone and licked the sauce off his fingers. "You know, you were really a great sport today," he said, sending her a warm look that slowly turned into a chuckle. He shook his head, his expression filled with fond exasperation. "I knew you were a determined woman, but good Lord, Cristen, today was a revelation. Do you ever give up?"

"No." She lifted her chin, forgetting for a moment her contorting stomach. But then she thought of Bob, and of marriage, and her defiant conviction faded a bit. She had given up on those long ago. "Well...almost never," she amended.

"After today, I can well believe it."

Cristen grimaced. "I guess I made a fool of myself, didn't I?"

"No, of course not. A lot of people took spills. You were just concentrating so hard that you didn't notice. Don't worry, you did just fine." Ryan selected another sparerib. Leaning forward, he pointed it at her. "But you probably won't believe that tomorrow when certain parts of your body start to protest."

"You mean like the part I'm sitting on?"

"Mmm. Maybe we can strap a pillow on you." Pure devilment danced in Ryan's eyes as he brought the sparerib to his mouth.

As Cristen watched his even teeth sink into the succulent meat, she felt a queer sensation in her chest. She waited for him to bring up what was on both their minds, but Ryan merely polished off the rib and picked up another one. It was then that it hit Cristen: he wasn't going to press her for an answer or even mention that scene in the garage. At least, not yet.

She narrowed her eyes. Advance and retreat. Now she realized it was the tactic he'd used all along, the clever devil. And very effectively, too. Indignant, Cristen picked up her knife and fork and attacked the plate of food in front of her. She took a bite of the barbecued beef and chewed it as though she were trying to pulverize rocks with her teeth. No, Ryan wasn't about to let the matter drop. He was just biding his time.

She was tempted to give him a good swift kick.

Ryan grinned at her mulish expression. "Did I ever tell you about the time I gave skating lessons to a dog?"

Cristen almost choked on the bite of coleslaw she was chewing. She grabbed a glass of water and took several quick swallows, scowling at him over the rim. Blast his ornery hide! She hadn't intended to speak to him, but who would resist an opening gambit like that?

"No," she said curtly.

"When I was in college I worked part-time one year at the local ice rink." Employing his Irish gift of gab to the fullest, Ryan launched into a tale about a woman who was so attached to her toy poodle that she couldn't bear to be parted from it for even a couple of hours a week. So she arrived for her first skating lesson with the dog in tow, demanding that they teach her Angelique, too.

"She'd even had skates custom-made to fit the animal," Ryan said with a wave of his fork. "Damnedest things you ever saw. Laced halfway up those skinny little legs, with blades about two inches long."

"What did you do?"

"Do? What could I do? I charged her double and taught the dog." Nonplussed, Cristen watched him take a bite of potato salad and chew thoughtfully. When he had washed it down with a swig of iced tea, he smiled reminiscently and added, "Turned out to be one helluva little skater, too. Much better than her mistress." He flashed Cristen a bland smile. "Took a silver medal at the Olympics that year."

Cristen's jaw dropped and, a beat later, snapped shut again. She tried not to laugh. Sucking in her cheeks, she speared Ryan with a censorious stare.

But it was no use. Her gaze met the unholy twinkle in his, and her lips twitched. A chuckle bubbled up and vibrated at the back of her throat. She gulped it down. It shot back up. Ryan's slow grin appeared, and her laughter burst free.

"Oh, you!" she sputtered finally. "You made that whole thing up."

"Just the last part. I really did teach her dog to skate. Honest," he swore with his hand over his heart.

"Liar." Cristen wadded up her paper napkin and threw it at him. Ryan batted it away and spent the next several minutes vociferously protesting the charge.

Resisting Ryan proved to be about as easy as trying to hold back the tide. All through the meal and during the drive home, the teasing, charming devil regaled Cristen with wild stories that kept her laughing and made her forget, for a while at least, that heart-stopping kiss and the decision she faced. As they entered the apartment he was only halfway through a story about how he had taught Jennifer to ride a bicycle, and she was already convulsed with laughter.

"It's not funny," he declared as Cristen plopped down on the sofa and leaned her head against the back, swiping at her eyes with the backs of her hands. "I huffed and puffed up and down that damned street for hours. I'll bet I ran five miles alongside that bike. But finally, *finally*, she got the hang of it. She was a bit wobbly, but she was so proud of herself," he said, smiling fondly at the memory.

He joined Cristen on the sofa, stretched his legs out in front of him and leaned his head back, also. "Well, anyway, I watched her ride around the block a couple of times, and when I was sure she could handle it, I went inside and turned on a Rams game. Every now and then I thought I heard something, but it didn't really penetrate until I turned off the set an hour later, just as Jennifer went by the house yelling 'Help! Help!' at the top of her lungs." Ryan shook his head. "I've never been so scared in my life. I swear, my heart tried to club its way right out of my chest. At the very least, when I shot out the door I expected to find her lying broken and mangled in the street.''

"What had happened?''

Rolling his eyes, Ryan chuckled in ironic amusement. "It seems she had learned to ride just fine, but she was afraid if she put on the brakes, she'd fall. So for an hour she'd been circling the block, screaming for me to stop her each time she passed the house.''

They laughed together again, but after a while the sounds became strained and faded away. Sprawled at either end of the sofa, each gazed at the ceiling and listened to the silence stretch out and thicken. Cristen could hear the mantel clock tick, the soft whir of cool air blowing through the air-conditioning vent, her own heart beating.

"Would you like some coffee?'' Ryan asked.

"No, thanks.''

"A drink?''

"No.''

Another ten seconds passed.

"How about dessert? There's some ice cream in the freezer.''

"No, I don't think so.''

Slowly, Ryan rolled his head on the sofa back. Cristen did the same. Their gazes met and held, and his mouth curved upward. "Wanna fool around?''

Though he'd posed the question in a teasing vein, both knew he was serious. Holding her breath, Cristen stared at him with wide, troubled eyes. She wanted to. Oh, how she wanted to. But she was afraid. Afraid of being hurt. Afraid of being inadequate. Good grief! Until just recently she hadn't even dreamed of being romantically involved with any man but Bob.

But most of all, she was afraid of failing again.

And nothing lasts forever, she reminded herself. Nothing. You know that.

Cristen also knew, with soul-deep certainty, that if she allowed herself to care for Ryan, losing him would devastate her. The pain she had felt over Bob's desertion would be puny by comparison.

She could see the passion smoldering in Ryan's vivid blue eyes, could sense it in the deceptive stillness of his body. It pulled at her, stirred within her a longing so intense that it was almost pain. Tears glistened in her eyes as she gazed at him. Her throat felt tight and achy. Her heart thudded with a slow, heavy beat.

With a strangled sound, Cristen bolted off the sofa and raced toward the kitchen. She pushed through the door and went to the sink, gripping the porcelain edge so tightly her fingers were bloodless.

Heaven help her, she had to be sensible about this. Everything was against its working. Ryan was happy-go-lucky and casual about most things; she was serious and determined. He was wealthy; she was struggling. He was worldly, experienced; in her thirty years she had known just one man intimately. There were high school girls more experienced, for heaven's sake.

The soft swish of the door alerted her to Ryan's presence. Frantic for something to do, Cristen turned on the water and snatched a paper cup from the dispenser. Before she could fill it, Ryan's hands settled on her shoulders, and she went perfectly still.

"You can't run from it, Cristen," he said tenderly. His breath stirred her hair, its moist warmth seeping through, making her scalp tingle. "Neither of us can. What we're feeling is real and strong, and it isn't going to go away." He bent his head and buried his face in the cloud of auburn curls at the side of her neck.

Cristen sucked in her breath. The paper cup slipped from her fingers. It hit the counter with a hollow clatter and rolled in a wobbly arc. "Don't, Ryan." Cristen tried to sound stern, but the command came out a little shaky. She hunched her shoulder against his gentle nuzzling, but her heart was suddenly playing leapfrog in her chest.

"Can you honestly say you don't like it when I do this?" Nuzzling aside the fragrant tresses, he nibbled her shoulder as far as the scooped neck of her blouse would allow, then worked his way back up to her ear. "Or this?" He nipped her lobe, then batted it playfully with his tongue.

A shuddering breath escaped Cristen, and she closed her eyes. "Ryan . . ."

"Or how about this?" he whispered, pressing his open mouth over the graceful shell. For a moment his breath filled her ear with moist heat; then the tip of his tongue traced each delicate swirl, and a delicious prickling sensation rippled over Cristen's skin.

Ryan's hands slid down her arms, slipped under them and pressed warmly over her abdomen. Cristen grasped his arms with every intention of removing them, but then, somehow, her forearms were resting atop his and her fingers were flexing around his thick wrists. His flesh was warm and hard, the silky hair covering it an erotic abrasion against her skin.

"Oh, Ryan." This time his name came out on a sigh, and she felt his smile against her neck.

Cristen's head fell back against Ryan's shoulder. She felt weak, her body burning with a delicious lassitude, her insides atremble. Were it not for his encircling arms she was not sure she could have remained standing.

All the arguments she had given herself for not getting involved with Ryan flew out of her head. For too long she had fought the attraction, but she could fight it no more. Her defenses breached she surrendered willingly to the sweet rush of passion. She was passive in his arms, absorbing his heat, his strength, greedily breathing in the heady masculine scent that surrounded her, reveling in the exquisite sensations created by his touch.

Her breasts were heavy and aching, and when Ryan cupped them Cristen spread her hands over his and pressed them closer. His thumbs swept back and forth over her nipples, and they peaked, pebble hard. Cristen moaned and rocked her head on Ryan's shoulder. He growled softly.

"Come here," he whispered, turning her in his arms.

He gazed down at her and smiled. Desire glittered in her green eyes beneath heavy, half-closed lids. Her breathing was deep and slow, her lips slightly parted, and as he watched, the tip of her tongue came peeking out and glided in a lazy circle. When it retreated her lips were wet, inviting.

The water was still gushing into the sink, and Ryan reached around her and turned it off. In the pulsing quiet that followed, Cristen was sure he could hear her heart thudding.

Watching her, Ryan cupped her cheek. His thumb brushed over her chin, her lower lip. Then, with slow, sure movements, he pulled her closer, tilted her face up and lowered his mouth to hers.

The first touch sent excitement streaking through Cristen like summer lightning. She moaned and pressed closer, her arms sliding up to encircle his neck of their own accord. Oh, Lord, she hadn't known until now how much she wanted this. Needed it.

Ryan's mouth rocked over hers with excruciating slowness. Tender. Tormenting. His sable mustache was a sleek, soft caress, as feathery as a whispering breeze against her skin. His tongue probed the corners of her mouth, the slick skin of her inner lip, the tiny serrations on her teeth, touched the tip of her tongue and pulled back.

Cristen couldn't hold in the small moan of frustration that rose in her throat and slipped between her parted lips, nor could she keep her arms from tightening around his neck.

Ryan smiled against her lips. And then, with a swiftness and power that was unbearably exciting, he obeyed her silent urging. Holding her tight, he kissed her with a dark, sweet fervency, the rhythmic thrusts of his tongue telling her of his desire, building hers.

The hand beneath her chin slid around her neck, his spread fingers spearing through her hair to cup the back of her head. His other hand began to move downward, sliding over her back and hips, cupping her buttocks and pressing her to him rhythmically, matching the undulating movements with the slow, deep thrusts of his tongue.

Cristen was bombarded with new, thrilling sensations. Needs, desires she had not even known she possessed were clamoring for fulfillment. There was a hollow, yearning ache growing between her legs. She wanted to get closer to Ryan, to writhe and clutch and coil herself around him.

Their clinging lips parted slowly as, with a small sound of pleasure, Ryan ended the kiss. Loosening his hold, he pulled away and eased her back until she was braced against the counter. Gently grasping her upper arms, he looked down at her.

She was flushed with passion, her expression bemused, yearning. Ryan's face was taut and his blue eyes seemed unnaturally bright, but the smile that curled up the cor-

ners of his mustache, though tender, held a touch of familiar devilment.

"Honey, for a gal who doesn't wanna fool around, your
kisses pack one helluva wallop," he murmured in a soft,
scratchy voice.

Cristen blinked, her heavy eyelids lowering and lifting
with sensuous lethargy. She was so aroused that it took a
moment for her to make sense of his statement. When she
did, warm color flooded her face. Flustered, she started to
speak, but Ryan placed his forefinger over her mouth.

"I know. I shouldn't tease you. Not now." He smiled
with gentle contrition, his gaze warm and caressing. His
blunt finger traced her mouth, then trailed along her jaw.
As he watched the movement his eyes darkened. "But,
sweetheart, the point is, the chemistry between us is too
explosive to ignore." He looked at her intently, his face
growing tense. His voice dropped to a husky pitch that
throbbed with want and sent a tingle feathering over her
skin. "I don't want to ignore it, Cristen. I want to enjoy it.
To lose myself in it. In you. And I think that's what you
want, too. Isn't it?"

It was true. From the very beginning the depth and
strength of the attraction she felt for Ryan had frightened
her. She had fought it, even denied it, but in her heart of
hearts she had known the truth: she wanted him, as she
had never wanted any man before.

Why else had she agreed to let him stay? Put up with his
teasing and not too subtle manipulating? All her complaining and resistance had been merely a smoke screen, a
bit of face-saving self-deception. People always did what
they wanted to do, given a choice. Deep down, she had
known what would eventually happen when she let Ryan
move in. It was time to face that.

With a pounding heart, she met the gentle demand in Ryan's direct gaze. "Yes. Yes, it is," she said honestly, if a bit shakily.

Something flared in Ryan's eyes, something hot and urgent...something deliciously, dangerously male. "Are you sure?"

Cristen swallowed. "Yes."

He stared at her for a moment longer, and then a slow smile curved his mouth. Without a word, he bent, slipped an arm beneath her knees, the other around her back, and lifted her high against his chest. She looped her arm around his shoulders, and for countless moments they remained that way, silent and still, looking deep into each other's eyes. Finally, still holding her gaze, Ryan shouldered through the swinging door and carried her to her bedroom.

The fading golden glow of sunset filtered through the sheer curtains at her window, bathing the room with a mystical light, as he set her on her feet beside the bed. In the hazy dimness, Ryan bracketed Cristen's face with his broad palms and tipped her head back. The waning light tinted her skin a rich apricot and created a fiery nimbus around her auburn curls. Her eyes glittered like emeralds from within their heavy fringe of lashes.

"You're so lovely," he whispered. "You bewitched me the first moment I saw you." His gaze dropped to her mouth, and slowly his head descended. Cristen's eyelids fluttered shut. "You've been driving me crazy ever since." He whispered the words against her lips, his breath striking her skin in warm little puffs. And then his mouth slanted over hers.

Never had Cristen experienced such a soul-stirring kiss. With exquisite care, his lips rocked over hers. It was the merest contact of flesh to flesh, but oh, so warm and tender. His tongue slicked over her quivering lips, probed the corners of her mouth, then swirled enticingly around its inner edge, without ever quite entering that yearning sweetness.

Cristen trembled beneath the sensuous assault. The excruciating gentleness aroused her almost beyond bearing.

One of Ryan's hands slid down and lightly cupped the side of her neck, his fingertips playing softly over the velvety rim of her ear and the sensitive skin behind it. His other arm looped around her back to hold her close.

At last he ended the tormenting caress, raising his head slowly and easing back a step. He smiled at her tenderly as he slid his hand down her neck, turning it so that the backs of his knuckles skimmed over her collarbone and chest to the button at the top of the scoop-necked blouse. His fingers deftly released it and sought the next one, his knuckles grazing the rounded tops of her breasts on their downward glide.

"You're trembling." Ryan's eyes flared as he felt her helpless response. He released another button...and another. Encountering the waistband of her jeans, he tugged her blouse free, watching her. "Do I frighten you, darling?"

"No. It's...not that," she said tremulously. "It's just..." Cool air feathered across Cristen's skin, sending another delicious shiver rippling through her as Ryan released the final button and eased the blouse over her shoulders, letting it fall to the floor.

"What? Tell me what's wrong."

"Nothing's wrong." Cristen looked at him, her expression soft and vulnerable, her green eyes misty with passion and just a touch of doubt. "It's just that it's been so long for me, and...and there's never been anyone else but my husband. It's . . . it's almost like the first time all over again.''

Ryan's hand stilled on the front clasp of her bra. "Oh, my love," he groaned in a voice that went low and rough with emotion. "Do you have any idea what it does to me to hear you say that?"

He took her mouth in a hungry, hot kiss that, when it was over, left them both shaken. With considerably more haste, he released the front clasp on her bra, and it joined the yellow blouse on the floor. Cristen sucked in her breath and gripped his shoulders as he cupped her breasts and swept his thumbs back and forth across her nipples. He bent and suckled a hardened peak, drawing her deep into his mouth. Each rhythmic tug seemed to pull at her womb, making it throb and yearn.

"Oh, Ryan!" Gasping, Cristen arched her neck back and clutched his head with both hands, burying her fingers in his hair, pressing frantically against his scalp to hold him to her as he lavished the same fierce attention on the other breast. Her heart beat against her ribs like a wild thing, while the rest of her body seemed to grow weak and liquid.

Hazily, Cristen heard the pop of a snap and the soft rasp of a metal zipper being lowered. His movements now frantic, Ryan hooked his thumbs under the top of her jeans and dropped to one knee, pushing them down around her ankles. Cristen held on to his shoulders for balance as he eased her shoes and socks and the soft denim over her feet and tossed them aside. The tiny triangle of lilac silk and lace quickly followed.

Ryan wrapped his arms around her hips and pressed his face against her stomach. "Oh, sweetheart, I've lain in that bedroom night after night, dreaming of this. Going crazy with wanting you," he said in a raspy whisper as he strung hot kisses over her silky skin.

Cristen trembled and held him close, her fingers buried in his hair. Her emotions overwhelmed her, and she closed her eyes against the sweet rush of feelings that surged up inside her—feelings she didn't want to put a name to. Instead she concentrated on the thrilling physical sensations within Ryan's embrace: the erotic brush of his mustache against the soft skin of her belly, the strength of his arms around her, the hot wetness of his mouth, the warm, silky feel of his hair.

The pleasure became so intense that it was almost pain, and finally, trembling, Cristen gripped his shoulders and urged him upward. "Please, Ryan. Oh, please."

He stood at once. His burning gaze roamed over her hungrily, sliding over every line, every dip and curve of her naked body, promising untold delight and sending Cristen's passion soaring. "Yes. Oh, God, yes," he said with throaty urgency.

Reaching around her, he tossed back the spread and covers, then eased her back onto the bed. As she stretched out languidly, Ryan snatched off his own clothes, his avid gaze never once leaving her. Then he was there beside her, pulling her to him, and their soft moans of pleasure blended together at the first thrilling touch of warm flesh to warm flesh.

His kiss was deep and penetrating, exploring her mouth with the same urgency that his hands explored her body. He traced the long, lush line of hip and thigh, the inward curve of her waist, the exquisite flare of her rib cage. Lovingly, he cupped his hand around her breast and flexed his fingers against the soft flesh.

Ryan kissed his way down her neck and collarbone to the scented valley between her breasts. Gently, he brushed his thumb across her aroused nipple, bringing it into swollen readiness, and Cristen moaned, her head moving from side to side on the pillow. With a soft growl of satisfaction Ryan's mouth closed lovingly around her nipple.

"Oh, Ryan!" she cried out, digging her nails into his back as a riot of sensations exploded inside her.

In restless passion, Cristen's hands ran over his shoulders and neck and back, her fingertips tracing the tiny knobs in his spine, then slipping around to explore his chest and twine in the coarse hair that covered it, tugging gently.

Every touch, every tiny incoherent sound of pleasure pulled their emotions tighter and tighter. Their breathing grew rapid, deep, labored.

Cristen trembled, her body awash with sensations and driving need. She had not known such voluptuous pleasure existed. It was sweet agony, and she gloried in it, greedily savoring each wondrous rush of emotion. The taut, throbbing ache that consumed her was nearly driving her mad, yet she wanted—demanded—more.

A whimper of pure pleasure escaped her as Ryan caressed the silky skin of her belly. The whimper became a moan when searching fingers slid lower and lovingly parted the warm, moist petals of her womanhood.

Her cry seemed to steal the last of Ryan's control. He raised his head and looked down at her, his face flushed and taut. "Oh, God, sweetheart. I can't wait any longer."

"I don't want you to." She gripped his shoulders and urged him to her. "Love me, Ryan," she whispered shakily. "Love me now."

It was all the encouragement he needed. He levered up and positioned himself between her soft thighs. Holding her gaze, he entered her in a smooth, silken stroke, smiling tightly as he watched her eyes glaze, her face soften with ecstasy.

He pressed deep, and when he was sheathed in her heavenly warmth, he threw his head back and went perfectly still. Strained muscles bunched and quivered in the arms braced on either side of Cristen's head. Eyes closed, his face contorted with passion, he clamped his teeth over his lower lip and fought for control.

But passion too long denied, desires too long repressed, could not be held in check. Ryan's self-restraint crumbled when Cristen's hands came stealing around his neck. With a groan he allowed her to tug him down, and they were quickly caught up in the age-old rhythm of love.

His thrusts were deep and strong, and Cristen's hips lifted eagerly to meet each one. Passion built and spiraled. Their movements became rapid, urgent, drawing the knotting tension tighter, ever tighter, until they were taut and eager, reaching...reaching...

And then the explosion rocked them both, and they cried out and clung to each other as the world seemed to disintegrate in a shower burst of ecstasy.

Chapter Ten

A lover. She had a lover. Standing beside the window, holding aside the sheer curtain, Cristen gazed out at the moonlit sky and the scattered lights of the city below. Even now, she could scarcely believe it.

Never in her wildest dreams had she pictured herself in such a situation. Her future had always seemed so clear, so...preordained. The pattern had been set early, and she had taken it for granted that she would spend her life with Bob. She wasn't prepared for a love affair.

Cristen looked over her shoulder at Ryan's recumbent form and felt the familiar warmth well up inside her. He lay sprawled on his back, one arm flung over his head. He had the look of a sated male—relaxed, satisfied, well pleased. Against the pale blue sheets his tanned skin looked darker than ever, his mussed hair a splotch of ebony. His rugged face was gentled in sleep, the strong jaw not quite so hard, the sensual lips slightly parted, revealing the edge of even white teeth. Cristen's gaze tracked downward over his brawny chest, following the path of dark hair that narrowed into a thin line over his concave belly and disappeared beneath the sheet that draped low across his hips. Heat coursed through her, and her breasts grew heavy, achy. Lord, he was so beautifully male.

Recalling the passion they had just shared, the hours of loving and intimacy, Cristen was shocked that she could be aroused again so soon by just the sight of him. She had never considered herself a particularly sensual woman, but with Ryan she was wild and wanton.

It was not a comfortable admission, but Cristen knew it was pointless to deny her feelings. She'd been doing that for months, and it had accomplished nothing.

With a sigh, she dropped the curtain and walked back to the bed. Her chest felt tight and her throat ached as she stared at Ryan with a mixture of longing and doubt. It was also pointless to deny the obvious: ready or not, like it or not, tonight had marked the beginning of a full-fledged, passionate affair.

Her heart seemed to do a little skip at the thought, but Cristen ignored it and let the satin robe slither from her shoulders, tossing it across the bedside chair as she slid back into bed. Careful not to wake Ryan, she pulled the sheet up over her bare breasts and stared at the darkened ceiling. Okay, so you're having an affair. So what? It was bound to happen sooner or later. After all, you're a normal, healthy young woman. So you're not prepared. You can handle it. Other women do. It's not as though you're making a lifelong commitment here. An affair is just that: an affair, a temporary liaison. Surely, if you go into a relationship knowing that it must eventually end, the parting won't hurt so much.

Cristen rolled her head on the pillow and felt a lump form in her throat as her gaze trailed over Ryan's profile. Oh, she would feel sadness, maybe even a little pain, but she would survive it as long as she didn't let things get out of hand.

All I have to do is keep things light, she told herself with firm conviction. No strings, no promises. That's the way to handle it. She turned on her side and closed her eyes, cupping her hand beneath her cheek. Just thank your lucky stars that Ryan O'Malley is not the marrying kind.

A patch of sunlight stretched across the floor, climbed up the side of the bed and painted a golden rectangle on the sheet draping Cristen's sleeping form.

Propped up on his elbow, his head resting against the heel of his hand, Ryan studied her with a profound sense of satisfaction and possessiveness.

God, she's beautiful, he thought, marveling at her creamy skin and the extravagant lashes that lay across her cheeks like tiny fans. Beautiful, fascinating, sexy, adorably stubborn and intense.

And mine.

Ryan released a contented sigh. After last night, there was no doubt about that.

Cristen stirred. The movement sent a curl tumbling across her cheek, its wispy end just touching her nostril. She twitched her nose and batted the air in front of it.

Smiling, Ryan gently pushed the tendril back behind her ear. His hand lingered there, his fingertips rimming the delicate shell, feathering over the tender skin behind it. He was impatient for her to wake up. He wanted to kiss her, to hold her close, to indulge in the nonsensical early-morning banter of lovers. He wanted to make love to her again.

But most of all, he wanted to say, "I love you," to see the look in her eyes when she heard the words...to hear them from her lips.

Was it too soon to propose? Lord, he hoped she didn't think so, because he sure didn't want to wait any longer. The past few months had been pure hell, lying in the other bedroom night after night, wanting her, loving her, until he was just one big ache.

But no more. He ran his fingers through her tousled hair and watched, fascinated, as the vibrant curls twined about them, then slipped away like strands of shimmering silk. The minute he got back to San Francisco he was going to have a ring made. An emerald, he decided, to match her eyes.

Cristen's breath made a whispery sound as it drifted in and out between her barely parted lips, drawing Ryan's gaze to their soft allure. He wanted to kiss her but resisted the temptation. After the night of loving they had shared he knew she needed the rest. He couldn't remember how many times they had made love, but it had been the small hours of the morning before their hunger for each other was appeased enough to allow sleep. God, it had been heaven.

Determinedly, Ryan dragged his gaze away from her enticing mouth, only to encounter the even greater temptation of her pert, bare breasts.

Cristen slept with the total abandon of a child, arms flung wide, blissfully unaware, and looking like a gorgeous Venus with the sheet tangled about her hips. Ryan stared at the lush feminine flesh, enthralled by the translucent skin, the tiny blue veins that rivered beneath it, the rose velvet nipples, puckered now by the cool air flowing from the vent in the ceiling. He longed to touch her, to draw a sweet nub into his mouth, to feel it harden against his tongue.

He fought it, but the sweet enticement was too much to resist. Leaning forward, he laved a dusky areola with his tongue, then drew back and blew gently. His eyes darkened as he watched it peak.

Ryan rolled forward and half covered Cristen with his body. With his forearms braced on either side of her rib cage, he cupped her breasts with his hands and buried his face in that soft, fragrant valley between. His tongue traced intricate patterns on the silken skin while his long fingers flexed around the tender mounds, lifting, weighing, squeezing, pressing them against his face. At last he trailed his mouth up over the soft flesh and captured a yearning nipple. He worried it gently, first with his teeth, then with his lips, and then, making a sound of satisfaction, he drew the aroused bud into his mouth and suckled deeply.

The feel of Cristen's fingers threading through his hair alerted him that she was awake, and he drew on her harder, slower. She arched her back and made a soft, purring sound, her nails lightly scoring his scalp.

The air felt cool against her wet flesh when he released her and looked up. His blue eyes were heavy-lidded and slumberous, his smile a wicked beguilement. "Good morning, beautiful," he said in a husky voice. "It's about time you woke up."

"Mmm. Good morning." Cristen stretched and rolled her head on the pillow, blinking languorously. "You're better than an alarm clock any day, you know that," she mumbled.

Ryan chuckled and nipped her playfully. "Great! I'm making mad, passionate love to the woman, and she compares me with a mechanical device. You're rough on the ego, babe." He nipped her again, then soothed the tiny pain with his tongue.

"Sorry. I'm not awake yet."

She watched him through slitted eyes, her look tender and passionate. Her fingers slid from his hair and down, tracing the broad, flat muscles that spanned his back, delicately trailing over his spine and shoulder blades. Everything about him pleased her.

Everything that was Ryan pulled at her senses like a strong magnet—the look of him, the feel of him, that wonderful masculine scent that was his alone. His mouth was warm against her skin, his tongue a velvet rasp that sent fire streaking through her. Even the slight abrasive rub of his beard stubble was oddly thrilling. She had never felt this way about a man before—not even Bob—and beneath the wonder of it ran a thread of fear.

Ryan switched his attention to her other breast, and Cristen's fingers dug into his back.

"How about now? Are you awake yet?" he teased before returning to his pleasant task.

"Not . . . not completely," she gasped as her body responded to his seductive ministrations.

Ryan raised his head and grinned. "Then I guess I'll just have to do something about that." Taking most of his weight on his forearms, he slid upward a few inches, his grin growing wider when the erotic friction between their bodies wrung another gasp from Cristen. Holding her gaze, he settled himself slowly, enjoying her little moan of pleasure as her sensitized nipples pushed up through the mat of hair and pressed against his chest. He rubbed against her, and with his mouth hovering just a hairsbreadth from hers, he murmured, "Because what I have in mind requires your full attention."

His kiss was pure seduction. Warm, slow, persuasive, his mouth rocked against hers, demanding a response. Cristen gave it willingly. With a long moan of pleasure, she went boneless beneath him and wound her arms about his shoulders, giving herself up gladly to the delicious sensations, to the heat and the power.

He lay cradled between her thighs, his body a wondrous heavy weight that pressed her deep into the mattress. She could feel his aroused manhood nudging intimately against her, seeking, yearning. Her body throbbed in answering need, and she kissed him back hungrily, sliding her hands down over his taut back to grasp his buttocks, urging him to complete the embrace.

Obeying her silent command, Ryan made them one, thrusting into her welcoming, moist warmth with a deep, sure stroke that wrung a cry of joy from both of them.

The time for slow seduction was past. Ryan loved her with bold sureness, demanding and giving with each powerful thrust. Cristen moved against him, matching his ardor, her hips arching and her long legs twining around him. The hours of loving they'd shared the night before might never have been, so great was their need. Their wild rhythm knotted desire tighter and tighter. Dark whispered words, stroking hands, incoherent sounds of pleasure, all fueled their passion.

Ryan inflamed. Cristen burned. And soon the fire consumed them both.

Cristen threw her head back and clutched his shoulders, chanting his name over and over as Ryan's hoarse shout sounded in her ear. A violent shudder shook him, and he collapsed against her, burying his face against her neck, while she hugged him tightly. Their hearts thundered in unison, and for several minutes the only sound in the room was the labored rasp of their breathing.

Replete and sated, Cristen stared at the ceiling and gently stroked Ryan's sweat-sheened back. Feelings swelled within her—delicious, warm, dangerous feelings that she knew could lead only to heartbreak. They made her chest tight and achy and filled her with the desire to weep, but she swallowed hard, widened her eyes and blinked back the threatening tears. You will not be foolish about this, she told herself as she struggled to bring her wayward emotions under control. You will not fall in love with this man. You will not.

After a while, Ryan rolled from her and lay on his back, eyes closed. At last, softly, he said, "I think I've died and gone to heaven." He opened one eye and grinned. "I don't think you can feel this good and live."

Cristen managed a lazy chuckle. "I know."

Turning on his side, Ryan propped himself up on his elbow and smiled down at her. "You awake now?"

"Hmm. Awake but not mobile. It's a miracle," she murmured drowsily. "Usually I don't even know there's a world until after the alarm blasts me out of bed and I'm up and moving. I— Oh, my Lord!" Cristen jackknifed to a sitting position and looked at the clock. "The alarm! I forgot to set it! I'm going to be late!"

She started to scramble for the side of the bed, but Ryan hooked his arm around her waist and hauled her back, pressing her down on the pillow. "Relax, will you? The shop won't fall apart if you're not there before opening. In a few minutes you can call Louise and tell her you're going to be late, but right now we need to have a talk."

"A talk? About what?"

Ryan smiled at her wary expression. "About last night. About us."

"What is there to talk about?" Cristen looked down and plucked at the hair on Ryan's forearm. Striving to appear casual and unconcerned, she said lightly, "After all, we're two adults. We both know that these things happen. Just because two people are strongly attracted to each other and are...uh...sexually compatible, that doesn't mean they have to make a lifelong commitment. You've been a bachelor all these years, so I know you're not interested in a permanent relationship. And I'm certainly not."

Ryan went very still. "Is that what we have? A strong physical attraction for each other?"

"Yes. Of course."

"I see," he said after a moment. "So how do you suggest we handle this 'attraction'?"

"Well, I don't have any experience with this sort of thing, and I haven't given it much thought, but..." A faint flush tinted Cristen's cheeks, and she shifted under Ryan's penetrating stare. "Well...given our living arrangement, I suppose an open relationship would be best."

"Open?" Ryan's brows cocked. "Define *open* for me."

"You know—no strings, no demands. No promises. We simply enjoy each other for as long as it lasts."

"What you're saying is no commitment of any kind. Right?"

"R-right," Cristen replied, suppressing the stab of pain the word brought. "And...and when it's over for either of us, we end it, with no recriminations."

Ryan stared at her in silence for so long that Cristen began to fidget and finally dropped her gaze back to her restless fingers.

"Why won't you tell me about it, sweetheart?" Ryan asked gently, and Cristen grew even more wary.

"Tell you about what? I don't know what you mean."

"Your marriage. I can only assume that it was a disaster. Otherwise you wouldn't be so gun-shy about a serious relationship."

Cristen stiffened. Her expression became remote. "Well, you're wrong. My husband and I got along quite well. We had a very... comfortable marriage."

Making an impatient sound, she shoved aside his arm and sat up. "I really don't have time for this, Ryan. I have to go to work." Self-consciously, she pulled on her peach satin robe and hurried toward the bathroom. At the door she stopped and turned to look back at him, her expression uncertain. "You do agree with me, don't you? About keeping things casual?" She held her breath, waiting for his reply. If he said no, she didn't know what she would do.

"Sure. No problem." With total disregard for his nakedness, Ryan pushed himself up in the bed until he was leaning against the headboard. He draped his wrist over his updrawn knee and flashed her a lopsided grin. "We'll just take it as it comes."

Relief poured through Cristen, but, strangely, along with it came a vague sense of disappointment, which she stoutly refused to acknowledge. "Good, then we— Oh, dear Gussie! Look at the time!" She whirled and dashed into the bathroom, calling over her shoulder, "Call Louise for me, will you, and tell her I'll be there in a half hour. Forty-five minutes at most."

Ryan's grin faded as the door closed behind Cristen. An affair. Hell and damnation!

He snatched up a pillow and hurled it across the room. It bounced off the wall and hit the carpet with a soft, unsatisfying plop, but it was enough to send Theda scurrying for cover.

Fists clenched, Ryan leaned back against the headboard and cursed a blue streak. When he started repeating himself he swung his feet to the floor, propped his elbows on his spread knees and cradled his head in his hands. Hell, it's probably poetic justice, he decided grimly.

Never in his life had Ryan deliberately hurt a woman. He had played the field for years, but he'd always been honest and straightforward about his intentions, or rather, lack of them. And all his relationships had been with worldly, experienced women who claimed to feel exactly the same, though he knew there had been a few who had cared more than they had let on.

No strings. Ryan gave a mirthless chuckle, then sighed heavily and pulled his palm down over his face. Hell, he wanted strings, all right. He wanted to bind Cristen to him in every way possible. He wanted to see his ring on her finger and, someday, his child at her breast. He wanted her in his life, in his home, in his bed. Permanently.

And all *she* wanted was an affair. Damn!

"We had a very comfortable marriage," Ryan mimicked nastily under his breath. What the devil did that mean? It sounded deadly dull.

But how could that be? To his way of thinking, marriage with Cristen would be exciting, stimulating and emotionally and physically satisfying. Anything but dull.

Even if her ex-husband was the world's biggest bore, that still didn't explain her aversion to marriage. What had gone wrong?

He wanted to storm into the bathroom and demand an answer, to give in to the uncharacteristic, primitive desire to rant and rave and pound his chest until she told him what he wanted to know. Ryan looked at the closed bathroom door and gritted his teeth. He wouldn't, of course. Caveman tactics were not his style. More important, however, he had a gut feeling that if he pushed her, she would take flight.

Well, it could be worse, he told himself as he stood and gathered up his scattered clothing. At least he was here. The arrangement did have that advantage. And now that some of the barriers were down, others would follow. He'd just have to chip away at them day by day. There was a hell of a lot more between them than just physical attraction, and somehow, some way, he was going to make Cristen see that. He'd been patient for months, and, though it went against the grain, he could manage to be patient for a while longer.

Ryan thought about the loving they had shared. It had been wonderful, beyond his wildest imaginings. A smile— part pleasure and part pure masculine smugness—tugged his mouth as he recalled Cristen's incoherent cries, the feel of her lying beneath him, the passion and eagerness in her face. And sweetest of all, her lingering shyness and her naive joy and astonishment at each shattering climax.

Affair, hell! Ryan thought, his jaw firming as he stalked toward the door. We'll see about that.

The crazy little fool! Cristen might not realize it, but she wasn't cut out for a shallow, temporary relationship. He didn't for one minute believe that she would have slept with him unless she loved him. And Cristen would love just as intensely, just as steadfastly as she did everything else.

It would take subtlety and patience and time, but he would win her over eventually. He had to. Being Cristen's lover was fantastic, but being her husband—that would be heaven.

Louise was frankly delighted with the turn of events. For days after she learned that Cristen and Ryan were lovers she walked around with a smug I-told-you-so smile on her face.

Cristen had had some vague idea that publicly she could just pretend that nothing had changed, and no one would be the wiser, but the moment she arrived at the shop that morning Louise had taken one look at her glowing face and pounced.

"Well, well, well. So it's finally happened, has it?"

"I don't know what you're talking about," Cristen had claimed loftily.

"Don't give me that. Those are stars in your eyes, if I ever saw them. Plus, you've got that look."

"What look?"

"The look of a woman who's been well loved. So come on, fess up."

The fiery blush that crept up Cristen's face had belied her denial, but she still managed to stonewall Louise's probing questions and endless speculation. Then Ryan had arrived and spilled the beans.

Not in the least reticent about proclaiming their new closeness, he had walked into the shop a little before closing, pulled Cristen into his arms and given her a long, passionate kiss that had had Louise whooping for joy and Dora gaping like a banked fish.

Denials had been pointless after that. Cristen had tried to muster some annoyance, but Ryan had merely brushed off her scolding with a grin and another kiss. Much to Cristen's surprise, once her initial embarrassment wore off, she found that she much preferred having everything out in the open.

The week that followed was the happiest, the most exciting that Cristen had ever known. They did nothing special, nothing out of the ordinary, but she breezed through each day on top of the world. She bounded into the shop every morning wearing a smile and left every evening full of eagerness and anticipation, her long, lithe stride eating up the five blocks between the shop and her condo so fast that it seemed her feet barely touched the ground. Even at that, there were times when it was all she could do not to break into a run. She worked as hard as ever, but now there was a constant light, buoyant feeling in her chest, a bubbling elation that gave the whole world a rosy hue and made even the most mundane or painstaking task a breeze.

At thirty, Cristen was experiencing for the very first time the euphoric, walking-on-air feeling that comes with falling in love. Of course, whenever the possibility occurred to her she promptly denied it, but all the signs were there: the fluttery heart, the knotted stomach, delight in the smallest things as long as they did them together, the underlying melancholy at being separated from the beloved for even a short time, the rush of joy at reuniting, the sheer pleasure and contentment of just sharing each other's company.

The highs and lows of loving were things Cristen had missed out on, had not even known existed. Bob Patterson had been such an integral part of her life that their feelings for each other had always just "been there," something that had developed over the years, something they had taken for granted. It hadn't come bursting in on them, bringing these extremes of emotion. Cristen despaired of it . . . and reveled in it.

She and Ryan made love often during that first, blissful week, whenever and wherever the mood struck them, and each time Cristen was awed anew. Once she came up behind Ryan while he was shaving, slipped her arms around his waist and ran a line of kisses down his spine. Within seconds she found herself stretched out beneath him on the bath mat, responding wildly to his driving urgency.

Afterward, as they lay side by side, too limp to move, Ryan opened one eye and promptly burst out laughing.

"What's so funny?" Cristen demanded. When his guffaws continued, her bafflement turned to indignation, and she gave him a sharp poke in the ribs.

For an answer, Ryan hauled her to her feet and turned her toward the mirror. Cristen gasped and dissolved into giggles.

Smeared over her face, breasts and abdomen was more shaving cream than was on Ryan's face.

Another time Ryan brought home two choice steaks for dinner, but in the midst of preparing the meal together a stolen kiss ignited into passion, and they ended up on a kitchen chair with Cristen astride Ryan's hips, oblivious to everything but each other and the wondrous ecstasy they shared.

So great was their absorption that it was several moments after reaching an explosive fulfillment that they noticed the smoke pouring out of the broiler.

"Our dinner!" Cristen shrieked.

"Dammit to hell! That's twenty bucks worth of choice beef!"

Panicked, Cristen jumped on one foot and then the other, flapping her hands. When she finally came to her senses she yelled, "The fire extinguisher! It's in the pantry!"

Ryan let out a string of curses that turned the air blue and dashed across the room.

Pandemonium reigned for the next thirty seconds. While Ryan sprayed the flaming meat, Cristen threw open the window and fanned the smoke-filled air with a dish towel.

When the crisis was past and the ridiculousness of it all hit them, they collapsed in each other's arms and laughed until they couldn't stand.

In the end, they dumped the charred steaks into the garbage and ate peanut butter sandwiches.

And neither cared in the least.

Chapter Eleven

Cristen gnawed on her thumbnail and stared at the phone. Her hand inched toward the receiver. At the last second she made a disgusted sound, snatched her fingers back as though she'd been burned and flounced away to resume her restless pacing.

A minute later she was back, staring at the phone with a mixture of longing and irritation. She felt as though she were being drawn to the edge of a precipice, about to lose control and tumble over into an abyss.

I won't call him, she told herself fiercely. I won't.

Foolishly, she had allowed herself to care too much, to become too emotionally involved. She had always missed Ryan when he was in California, but she was not prepared for this despondency, this terrible yearning ache. It angered her. It frightened her.

Cristen turned away again and stalked back across the room. She wouldn't give in to it. She wouldn't call him.

She wouldn't make more of a fool of herself than she already had.

Closing her eyes, she shoved her hands through her hair and pressed her palms tight against her temples, moaning softly as she recalled her behavior the past weekend.

As Sunday, and thus Ryan's departure time, approached she had been eaten up with dread. She told herself over and over that she was being foolish. He would be back on Friday. That it was only five days, after all.

It didn't help.

With every passing hour she had grown tauter, more distracted. She had not been able shake the disturbing feeling that he would not be back. It was irrational, she knew. There was no basis for her fear. She'd kept telling herself that just because Bob had walked away without a word didn't mean that Ryan would. He simply had a business to run.

Yet on Saturday night, when Ryan had taken her into his arms, she'd clung to him, fighting back tears.

Even now, Cristen blushed when she recalled her wanton response to Ryan's lovemaking. His kiss had begun as a slow seduction, but she had been driven by desperation, responding wildly, pressing herself against him and kissing him back with heat and passion. When he had taken her to bed she had writhed and twisted in his arms, frantic for his lovemaking.

It had been the same the next morning. Afterward she'd been horrified to see that her nails had left angry red marks on Ryan's back, but he'd merely flashed his teasing grin and called her a sexy wildcat.

Lord. What must he think of me? Cristen wondered, chagrined at the memory. She had worn her heart on her sleeve like an adolescent. And she hadn't handled the remainder of the day any better.

They'd spent Sunday lazing around the apartment, talking, reading the paper, listening to music. Cristen had tried to enjoy the quiet time together, but she couldn't, for dreading what was to come. The hours had seemed to race by. By the time Ryan was ready to go he had caught her somber mood.

Standing with her hands clasped behind her back, too miserable to speak, Cristen watched him pat his pockets to check for his wallet and keys. Ryan kept clothes in both Houston and San Francisco so that the only thing he carried with him was a briefcase. He riffled through its contents before snapping the lid shut, then looked at Cristen, his eyes reflecting the longing and dread she felt.

"Would you ride to the airport with me?" he asked quietly.

It was a foolish extravagance. Cab fare back from the airport cost an arm and a leg, but not for a moment did she even consider refusing. She would have paid ten times that amount to spend another hour and a half in his company.

It wasn't enough. Far too quickly, Cristen found herself standing at the outer glass wall of the terminal, watching Ryan's plane climb toward the setting sun until it was no more than a speck against the rose-streaked sky.

Heavy-hearted, she trudged through the days that followed on feet of lead. She had no enthusiasm for anything, but she still put in long hours, arriving at the shop early and staying late. Anything to avoid going home to that empty apartment ... and even emptier bed.

"Well, it's time you pulled yourself together and quit acting like a lovelorn teenager, for heaven's sake," Cristen scolded, glaring at the silent telephone. "And you will not call him."

A half hour later and ten arguments to the contrary, Cristen shakily dialed Ryan's office number. It was answered on the second ring by the sultry-voiced secretary, who informed her throatily, and with what seemed to Cristen to be a great deal of relish, that Mr. O'Malley had left for the day.

She called his apartment, and at his "Hello" her heart leaped, only to plummet again when she realized it was merely a recorded voice on his answering machine.

Another call, two hours later, produced the same results, and Cristen hung up the phone slowly, feeling as though there were a lump of wet cement sitting on her heart.

Was he with another woman? The thought sent pain searing through her, but she pressed her lips together and struggled against it. It was entirely possible. Ryan was, after all, free to do as he pleased. They might, by tacit agreement, see only each other when he was in Houston, but nothing had been said about those times when he was in San Francisco.

No strings. No commitments. It was the best way. The only way, she told herself stoutly as her listless steps carried her into the bedroom.

One of Ryan's tennis sweatbands lay on the bedside table. Cristen picked it up and curled into a ball on top of the bedspread, absently stroking the soft terry cloth. Her throat ached, and her chin wobbled. Pressing her lips into a tight line, she gazed across the dimly lit room and fought the foolish desire to weep.

The next night Cristen worked even later, staying at the shop until well past eleven, and returned the next morning at eight. If Ryan wanted to call her, he had the shop number, she reasoned. But she'd be darned if she would call him again. Or even sit around waiting to hear from him.

On Thursday she planned to work late again, but just before closing, Louise's husband breezed in and announced his intention of taking them out to dinner, and all Cristen's protests fell on deaf ears.

"You are not going to work again tonight," Louise informed her. "You'll make yourself sick if you keep on at this rate. Now I won't take no for an answer. You're coming out to dinner with us."

Before Cristen knew what hit her, Louise had closed out the register, hustled everyone out and locked the door.

Lord, he was tired.

As Ryan stepped from the conference room into the corridor the scene behind him was disaster. Overflowing ashtrays, wadded pieces of paper, dirty cups containing the cold dregs of countless gallons of coffee, bent paper clips, empty cigarette packs and cigar wrappers littered the long walnut table, whose glossy surface was speckled with sticky spills and dropped ashes. The air in the room was stale. Overhead, a cloud of blue smoke clung to the ceiling. With the exception of Marsha Townsend, the dozen or so people around the table were rumpled and weary, their disgruntled faces reflecting the strain of hours of fruitless negotiation.

Dark looks and harsh words still flew between the opposing sides, but Ryan closed the door on the bickering. Carrying his suit coat slung over his shoulder, he walked toward the double doors at the opposite end of the hall.

In his office he tossed the jacket over the back of the first chair he came to and sat down at his desk. Relishing the quiet and solitude, he raked both hands through his hair, leaned back and released a sigh that was very near a groan.

Beard stubble shadowed his jaw. Lines of fatigue etched his face, and his eyes were red rimmed and bloodshot. His clothes looked as though they'd been slept in—the shirt wrinkled and blousing over his trousers, sleeves rolled up, collar unbuttoned, the loosened necktie hanging askew beneath it.

Ryan rotated his head and sighed when his neck popped. Wearily, he rested his head on the high-backed leather chair and wondered what to try next. He had stepped off the plane Sunday night to find everything in chaos: management in an uproar, the factory workers threatening to walk out, the union reps hostile and uncooperative. Now, after four days of trying to avert a strike, they were still at an impasse, with no solution in sight.

Making a frustrated sound, Ryan arched his back and rubbed his eyes with the heels of his hands. What he needed was a meal, a hot shower and twelve hours of uninterrupted sleep. But more than any of those, he needed Cristen. He wanted to hold her close, to breathe in the sweet fragrance of her hair, her delicious woman scent, to feel her soft skin against his, to sample its taste and texture. He wanted to kiss her and make love to her and hold her through the night.

A stirring warmth surged through his loins at the thought, and he shifted, his mouth twisting wryly. Thinking along those lines was downright foolish, not to mention painful. There was no way he could be with Cristen until this labor problem was settled.

Ryan straightened and looked at the phone, then at his watch. A little after nine—eleven, Houston time. She would be asleep, but maybe she wouldn't mind. He just needed to hear her voice, to talk to her for a little while, he told himself, picking up the receiver.

A few minutes later Ryan scowled as he counted off the rings at the other end of the line. The telephone was right beside Cristen's bed. Even taking into account what a sleepyhead she was, she'd had plenty of time to wake up and answer.

Finally, after a dozen rings, Ryan muttered a curse and hung up. On an off chance, he dialed the shop, but there was no answer there, either.

He checked his watch again, and his frown deepened. Where was she at this hour? Surely she wouldn't go out with another man. Not after what they had shared.

Ryan's hands knotted into fists, and his jaw grew rigid. He wouldn't put it past her. By now she'd had time for second thoughts. Dammit! It was just the sort of stunt Cristen *would* pull, if for no other reason than to prove to herself that there was nothing serious between them.

During the next twenty minutes he tried both numbers three more times. With each ring of the phone the wrenching ache in his gut grew steadily worse.

He was staring pensively out his window when the door to his office opened. Ryan looked around as Marsha Townsend entered.

"Hi. Am I intruding?"

"No, of course not. Come in." Ryan watched her glide toward him across the slate-blue carpet, amazed anew that Marsha always managed to stay fresh-looking and immaculate. She, too, had been at the bargaining table since early this morning, yet while everyone else looked as though they'd been jerked through a knothole backward, Marsha's trim, wine-red suit and pearl-gray blouse were wrinkle free, her makeup was perfect, and not a single black hair had escaped the intricate chignon at the back of her head.

Settling into one of the leather chairs in front of his desk, Marsha smoothed the pencil-slim skirt over her thighs and knees and crossed her shapely legs, every move slow and deliberate.

Ryan's mouth quirked. Marsha was an intriguing, complicated woman. In a courtroom or at a negotiating table she was a tough-minded attorney; in a social situation, a witty sophisticate; and in the bedroom an insatiable tigress. Yet, even there, she managed to always appear immaculate.

He thought of Cristen lying beneath him, her face flushed and glistening, sweetly contorted in passion, her wild Gypsy curls spread out on the pillow in fiery disarray. A sharp stab of longing pierced his chest, and he barely stifled a sigh.

"How's it going?"

"At this point, it's hard to say. I left them hashing over our offer."

"Which means we'll be here most of the night. That group doesn't seem to be able to agree on anything." Ryan muttered a rude word and rubbed the nape of his neck, then pulled a hand down over his face, his beard stubble making a rasping sound against his palm.

Tipping her head back, Marsha studied Ryan through half-closed eyes. "You need some rest. You look beat."

"Hmm. Aren't we all."

Marsha rose languidly and perched on the corner of Ryan's desk. She leaned back on one palm and gave him a sultry smile. "What do you say we knock off for the night? You could come to my place and soak in my hot tub," she said in a throaty voice. "Afterward, I'll give you a rubdown. I might even be persuaded to grill a couple of steaks."

For a long moment, Ryan looked at her in silence. She was offering much more than a meal and a hot soak, and they both knew it. The brief, torrid affair they'd enjoyed had ended over a year ago, but Marsha was a true hedonist, taking her pleasure when and where she found it. She was perfectly capable of enjoying a night of passion without one iota of emotional entanglement. He suspected that she preferred it that way.

Ryan wouldn't have been human if he hadn't been tempted. Marsha was a beautiful woman and a sexy, imaginative bed partner. He was tired, hungry and frustrated, and his body clamored for the sensual satisfaction she offered.

His gaze slid to the telephone. Was Cristen out with someone else? Would she even care if he took Marsha up on her offer? Ryan sighed and met Marsha's seductive gaze with a rueful grimace. The trouble was, *he* cared. Despite his body's demands, his heart needed more than just a warm, responsive woman. He needed love. He needed caring.

Dammit! He needed Cristen.

"Sorry, Marsha," he said, softening the rejection with an apologetic smile. "I don't think so."

Marsha arched one dark brow but after a moment merely shrugged and slid off the desk. "Okay. It's your loss. If that's the way you want it, then I guess I'll go back and butt heads with the opposition some more."

Watching the deliberate provocative sway of her hips as she sauntered across the room, Ryan grinned. So help me, Cristen, if you've been out with someone else, I may just beat you.

All day Friday Cristen was so jittery that she could barely work. Half expecting Ryan to come directly to the shop from the airport, she tensed and looked up whenever the bell over the door jingled. Each time she told herself to stop acting like an idiot. Just because she'd been eaten up with longing and loneliness didn't mean that Ryan felt the same. He'd certainly been quick to agree to an open relationship, she reminded herself irritably. No doubt he'd been out with some gorgeous California blonde every night.

Even so, after the shop closed Cristen all but ran home. Her disappointment at finding the apartment empty was immense. She told herself that he'd probably just missed his flight, but even so, it was all she could do not to weep.

Six hours later she no longer even tried to hold back her tears. Sitting in the dark, curled up in a ball of misery in the corner of the sofa, she finally accepted that Ryan wasn't coming.

It serves you right, she told herself miserably. You knew better than to fall for that handsome charmer. You were just asking to get hurt. Theda rubbed against her legs, meowing her sympathy, and Cristen absently stroked the cat's back. This was probably his way of telling her it was over. Her laugh was short and mirthless. She was no expert on affairs, but surely theirs had been the shortest on record. Ryan was obviously a man who enjoyed the chase much more than the victory.

Abruptly, she scrubbed at her wet cheeks with the heels of her hands. "Well, I don't care if he never comes back," she vowed, lurching to her feet and dumping a protesting Theda in the process. She stomped from the living room and down the hall to Ryan's bedroom like a storm trooper on the rampage. The man was a faithless, feckless wretch, and she was better off without him. "If he wants out, I'll make it easy for him," she muttered as she scooped up the contents of his dresser drawers and dumped them onto the bed.

At eleven forty-seven Sunday night Ryan stepped into the apartment, flipped on the light, reset the burglar alarm, turned and promptly barked both shins on the mountain of luggage piled in the entryway.

Cursing, he staggered forward through the toppling cases, flinging his arms wide in a desperate effort not to fall flat on his face. The cases crashed to the floor, skidded across the slick surface, slammed into the walls and bounced off again. One hit Ryan in the ankle, and he roared like an enraged bull. Holding his injured leg, he hopped around on one foot and spewed out a stream of imaginative curses that should have blistered the paint off the wall.

In the midst of the unholy racket, Cristen came running in from the bedroom, sleep rumpled, wide-eyed and wearing a black nightgown that was made of a little silk and lace and a lot of imagination.

"Ryan!" She stopped short, joy surging through her at the sight of him, but she quickly squelched the traitorous emotion.

At the sound of her voice, Ryan looked up and glared, his irritation not in the least mollified by the alluring sight she made. "Cristen, what the hell is all this?"

His tone brought Cristen's chin up. "Your luggage," she replied succinctly.

"I can see that. But what the devil is it doing here?"

"I packed your things for you."

"What do you mean, you— Ouch! Dammit," he swore when he took a step toward her. He hobbled another couple of steps, then stopped and put his hands on his hips and pinned her with a narrow-eyed stare. "Are you saying you're throwing me out?"

"I'm merely making things easier for both of us."

"Easier! What the hell does that mean?"

Cristen flinched at his explosive tone, but she held her ground. "Oh, come on, Ryan. I don't need a house to fall on me to get the message. You traipsed off to California and got so wrapped up in your life out there that you didn't even spare me a thought, much less a five-minute phone call. And to top it off, you didn't even bother to let me know that you wouldn't be back on Friday, as usual."

"Didn't my secretary call and tell you I'd probably have to work straight through the weekend?"

"That sultry-voiced sexpot who works in your office? No, she didn't."

"Maybe if you'd stay home once in a while so a person could reach you—"

"You expect me to hover around the phone like some lovesick teenager, waiting for you to remember that I exist? Well, think again, buster!"

"Dammit, Cristen! I was working!"

"Ha! Don't give me that. I called your office."

"And I called you. Several times, quite late at night." He started toward her, menacing despite his limp. "I want to know where you were."

He was angry. Truly angry. Cristen's eyes widened as it hit her for the first time that Ryan—easygoing, devil-may-care Ryan—was actually seething. The knowledge sent a little thrill of fear racing down her spine, but she would have died before letting him know it. She faced him belligerently, her hands on her hips. "Well, that's just too bad. You have no right to question me about what I do. We have an agreement—"

"You can forget that 'open relationship' crap," he roared, slicing his hand through the air and making her jump. "That whole deal is off, as of right now."

"What! Y-you can't—"

"I can and I will." Coming to a stop in front of her, he grasped her shoulders and gave her a little shake. His face was set and implacable, and his eyes blazed like blue fire. "Don't talk to me about no strings and no demands. I just spent the most god-awful week of my life, working my tail off and all the time worrying myself sick, wondering if you were seeing someone else or if you'd had second thoughts about us."

All the fight went out of Cristen, and she looked at him with amazement. "Really?"

With that one breathless word, Ryan's anger melted. He looked into her sweetly vulnerable face, filled with hope and longing and just a lingering trace of fear, and felt his heart contract.

"Really." With a groan, he pulled her tightly against his chest. As her arms wrapped around his back and she nestled against him, he tilted his head to one side and rested his cheek against her hair.

"God, how I missed you," he murmured, rocking her gently. "And I did try to call you, sweetheart. Several times, but you were never here."

"I . . . I tried to call you, too. At your office and your apartment."

"I was tied up in meetings with union reps most of the time, trying to avert a strike. That was why I had to stay over. And I did ask my secretary to call you and let you know. Honest."

"When you didn't show up on Friday, I thought that you'd lost interest," she confessed softly against his dark suit vest.

"Ah, love." Ryan closed his eyes and tightened his hold and continued his gentle swaying. Where did this insecurity come from? Never would he have guessed that his determined, intense, self-assured Cristen would suffer from such doubt, be so heart-wrenchingly vulnerable. It went totally against her nature. The only answer was that she had been hurt badly in the past. Most likely by that damned ex-husband of hers, Ryan thought grimly.

Cristen looked up and touched his jaw with the tips of her fingers. "I didn't see anyone else while you were gone," she assured him, her eyes soft and earnest. "On the evenings I wasn't working I was with Louise and John."

Ryan grinned. "Good." He bent and kissed her long and hard. When he finally raised his head, his smile and the glint in his eye held pure devilment. "But while we're still on the subject, I think we'd better discuss this relationship of ours."

"Oh?" Cristen's heart hammered.

Without releasing his hold, Ryan began to walk her backward, through the door and down the hall. "Uh-huh." He nibbled a line of kisses down her neck as he maneuvered her into her bedroom and across to the bed. "It's time to renegotiate our contract." The backs of Cristen's knees struck the mattress, bringing them to a halt.

Ryan nipped her earlobe with gentle savagery. "Actually, I'm getting pretty good at it."

"Oh, really?" Cristen managed breathlessly.

"Yeah. So listen up." He cleared his throat; then his warm breath wafted across her skin. "First of all, forget that 'keep it light' junk. I'm crazy about you, woman, and I'm through pretending otherwise." With the tip of his tongue, he traced each delicate swirl of her ear. Cristen shivered and clutched him tighter as her knees turned to mush. "Second, from now on our agreement has an exclusivity clause. You're mine and I'm yours, and that's the way it is. Period. I refuse to spend another day eaten up with jealousy, wondering where you are and what you're doing and who you're doing it with.''

"Oh, is that so?'' Cristen tried to imbue her voice with haughty indignation, but it came out all breathless and quavery. Anyway, she was finding his terms very much to her liking. And the thought of Ryan actually jealous of her sent warmth streaking through her veins.

"Yep. If I catch you so much as looking at another man, I'll turn you over my knee. Right after I deck the jerk.''

"Primitive beast.''

"Hmm. You bet.''

Ryan kissed his way across her cheek to her mouth. He probed its corners, then drew her lower lip into his mouth and sucked gently. "And third,'' he whispered as his hands charted her shape, "from now on, we'll be open with each oth—''

He stopped abruptly when his hand encountered the fragile lace that molded her breasts. He backed up a half step and looked her over, his eyes going wide as he took in the skimpy wisp of black silk and lace that skimmed her body. "What is this thing you've got on?'' he asked in a raspy voice.

"It's a nightgown.''

"The hell you say.''

He bent and kissed the rounded tops of her breasts and the scented valley in between, then worked his way downward, following the plunging V neckline all the way to her waist. "Honey, what this thing is, is an invitation,'' he murmured against her skin with a wicked chuckle as he slipped the tiny straps off her shoulder and began to peel the provocative garment down over her hips. "One that I accept.''

Chapter Twelve

Summer sizzled on through July and August, then waned as September lengthened into one of those brilliant, perfect autumns that were so rare along the Gulf Coast. Trees burst into flame. The air was crisp and dry with a faint nip, the sky a clear cobalt blue.

It was a halcyon time for Cristen. Never had she been as happy, as contented. Never had life been so sweet.

The expansion was complete, and business was great. Her personal life was wonderful and exciting. The love she had fought so hard to deny, then to contain, burgeoned and grew day by day. It filled her heart and colored her life and made her happy beyond measure.

When Ryan was in Houston, they spent every spare minute in each other's company, loving, laughing, sharing everything; fun times, quiet moments, mundane chores—it didn't matter as long as they were together. And with each passing day they grew closer and their relationship deepened.

He learned that her favorite color was blue and that she cried at sad movies. She learned that two things he absolutely would not eat were liver and Brussels sprouts. He learned that Cristen's secret fantasy was to play the banjo. She discovered that he was a voracious reader of mystery novels and had a ticklish spot just below his third rib.

They went to an open-air concert at Miller Theater and a baseball game at the Astrodome. He helped her pick out new draperies for the living room, and she helped him wash and wax his car. Ryan liked country-and-western and bluegrass music, but for her he donned a tux and took her to the ballet and the symphony.

Because Ryan adored sports of all kinds, Cristen tried to develop an interest in them, too, and to participate whenever possible. She was game to try anything and gave it her all, but it soon became apparent that sports were not her forte.

When Ryan took her golfing, she dug a hole in the ground with her club every time she swung at the ball, beaned another player with a wild drive and scored in the high two hundreds. On the tennis courts she hit the ball like Babe Ruth swinging for a homer, usually sending it sailing over the backstop. When they went fishing, she hooked an old shoe, a cottonwood tree and the seat of Ryan's pants.

He didn't even consider letting her on a handball court.

After she skinned her knees playing softball and scored for the opposition in a touch football game, Ryan tried to gently dissuade her from trying anything else, but by then Cristen was determined to find at least one sport at which she could excel. Ryan considered—and rapidly discarded—archery, skeet shooting, skydiving and hang gliding. In the end he finally decided he would teach her to bowl. The worst she could do there was throw gutter balls, he reasoned.

"Now then, you put your thumb and two middle fingers in the holes and place your left hand under the ball, like so," Ryan explained, demonstrating.

"Like this?"

"Yes. That's fine." He stepped behind Cristen and reached around her, covering her arms with his. "Now, I want you to concentrate on that little blue spot on the floor while you glide forward—" he gave her a little nudge "—taking one, two steps, you bring the ball back, swing forward on the third and release, keeping your wrist locked as you do, all in one continuous motion. Got that?"

"Yes. Yes, I think so."

Ryan walked her through it once more, just to be sure, then stepped back a few paces to watch.

With her lower lip clamped between her teeth, Cristen cradled the ten-pound ball in her hands and stared down the alley at the triangle of pins. *Three steps. Swing back. Swing forward. Let go. Three steps. Swing back. Swing forward. Let go.*

She repeated the litany several more times, drew a deep breath and took a step. Concentrating for all she was worth, she took the second step, swung her arm back . . . and the ball went flying out of her grasp, straight out behind her like a cannon shot.

"Holy shi— Arghhh!"

Cristen gasped and spun around, just in time to see the bowling ball come down on Ryan's right foot.

"Ow! Ow! Ow! Ow!"

"Oh, Ryan! Oh! I'm so sorry!"

Cursing like a sailor, Ryan hopped around in a crazy circle, his face screwed up in an agonized grimace. Cristen dithered around him, flapping her hands and making sounds of distress.

Finally he collapsed on the players' bench. Cristen dropped to her knees at his feet and reached for his injured foot. "Here, let me take your shoe off so we can see how bad it is."

"No! Don't touch it!" Ryan yelled, but Cristen was already unlacing the shoe. "Ow! *Ooooww!* Watch it!"

Cristen tossed his shoe aside and peeled down his sock with as much gentleness as haste would allow. When his toes emerged she gasped and sat back on her heels.

His big toe and the area just above it were already swelling and beginning to discolor. "Oh, Ryan," Cristen whispered mournfully. She looked up at him with tears in her eyes. "I'm so sorry, darling. I didn't mean—"

"I know. I know," Ryan said through clenched teeth. "Don't . . . worry about it. The important thing . . . now is to . . . get to a doctor."

"Oh! Yes, of course!" Cristen shot to her feet and snatched up her purse. "I'll get someone to help you to the car."

"No. Don't . . . do that. Just give me a hand up. I . . . can make it."

Cristen tried to argue, but Ryan was insistent. Reluctantly, she helped him to his feet and slipped her arm around his waist. It was a slow struggle, and several times they both nearly toppled over, but with Ryan leaning heavily on Cristen and hopping on one foot they finally made it to the parking lot.

As they approached the Jaguar Cristen asked for the keys.

"Keys?" The one-word question reflected wariness that bordered on horror.

"Ryan, I have to unlock the car."

"Oh," he replied sheepishly.

"And I'll need the keys to drive."

"*Drive!* You're going to drive? Oh, no. Not *my* Jag. Absolutely not. I've seen the way you drive."

"Will you be sensible? It's that or call an ambulance. You certainly can't drive. Why, you can't even bear to put your foot on the ground."

"But, Cris, this is my Jag" he said plaintively.

"Yes, darling. I know." Cristen propped Ryan against the side of the car and dug into his jeans pocket for the keys.

"It's a 1975 XKE."

"I know that, too," she said soothingly as she unlocked the car door. Taking advantage of his temporary shock, she gently but firmly maneuvered him into the passenger seat.

"It's a classic."

"Uh-huh."

She slammed the door and hurried around to the driver's side. When she slid in under the wheel and put the key into the ignition, Ryan's shock turned to panic. "Cris, I don't think this is a good idea."

Mentally giving thanks that Ryan had backed into the parking space, Cristen ignored him, gripped the wheel with all her might and stomped on the accelerator.

The car died with a shudder.

"Dammit! You don't just give it gas!" Ryan yelled. "You've got to use the clutch and put it in first gear."

"Oh." Cristen did as he said and hit the gas again...and the Jaguar shot backward, tires squealing.

Luckily, there wasn't a car in the slot behind them.

"You're in reverse! Hit the brakes! Hit the brakes!"

Cristen did—with both feet. The car screeched to a halt and died, and Ryan pitched forward, hitting his head on the windshield and his injured foot on the underside of the dash.

"Ahhhhhh!" Ryan grabbed his abused foot and propped it on his other knee. While he rocked back and forth over it, moaning, Cristen restarted the engine and struggled with the gearshift. Finally finding first, she hit the gas pedal again. This time the car moved forward in a series of jarring, erratic little hops.

"The clutch!" Ryan groaned. "You've got to synchronize it with the gas!"

"Of all the stupid... Why don't they make these things with automatic transmissions?" Cristen grumbled.

This time Ryan's groan had nothing to do with pain.

It took three more tries for her to get the hang of it, but when everything finally meshed they peeled out of the parking lot as if they were rocket powered. Cristen burned rubber for a half a block before the tires got traction. Then she really poured on the speed.

"No! Not the freeway! Cris, I don't think you should—Oh, my God!"

Cristen zoomed up the entrance ramp doing seventy. She cut across four lanes of traffic, drawing a blast from the air horn of an eighteen-wheeler and missing a station wagon by a hair. Ryan turned pasty gray and mumbled something that sounded like a prayer.

A mile down the road she spotted the interchange, but there wasn't a break in the traffic. Cristen held her hand down on the horn and brazened her way through.

"Oh, God. Oh, God. Oh, God," Ryan chanted.

Behind them, tires screamed and horns blared as the Jag tore around the looping underpass onto another freeway.

Two exits later she sent the car hurtling down the ramp at the same death-defying speed and began to make her way through an older, sedate part of town, heading for the medical center.

Clutching the armrest with one hand and his foot with the other, Ryan alternated between cursing, praying and moaning as Cristen careered through traffic, grinding gears, skidding around turns and striking terror into the hearts of other motorists.

At the hospital she turned too sharply and bumped over a corner, then scraped the right tires along the curb before coming to a screeching halt at the emergency entrance. Pale and shaken, Ryan breathed a heartfelt "Oh, thank you, Lord" and leaned his head back against the seat as Cristen cut the engine and scrambled from the car.

In no time the hospital attendants emerged, bundled Ryan onto a gurney and whisked him away to a treatment room, leaving Cristen to deal with the emergency room nurse and her endless forms and questions.

Once that chore was handled, Cristen paced the floor of the waiting room for what seemed like hours, riddled with guilt and worried sick. Oh, you fool. How could you have been so careless? she berated herself. You've probably maimed him for life. Oh, Lord. What if it's serious? What if he ends up walking with a limp? He'll never forgive you.

After another restless circuit of the room, Cristen stepped to the door again, just in time to see Ryan being wheeled down the hall in a wheelchair.

His right leg was encased in a cast from toe to knee, and he looked a bit peaked, but when he saw her hovering uncertainly in the doorway, a lopsided grin kicked his mustache up at a rakish angle. "Hi, slugger. Ready to go another round?"

Relief poured through Cristen at his teasing tone, and she rushed forward to meet him. "Oh, darling, how do you feel? What did the doctor say? Is it bad?"

Ryan chuckled and took her hand. "One broken bone and a massive bruise. I have to stay off it as much as I can. But it should be good as new in six to eight weeks."

"Are you in any pain?"

"No, they gave me something. But I am bushed. What I really need is a comfortable bed, someplace where I can elevate this leg."

"Oh! Of course. You just wait right here and I'll go bring the car around."

"Oh, no. Not that again." Ryan closed his eyes briefly and gave an eloquent shudder. "Cristen, my love, I adore you, but I'd rather run naked through a pit full of hungry alligators than get back in that car with you driving. Now why don't you just go call Louise and John and see if they'll come get us. I can stretch out in the back of Louise's van, and John can drive the Jag back to the apartment."

Cristen protested just on principle, but it was a halfhearted token at best. She didn't relish maneuvering that powerful machine through Houston traffic again. When it came to cars she had only two speeds: stop and wide open. And wide open in that beast was supersonic.

Their friends were happy to help, though they did tease both Cristen and Ryan unmercifully.

"For heaven sake's, didn't you explain to her that you throw the ball *toward* the pins?" Louise scolded as she and John assisted Ryan into the back of the van.

"I think so," Ryan said solemnly.

"Louise! It was an accident. The ball just slipped out of my fingers."

John clapped Ryan on the back. "In the future just remember that you have to be quick on your feet when you're teaching Cristen anything physical, because she goes at everything like fighting fire."

"So I've learned." Grinning at Cristen, Ryan gingerly lowered himself onto the bench seat at the rear of the van.

"Well, at least two good things have come out of all this. I finally get to drive a Jaguar, and—" John paused and winked at Ryan "—you've become a member of a very exclusive club."

"What's that?"

"The I-survived-Cristen's-driving club," both Louise and John said in unison, then burst out laughing, with Ryan quickly joining in.

"Very funny," Cristen grumbled.

It took some doing, but they finally got Ryan home. Once they had him settled in bed, Louise and John left, promising to return the next day with a pair of crutches. As they went out the door, John couldn't resist adding, "And a club T-shirt."

Cristen fussed over Ryan like a worried mother, straightening his blanket, fluffing his pillow and asking him every five minutes if she could get him anything. Even though it had been an accident, she couldn't help but feel guilty, and she was anxious to make it up to him, but Ryan thwarted her efforts when he succumbed to the pain medicine the doctor had given him and fell asleep.

Cristen paced. Every twenty minutes or so she peeked in at Ryan, but he slept on peacefully. She made herself an omelet for dinner, then put on her nightgown and tried to watch television, but she abandoned that after a while in favor of one of Ryan's mystery novels.

Around ten, just as she reached a hair-raising passage, Ryan nearly scared her out of her skin when he awoke and bellowed her name. After helping him to the bathroom, she brought him a dinner tray containing three hearty roast beef sandwiches, a huge bowl of vegetable soup and a tumbler of milk, all of which he devoured with his usual healthy appetite.

When Cristen had dealt with the dishes she returned to Ryan and sat down beside him on the bed. "How do you feel?" she asked, reaching out to touch his cheek with her fingertips.

"Fine."

"Is there any pain?"

"Hardly a twinge."

"Ryan, I am so sor—"

"Shh." He hushed her with a forefinger against her lips. "It wasn't your fault, so no more apologies. Okay?"

Reluctantly she nodded, and he removed his finger.

"Is there anything else you want?"

A hint of a smile played about Ryan's mouth, but there was no amusement in his hot, hooded gaze. It skimmed downward over her neck and shoulders and came to rest on her creamy breasts, swelling above the low-cut apricot lace gown. When he looked up, his eyes were a dark, stormy blue. "Yes," he said in a low, husky voice. "You."

A surprised giggle shot up out of Cristen's throat. "Ryan! You know we can't."

"The hell we can't."

"But . . . but your foot—"

"You just let me worry about my foot."

Ryan reached out and traced one long finger along the lacy edge of her nightgown, leaving a trail of fire on her skin. Cristen's eyes grew cloudy as a delicious shiver rippled through her. Smiling, Ryan slipped the finger into her cleavage, hooked the low neck of her gown and tugged her closer.

Cristen did not even try to resist. When Ryan touched her like that her common sense flew out the window and her will and her flesh turned as weak as mush.

"We'll take it nice and easy," he murmured.

Very deliberately, he eased first one, then the other strap from her shoulders. At his urging, Cristen obediently slipped her arms free, and the lacy garment fell in soft folds about her waist. Bracing himself up on one elbow, Ryan touched the tip of his tongue to her nipple. When it peaked he mouthed it gently. Over and over. The sweet torment made Cristen cry out, and she clutched his shoulders, digging her nails into firm muscles. At last he drew the tender bud deep into his mouth and suckled with slow, strong suction.

Cristen threw her head back and gasped. "Oh, darling! Darling!"

Cold air hit her wet flesh as he abandoned it to lavish the same attention on the other breast. Cristen arched her spine and clasped his head, wanting, needing more.

When she was almost incoherent with pleasure, Ryan eased back on the pillow, pulling her with him. "Lift up your hips, love," he murmured as he pushed her nightgown downward. "There, that's it."

As the nightgown slithered to the floor, Cristen found herself lying half over Ryan. He felt warm and wonderful and masculine and sexy, and her heartbeat felt like a triphammer when her breasts pushed into the crisp mat of hair on his chest. But then her toe bumped against his cast, and she stiffened. "Ryan, I don't think—"

"Don't think," came his urgent whisper. "Just feel. Feel how much I want you. How much I need you." He took her hand and guided it downward, and as her fingers enclosed his velvet hardness he moaned.

"Did I hurt you?" Cristen jerked her hand away and tried to pull back, but Ryan tightened his hold and chuckled.

"Hardly. Just relax, sweetheart. Everything will be fine."

He lifted her more fully atop him and rocked his hips against her, chuckling again at her gasp of pleasure. "Now then. I want you to do exactly as I say."

As his mouth played with her ear he murmured his instructions in a deep, dark voice that sent a hot flush sweeping over Cristen from her toes to the roots of her hair.

"Ry-an!"

His wicked chuckle made dust of her weak protest, and, shyly at first, then with growing boldness, she complied.

"Yes, that's it," Ryan gasped. "That's it. Yes. Oh, God, yes."

"Ahhhhh, love."

For the first few weeks Ryan lazed around the apartment, staying off his foot as much as possible and conducting a great deal of his business by phone. Cristen fussed over him like a banty hen with one chick, seeing to his every need, coming home at noon and preparing a hot lunch and rushing back the minute the shop closed. More than once Louise got so exasperated with her anxious clock-watching that she shooed her out early just to get rid of her.

Ryan mastered the crutches quickly. By the fourth week the doctor gave him permission to return to the construction site, provided he didn't overdo. Transportation was a problem, but Ryan solved it by hitching a ride with his foreman.

To spare himself the rigors of air travel he continued to confer with California office by phone daily and had one of his executives shuttle back and forth with papers that needed his signature and whatever else that required his personal attention.

Cristen was delighted with the arrangement. It was heaven not to face those partings and those long, lonely days without him. She adored knowing Ryan would be there when she got home, sharing her life with him, going to sleep in his arms and awakening to his soft, persuasive kisses.

"If I'd known it would keep you here, I'd have broken your foot sooner," she teased one night as she lay with her head on Ryan's chest.

He chuckled and ruffled her hair. "Yeah, well, don't get any ideas. I happen to be quite fond of my bones just the way they are."

Cristen sighed dramatically. "Honestly. I get no cooperation out of you." She pursed her lips and blew out a gentle stream of air, ruffling his chest hair, then turned her head and nipped the small bud nestled there.

Ryan's reaction was swift and masterful and thoroughly satisfying. In a blink, he rolled her to her back and blanketed her body with his. He propped himself up on his elbows and cupped her breasts in his palms, pushing the lush mounds together. "You want cooperation?" he growled lovingly as his head descended. "I'll show you cooperation, woman."

The only clouds on the horizon were those occasional times when she allowed herself to wonder what the future held. Cristen was happy with things just the way they were, but she knew, deep down, that no relationship remained static. Eventually, they had to make a real commitment to each other...or part. Both possibilities terrified her.

For the most part, though, she pushed those thoughts to the back of her mind. With her usual single-minded determination, she concentrated on the present, reveling in the joy that was hers now.

Cristen had hoped to have the full eight weeks, but it wasn't to be. At the beginning of the sixth, Ryan's top executive called with news that they had been asked to bid on providing and installing a sophisticated security system in an enormous petrochemical plant in Oklahoma. Within minutes Ryan was packing a bag and making flight reservations.

"But I don't see why you have to go," Cristen complained. "Why can't you send someone else?"

"Because this is the biggest account my company's ever had a shot at, and I'm going to make sure no one else goofs it up." Ryan snapped his case shut. "If you'll carry this down to the lobby for me, I think I can manage my briefcase." He swung around on his crutches and started for the dresser, but then he caught sight of Cristen's woebegone expression.

Changing course, he took two thumping steps that brought him up in front of her, and with the crutches braced firmly under his arms, he reached out and grasped her shoulders. "It won't be for long, sweetheart. Just a few days at most. I'll be back before you know it." He dropped a soft kiss on her mouth, but when he raised his head she was still the picture of dejection.

When his coaxing smile didn't work, Ryan took a deep breath and said weakly, "Look...uh...why don't you come to the airport with me. You..." He stopped and swallowed hard. "You can drive my car and bring it back."

That did bring a smile to Cristen's face. "Oh, Ryan," she said, laughing. Looping her arms around his waist, she pressed her cheek against his chest. "I wouldn't ask that kind of sacrifice from you. I'll take a cab, as I usually do."

But she was touched. Touched . . . and a bit frightened. For the offer spoke plainly of the depth of Ryan's feelings, and that was something she wasn't ready to face yet.

At the airport, Cristen tried to convince Ryan to use a wheelchair, but he wouldn't hear of it. Consequently, the walk down the concourse took twice as long. They reached the gate just as the passengers from the previous leg of the flight were deplaning. Cristen was so intent on getting Ryan safely through the crowd that she didn't see the couple coming toward her until she bumped into them.

"Oh! I'm terribly sorry, I—" She stopped short as she focused on the man, and all the color drained from her face.

"Bob!"

Chapter Thirteen

After a stunned moment, Bob smiled uneasily. "Hello, Cris."

Too numb to speak, Cristen merely stared at her ex-husband. What did you say to a man who had walked away without a word?

Beside her, Ryan grew very still, his narrowed gaze moving from one to the other.

Cristen didn't notice. At that moment she wasn't aware of anything but Bob Patterson. It seemed so strange, after a two-year separation, to be looking at that face she knew as well as her own. He hadn't changed outwardly, except that his sandy hair had receded a bit more. He was still too thin, still had that diffident, nervous air about him. And he still dressed in ultraconservative clothes.

Bob's naturally ruddy complexion turned a shade redder under her steady gaze, and he shifted his feet. "Uh...how've you been? You're looking good."

"Fine. I've...I've been fine. And you?" The banal chitchat tightened the vise that was squeezing Cristen's chest. Sweet heaven! We're talking as if we barely know each other, and we spent our entire lives together. We were married, for Pete's sake!

"Actually, I'm terrific," Bob said sheepishly. He hesitated, then took a deep breath and seemed to draw himself up taller.

Cristen had been so spellbound by the sight of him that she hadn't noticed the woman next to him until he put his arm around her shoulder and drew her nearer. Cristen's gaze shifted, and once again shock hit her like a fist to the solar plexus.

"Cris, I'd like you to meet my wife, Vicki." Giving the petite woman a tender look, Bob squeezed her arm and said gently, "Darling, this is Cristen."

"Hello, Cristen. It's very nice to meet you. I've heard so much about you from Bob that I feel I already know you."

As though in a trance, Cristen accepted the proffered hand and mumbled a reply. It struck her that the woman was her opposite. In her heels Cristen was a couple of inches taller than Bob, but Vicki's head barely reached his chin. The sleek dark cap of hair framing her heart-shaped face in no way resembled Cristen's own riot of fiery curls. Vicki was petite, doll-like, with big brown, spaniel eyes and that soft, fragile look that men found so appealing.

And she was at least seven months pregnant.

Ryan coughed discreetly, drawing Cristen's attention.

"Oh, I'm sorry," she said quickly. "Ryan, this is Bob and...and Vicki Patterson. Ryan O'Malley."

Greetings and handshakes were exchanged. From Ryan's expression, Cristen knew he hadn't made the connection between her and Bob, though he was still looking at both of them strangely.

When the amenities were over an awkward silence began to build, and Bob grew more discomfitted. "Well, uh, so how's the shop going?"

"Very well. We've even expanded." Cristen tried to focus her attention on Bob, but over and over her gaze kept straying to Vicki . . . and her protruding abdomen. Bitterly Cristen recalled how in the past, whenever she brought up the subject of starting a family, Bob had had a dozen excuses why they should wait.

"Good. Good. And are you still living in the condo?"

Damn you! she silently fumed. In two years you haven't even bothered to call to see if I was alive. Why ask these inane questions now? "Yes, of course. It's convenient. And I have a roommate now."

Her failure to identify him as that roommate drew a sharp look from Ryan. "Look, I hate to break this up, Cristen," he said, tugging her elbow, "but if I don't get a move on, I'm going to miss my plane. All the other passengers have already boarded."

Bob was clearly happy to escape the tense situation, and after a flurry of hasty goodbyes, the next thing Cristen knew they were heading in opposite directions.

She walked alongside Ryan in a stupor. Mercifully, some deep, primal instinct for survival had taken over, and her mind and her emotions were numb. But a tight knot of pressure was building in her chest, at its core a hurt so deep that it could not be acknowledged. Not yet. Not here.

At the entrance to the boarding tunnel, Ryan braced his weight on one crutch, hooked his hand around Cristen's neck and pulled her close for a hard kiss. She was barely aware of it.

Concern and a touch of panic marked his expression when he raised his head. "What is it, darling? What's wrong?"

"Nothing. I . . . nothing," she managed, staring at him distractedly.

"Cristen, dammit, something—"

"Sir, you really must board now," the flight attendant called. "We're ready to leave."

Frustrated and worried, Ryan cursed under his breath and shot the woman a blistering look. "Look, I'll call you as soon as I get to the hotel, and we'll talk." He kissed Cristen again and grimaced at her blank expression. Then he swung away down the tunnel, his crutches thumping on the thin floor.

Usually Cristen watched until Ryan's plane taxied out onto the runway, but before he was out of sight she turned and walked away. Like a wounded animal going to ground, she instinctively headed for home.

Forty-five minutes later, when she entered the apartment, it was dark. She didn't notice. She didn't care. With zombielike movements, she crossed the shadowy living room and sank down into a chair.

Sitting absolutely still, she stared into the darkness. The pressure in her chest was growing, and her throat was so tight that she could barely swallow. The only sounds were the tick of the mantel clock and her slow, measured breathing.

For a long time she struggled to hold on to the blessed numbness, but it was impossible to keep at bay all the raging emotions that churned just below the surface. Gradually, inexorably, they pushed their way through the unnatural calm, bringing a rush of pain that welled up inside her, searing her to her very soul.

She felt like such a fool. All this time she'd been telling herself that Bob had needed freedom. All their lives she had always been the leader, the stronger of them, and when he left she had assumed that he had gotten fed up with going through life as part of a pair, that he needed time and space to try his wings, to be on his own. It had hurt, terribly at first, but after a while she had been able to accept it.

But now... Now, after seeing him very obviously happily married to another woman, Cristen knew that she had only been fooling herself. It wasn't marriage that Bob had rejected. He had rejected her.

She no longer loved Bob. And she certainly didn't want him back. But that didn't make it hurt any less. By leaving the way he had, by not being honest with her, he had dealt a crippling blow to both her pride and her self-esteem.

Beside her, the telephone rang, shattering the silence and making her jump. She glanced at it, then looked away. It shrilled several times, then stopped, only to start up again a couple of minutes later. This time it rang a full five minutes before the caller finally gave up. Cristen simply tuned it out.

Where had things gone wrong? she wondered. When had Bob stopped loving her? Or had he ever loved her? If he had only told her how he really felt years ago, they could have avoided all this heartache and salvaged a friendship. Did all those years they shared mean so little to him?

For over an hour Cristen sat in the dark, torturing herself with endless, unanswerable questions. Finally she turned on the lamp beside the chair. In a haze of pain, she walked into the hall and retrieved a scrapbook from the back of the storage closet.

Cristen ran her hand lovingly over the front of the album as she returned to the living room and sank down on the floor in front of the sofa. Age had mottled the finish, and the binding was split from years of use. Crammed with much more that it was ever intended to hold, it bulged like an old woman who has gone to seed, tattered edges of worn photographs, bits of paper, snippets of ribbon protruding from the yellowed pages.

Lovingly put together over the years by both her mother and Bob's, the album was filled with pictures and mementos that chronicled the various stages of their children's life together. Memories swamped Cristen as she slowly turned the pages, bringing a fresh wave of pain and shattering her fragile control. Her throat grew so tight that she couldn't swallow, and tears pooled in her eyes.

There were snapshots of them as babies, sitting naked in a wading pool; of three-year-olds making mud pies; of them trudging off to their first day of school, holding hands and carrying their lunch pails; of two gangly, scabby-kneed ten-year-olds with brand-new bikes; as self-conscious teenagers, dressed for a prom; of graduations; and finally, their wedding. There were childish drawings and report cards, old programs and scholastic awards, pressed flowers and pom-pom ribbons, ticket stubs and clippings from the school paper.

A tear welled over and spilled down Cristen's cheek as she took the first picture from the album and ripped it in two. She did the same to a second and a third. By the time she reached the fourth one tears were streaming down her face. Slowly, methodically, she worked her way through the album, tearing the photos to bits and crushing the pressed flowers, letting the fragrant petals sift through her fingers like all the treasured years that now had no meaning.

That was how Ryan found her.

Cristen didn't hear the key in the lock, but when the front door was shoved open so hard that it hit the wall, she started and looked up.

Ryan came thumping into the room a second later, swinging on his crutches as if he were running a race. "Cristen?" He halted just inside the door, chest heaving. When he spotted her huddled on the floor he started forward, then stopped short, his anxious look turning to deep concern at the sight of her pale, tear-streaked face. "Oh, God, love, what is it? What's wrong?"

"Ryan." Her tears spurted anew at the sight of him. She had not realized until that moment how badly she needed him, his comfort and strength, the solace of his caring. Instinctively she rose to her knees and held out her arms. "Oh, R-Ryan...hold m-me. Please...ho-hold me."

When Ryan reached her he slung his crutches aside, dropped down onto the sofa and snatched her into his arms. He crushed her protectively against his chest. "Sweetheart, are you all right? What is it?"

The tears she'd held in check earlier now came pouring out of her in a torrent. The racking sobs shook her body so, a reply was impossible. Waiting for the storm to pass, Ryan pressed a kiss against her crown and rocked her gently as hot tears plastered his shirt to his chest.

Cristen burrowed against him, seeking the strength he gave so willingly. He was the bedrock of her life, her only source of comfort, and she clung to him with all her might.

She was so grateful for his presence that it didn't strike her until she had calmed a bit that Ryan should not be there at all. "Ryan?" she sniffed against his neck. "Wha...what are you doing here? You're supposed to be in...Tulsa."

"I was worried about you. I knew when I left you that something was wrong, so when the plane stopped in Dallas I got off and called. When I didn't get an answer, I caught the next flight back."

"Oh, Ryan." The depth of his caring was a balm to her soul. Cristen was so touched that tears spouted afresh.

"Shh. Don't cry, love." Cradling the back of her head with a firm hand, he held her close and rubbed his cheek against her hair. "Just tell me."

Over her shoulder Ryan surveyed the damage she had wrought. The shredded photos and crumpled mementos spoke eloquently of her pain, and he ached for her. He recognized Bob Patterson from one of the torn pictures and was fairly certain he already knew the cause of her distress, but he needed to hear it from her.

"He was...my...my husband," she choked as Ryan stroked her hair.

"Bob Patterson?"

Cristen nodded, then pulled back. "How did...did you know?"

Still cradling her with one arm, Ryan stroked the tears from her cheeks. "I recognized him from those pictures," he said, nodding toward the scattered debris on the carpet. "Now, don't you think it's time you told me about it?"

Cristen sought again the haven of his embrace and pressed her face against his chest. She didn't want to talk about it, but she knew that Ryan deserved the truth. Strangely, once she began, the whole story, from their childhood together to Bob's desertion, came pouring out of her. By the time Cristen had finished she was again crying, though quietly this time.

For several moments Ryan just held her close. Then he asked sadly against the top of her head, "Do you still love him that much?"

"No. No, it's n-not that. It's just that...I...I feel so...so foolish...a-and so...so inadequate. So worthless."

"Worthless! Oh, sweetheart, don't say that. Don't even think it," Ryan whispered thickly. "You're the most wonderful woman in the world to me. Don't you know that?"

The words should have comforted her, but instead they tore at her heart, because she wanted so badly for them to be true, and they weren't. They weren't. Ryan had known her only a short time. Bob had known her all her life, and he had not thought she was worth loving.

The thought brought a fresh spasm of pain, and Cristen's shoulders began to shake again. Ryan's arms tightened around her, hugging her to his chest in a bone-crushing embrace. "Oh, don't, sweetheart. Don't do this to yourself. You're not to blame."

"But I a-am. I am. Don't you s-see? I've been...blind and stupid. All my...life I've been living in a dream world that didn't exist. I...I thought Bob loved me, b-but he didn't. He never h-has."

Ryan released his hold and raised her head, framing her tear-streaked face between his palms. "You're wrong, darling. I'm sure Bob loved you in a way. He probably still does. The problem is that neither of you ever had any other options. You drifted from being childhood playmates into being teenage sweethearts, and from there into marriage. You were such a part of each other's life that you never stopped to question if what you felt was love or just a deep fondness based on years of shared memories." His eyes full of sympathy, Ryan shrugged. "It took him a while, but Bob obviously started to question."

"And discovered the answer was he didn't love me after all," Cristen murmured in a wavering voice.

"Not the way a man should love the woman he marries, no." Ryan paused, then added softly, seriously. "Not the way I love you."

Cristen caught her breath as she read the silent message in his blue eyes. A panicky feeling rose inside her, suffocating her, and she tried to move away, but Ryan was having none of it.

His hand shifted from her face to her upper arms, and he held her in place, his eyes boring into her, refusing to let her look away. "Do you love me, Cristen?"

She gave him a desperate look, silently pleading with him to stop. "Ryan, please..."

"Do you?"

"You know I do, Ryan, but..."

"Then marry me."

Cristen closed her eyes, pain overwhelming her. Slowly, one by one, fresh tears squeezed from beneath her lids and streamed down her face. "I...I can't," she whispered in anguish. "I just...can't."

"Why not? We love each other. *Really* love each other. We can make it work, darling."

Cristen pulled herself out of his arms and retreated to the other side of the room. She felt brittle, ready to shatter. As though forcibly holding herself together, she folded her arms across her middle. "Ryan, please don't do this."

"Don't do what? Don't ask for commitment? Don't expect a future? I can't do that, Cristen. You must have known it would come to this eventually, feeling as we do about each other."

"But why can't we just continue the way we are?"

"The way we are? You mean just live together a few weeks out of the month, then go our separate ways the rest of the time?" Ryan gave a short, mirthless laugh. "Not good enough, sweetheart. Oh, I'll admit we've had good times. The company's great, and the sex is fantastic. But I want more than that from you, Cristen. I want you to be my wife, the mother of my children. I want to grow old with you by my side. I want marriage and all it implies."

"Ryan, please. Don't you understand? I tried marriage, and I couldn't make it work, not even with a man I'd known my whole life. I can't go through all that again." Unable to bear his bleak expression a minute longer, she turned away.

When Ryan next spoke he was standing behind her. His voice was soft, heavy with sadness. "Cristen, trust is part of love. If you really love me, you have to believe that I'd never willingly hurt you."

Cristen turned slowly. She reached up and touched his cheek with the tips of her fingers, her face tight with pain. "I *do* love you, Ryan. I do. It's just that I . . . I can't handle marriage right now. I just can't."

He removed her hand from his face and held it in a gentle grip. For a moment he just stood there, staring at her hand, brushing his thumb back and forth across her knuckles. He looked up, and his eyes held a world of sadness and hurt as he said softly, "Well, I guess that about says it all."

Cristen stared at him, fear coursing through her. "Ryan, I love you."

Pain and weariness etched his features. He edged closer and, bracing himself on his crutches, framed her face with his hands. He studied her anguished expression, his own heavy with regret. "I know," he said tenderly before dropping a soft kiss on her parted lips.

He gazed into her frightened green eyes, touched one corner of her mouth with his thumb, then turned and made his way across the room and out the door.

Numb, Cristen stared after him, stricken with loss.

* * *

He'll be back, Cristen told herself repeatedly all during the following week. Of course he will. After all, he left his clothes, so he has to come back. *He has to.*

Yet the awful feeling that Ryan wouldn't return never quite left her, and by closing time on Friday she was a bundle of raw nerves. Riddled with both dread and anticipation, she rushed home, only to have her worst fear realized: Ryan wasn't there.

After the first slump of depression Cristen roused herself enough to check Ryan's room and was immensely relieved to find his things still there. He'll be back, she told herself. He probably just had to take a later flight.

But as the hours passed and Ryan still didn't appear, Cristen's shaky confidence began to dissolve. By the time ten o'clock came, she had all but given up hope.

She was huddled in a dejected ball on the sofa, arms wrapped around her legs, her chin propped on her knees, staring at the television news commentator and not taking in a single word, when the unmistakable sound of a key in the lock sent her spirits soaring. Cristen jumped up and swung around to face the door, her heart thumping and her face alight with joy.

Ryan swung into the room on his crutches, followed closely by Charley Hawkins, their doorman, who carried his suitcase. "Just put it down anywhere, Charley," Ryan instructed as he reset the alarm. "I can handle it from here."

"Sure thing, Mr. O'Malley." Charlie accepted Ryan's tip, doffed his cap, muttered a quick "Evening, Ms. Moore" to Cristen and left.

When Ryan turned from closing the door, his gaze met Cristen's for the first time. He smiled politely. "Hi."

"Hi." Cristen felt as jittery and tongue-tied as a schoolgirl. She twisted her hands together behind her back and groped for something more to say. "How was your trip?"

"Fine."

"Good, good."

Giving her another distant smile, Ryan turned and began to flip through the stack of mail on the small table by the door.

Cristen fidgeted. "You're, uh, you're late tonight. Did you miss the early flight?"

"No. I just decided to take the late one."

"Are you hungry? Would you like something to eat?"

"No, thanks."

Bracing his weight on one crutch, Ryan bent and picked up his suitcase.

"Oh! Here, let me get that," Cristen said as she leaped forward to take it from him.

"That's okay. I can manage." With the case resting against his crutch, his hand wrapped around the handle and the crutch grip, Ryan started across the living room. At the hall door he paused and gave her another of those damnable polite smiles. "If you'll excuse me, I think I'll say good-night. I'm bushed."

"Of course," Cristen said faintly. "Good night, Ryan."

She trailed along behind him as far as her bedroom door, where she stood and watched with a heavy heart as he clumped on down the hall to his old bedroom, the room he hadn't slept in since the night they first became lovers.

All the next week, Saturday and Sunday included, Ryan worked at the construction site, rising early and not returning until late at night. The only way Cristen got to see him at all was by waiting up until he came in, and then he always excused himself immediately and went straight to his room. He was polite, even amiable, but there was a feeling of constraint between them, a distance that could not be breached.

The following Friday, Cristen could have wept when she returned home to find a note from Ryan telling her that he had caught an early flight back to California.

It was a pattern that repeated itself over the next few weeks, only now, instead of spending his weekends in Houston, Ryan flew in late Sunday night and flew back early on Friday. Cristen saw him so rarely, he'd had his cast removed for over a week before she even knew it.

They no longer shared meals or chores or anything else. Ryan stopped leaving coffee and juice for Cristen in the bathroom. She no longer bothered to buy his favorite beer because Ryan was never there to drink it. On the few occasions when they bumped into each other they were so excruciatingly courteous it made her wince inwardly.

One Friday Ryan left her a check for his rent, along with a note explaining that he had included an extra hundred dollars to make up for his inability to help with the housework. Cristen's heart seemed to crack when she read the formal little missive, and she closed her eyes and bit back tears, distressed to her lovelorn soul that they had become merely two strangers sharing the same roof.

To Cristen's dismay, Ryan no longer seemed in the least interested in her as a woman. Once, when he came home earlier than usual, she was lounging on the sofa watching television, clad in one of her most revealing nightgowns. Cristen's heart pounded in anticipation when Ryan drew near, but he didn't even pause as he said, "Hi, Cris. Enjoying the movie?" Stricken with an acute sense of loss, she watched him disappear down the hall.

Cristen yearned so for the love they'd had that she thought her heart would surely break. She spent most evenings wandering through the apartment like a wraith, too unhappy and restless to settle anywhere for long. Her longing became so sharp that she found herself doing utterly foolish things: burying her face in Ryan's terry-cloth robe and breathing in his scent, running her fingers over his hairbrush, sniffing his cologne.

It was, of course, impossible for Cristen to hide her misery from Louise, and once her friend had ferreted out the whole story she put the blame squarely in Cristen's lap.

"I always knew you were mule stubborn, but I didn't know you were stupid, too. How could you be so foolish? That man loves you and you love him, yet you're going to throw all that away, just because Bob Patterson didn't have the gumption to act like a man." She threw her hands up in disgust. "Lord have mercy, you're not just stupid, you're a coward."

"I am not! Louise! How can you say that?"

"Easy. The only reason you turned Ryan down is because you're afraid he'll desert you like Bob did."

"It could happen," Cristen said defensively, giving her a wounded look. "Sometimes love dies."

"That's hardly likely. Not with a man like Ryan. Besides, I doubt that Bob stopped loving you. I think he just finally realized that it wasn't the kind of love you build a marriage on." Louise sat down and took Cristen's hands. "Oh, Cris, don't you see? Growing up together the way you did, neither of you ever had a chance to find out if there was more to life and loving, if there was something richer, deeper."

A look of faint surprise flickered over Cristen's face. "That's basically what Ryan said."

Louise gave her hand an encouraging squeeze. "Then believe him, Cris. And give your love a chance. If you don't, you're going to lose him."

* * *

Over the next few days Cristen gave a lot of thought to what Louise had said, particularly her warning about losing Ryan. It was an unbearable thought. Even the sterile existence they had now was better than an endless future without Ryan. Yet Cristen knew that Louise was right. They couldn't go on in this miserable limbo, and they couldn't go back to being just lovers. She had to make a commitment to Ryan, had to entrust him with her heart and her future, for without him she had none.

She also thought a great deal about Bob. Had they really just drifted into marriage out of habit? Had he realized it finally and begun to feel trapped? Or had he known before their marriage and just lacked the fortitude to tell her? Knowing Bob, she was aware that it was entirely possible.

He was basically a weak man. She had always known that but had never wanted to admit it. To do so would have tarnished all those cherished memories she had held so dear. Which, Cristen realized, explained why she had never confronted him in the past two years. Cristen knew she could have contacted Bob at any time. She had simply to call his mother and get his phone number. Yet she, who always saw everything through to the bitter end, had chosen to put it out of her mind, to leave that episode in her life unresolved, rather than face the truth about Bob.

All along Cristen had known why he had walked out without a word. Bob had always manipulated and schemed and played on her sympathies to get his way, but he had never been able to oppose her openly.

No doubt he was much happier with Vicki. Cristen could see now that Bob needed a fragile little flower, someone who would make him feel strong, someone who would look up to him, lean on him, defer to his wishes and opinions in all things.

It was not the kind of relationship she could have endured herself, Cristen admitted, which, she supposed, just proved that she and Bob had been sorely mismatched.

The past few months had taught her that she did not want a man who would dominate her or constantly yield to her, but a man who was her equal. Cristen needed someone who was secure within himself, who would stand up to her when it mattered, yet who would applaud her strength and cherish her for it, a man who would cosset and comfort her when life had dealt her a blow, and stand back and cheer when she triumphed on her own.

Darn it! She needed Ryan!

Even knowing that her happiness lay with Ryan, Cristen was not quite able to put her old fears to rest. After mulling it over for several days, she began to feel that before she could get on with her life, she had to deal with the debris in her past, which meant she had to see Bob one last time and clear the air.

She had no trouble getting Bob's phone number from his mother, but before she could set up a meeting with him, disaster struck.

The phone call came around midnight on a Tuesday night, during a week when Ryan was in Houston. By the time Cristen finally stumbled from the bed and came to her senses, Ryan had already answered it. The minute she entered the living room and heard his terse tone, she knew something was terribly wrong.

"How bad is it?" he asked, as he waited for an answer Cristen stood behind him, nervously staring at the tense set of his shoulders. "I see. All right. Cristen and I will meet you there in ten minutes."

"What is it?" Cristen demanded the instant he replaced the receiver.

Ryan turned to her, his expression grim. "That was Louise. Cristen, there's been a fire in your shop."

Chapter Fourteen

Dora did *what*!"

"Now, Cris, don't get so upset. It was a simple mistake that anyone could have made," Lousie insisted. "Dora heated a pot of soup for dinner, then forgot to turn the hotplate off. After we closed at nine it simmered for hours until there was nothing left but the meat and vegetables, and they caught on fire."

"Louise. Dippy Dora's *simple* mistake may have just put us out of business."

With a sick feeling of despair, Cristen looked around the ruined shop. The smoke had set off the sprinkler system, which had doused the flames before the fire truck had arrived, but the water damage was extensive. Shelves were buckled, and the carpet and wallpaper were ruined, along with the dolls and dollhouses and all the painstakingly crafted wooden miniatures. Only the items in the cases and the ones made of metal or glass were undamaged.

"Surely you have insurance," Ryan said.

"Some. But not enough to cover this. We've been meaning to increase our coverage ever since we expanded, but we never got around to it. Anyway, even if we had the money to make the repairs, it would still take months of work to replace our stock. It's going to be like starting all over again."

"I'm sorry. That's rough."

Cristen wandered around, disconsolately inspecting the damage, until the firemen gathered up their equipment and left. Since there was nothing more they could do that night, they locked up the sodden shop and went home.

During the short ride, Ryan said nothing, and Cristen leaned her head back against the Jaguar's plush leather seat, too depressed to care.

When they entered the apartment Ryan turned to her, his expression serious and sympathetic. "Cristen, I'm sorry about tonight. I hope everything works out all right for you and Louise."

Cristen's lips twitched in a wan smile. This was the closest she had been to him in weeks, and it had taken a disaster to make it happen. His scent drifted to her, so wonderfully familiar that saliva gathered in her mouth. His short-sleeved sport shirt was buttoned only halfway, and the sight of his furry chest, his muscular forearms, the familiar way he hooked his thumbs in his belt loops, set off a quivering awareness in Cristen's stomach.

"Thank you, Ryan. And thanks for taking me to the shop."

"You don't have to thank me. I was glad to help." He smiled that bland smile and edged toward the door. "Well, I guess we'd better turn in and get what sleep we can. Good night, Cristen."

"Good night." She watched him go with a heavy heart, painfully aware that he had not offered to help further. Oh, Ryan. Ryan. I still love you so. How can you be so distant and cold?

The next morning Cristen and Louise met with the insurance adjuster, who merely verified what they already knew: their coverage was inadequate, which meant that to reopen, they were going to have to borrow more money.

Since there was no point in putting off the unpleasant task, Cristen left Louise and John to clean up what they could of the mess and went to meet with their banker.

Cristen entered Mr. Donaldson's office with a great deal of trepidation, knowing her chances of obtaining another loan, on top of the one they already had, were slim to none. This time she had practically no collateral and no willing cosigner.

To her utter astonishment, she had barely begun to explain their situation when Mr. Donaldson assured her that the matter of another loan had already been taken care of.

"Mr. O'Malley has agreed to cosign for whatever additional amount you need," Mr. Donaldson told her with a satisfied smile.

"He has?" Cristen was stunned and mystified, then doubtful. It occurred to her that Ryan could have made the offer months ago. She looked at the banker warily. "When, exactly, did Mr. O'Malley tell you this?"

"Why, this morning. The doors had barely opened when he came in to see me about the matter."

Joy poured through Cristen. All through the remainder of the meeting, while she and Mr. Donaldson discussed money and terms, she couldn't seem to stop grinning, and when she left she was practically walking on air.

Oh, Ryan, Ryan. You sweet, wonderful, absolutely adorable man. You do still care.

She should have known that Ryan would never abandon her. Even though she refused to marry him, he had stayed. He had kept his distance, true, but he had stayed. And when she had needed him, he was there for her. In her heart, she knew that he always would be.

Cristen was so happy that she could have jumped up and clacked her heels together, right there on the sidewalk. It no longer mattered why Bob had left her, or if he had loved her, or not loved her. She simply didn't care.

Who needed him? Not her. She had the man of her choice. She had Ryan.

Or at least I will have after tonight, she told herself. Still smiling, her green eyes glinting with determination, she strode jauntily toward the mall.

She was ready for him. The small table for two before the fireplace gleamed with her best china and silver. Candles were ready to be lit, soft music drifted from the stereo, the lamps were turned low. Wine was chilling. In the oven a roast was nearing perfection, and Ryan's favorite chocolate pie sat on the kitchen counter, waiting to be cut.

Cristen smoothed the linen tablecloth and needlessly adjusted the silver and stemware for the fifth time. Theda sat in a chair, watching her mistress's nervous fidgeting with feline curiosity, her head tipped to one side. Catching the cat's disdainful stare, Cristen grinned.

"Well, Theda, what do you think? Will it do?"

Theda answered with a bored meow.

"And does that go for me, as well?" Cristen asked, holding her arms out and turning in a slow circle so that her silk caftan flowed against her curves.

Not deigning to reply, Theda curled into a ball and ignored her.

Laughing, Cristen walked to the mirror that hung over the stereo to check for herself. Her makeup was still perfect, and her freshly shampooed hair billowed around her face and shoulders in a cloud of shiny curls. Leaning close, Cristen ran a smoothing fingertip over her eyebrows and rubbed her glistening lips together. She was giving her hair one final fluff when she heard Ryan's key in the lock.

Cristen spun around and fixed her eyes on the door, one hand pressed against her fluttering stomach, the other gripping the edge of the stereo cabinet behind her.

His gaze downcast, Ryan stepped inside. He carried his overcoat slung over one shoulder. The top two buttons of his shirt were undone, and his loosened tie hung limp and askew. There were lines of fatigue etched around his eyes and the corners of his mouth. A faint shadow along his jaw revealed the beginnings of a beard. He looked utterly weary... and heartbreakingly dear.

He locked the door, reset the alarm, and took a step into the living room.

"Hi."

Cristen's soft greeting brought Ryan to a halt, his head snapping up. His wary gaze swept over her, then scanned the dimly lit room, taking in the table set for two before the cozy fire. He looked back at her, his expression even more guarded. "Hi. I didn't expect you to be up."

"I've been waiting for you." She waved her hand toward the table. "I thought we could have dinner together and talk."

Ryan's mouth quirked. "Thanks, but I've already eaten. Anyway, I'm really too beat for conversation tonight."

"Oh, but I made your favorite meal," Cristen protested with just a trace of panic in her voice when he started for his bedroom. "I even made a chocolate pie."

"And it all smells heavenly, Cris, but I'll have to pass. All I want is a hot shower and about eight hours of shuteye." He paused just before turning into the hall and looked back at her. "Thanks for the offer, though. Good night."

Cristen stared after him, so frustrated that she could have screamed. She looked at the romantic fire, the perfectly laid table, the lovely tapered candles still waiting to be lit and did the next best thing: she hauled off and kicked the dainty tufted hassock her aunt had given her, sending it tumbling across the carpet.

Theda yowled and streaked away.

Mumbling under her breath and limping, Cristen stomped over the fire and jabbed it savagely with a poker. When she had it banked she replaced the screen, banging and rattling it against the hearth with no compunction whatsoever. "Sleep through that if you can," she muttered, casting an angry glance toward the bedrooms.

She marched into the kitchen and turned off the oven and the burners under the simmering pots. "And to think my mother always said that the way to a man's heart was through his stomach," Cristen snarled as she shoved the chocolate pie into the refrigerator and slammed the door. "She obviously never met a blockheaded, obstinate, ornery jackass like Ryan O'Malley. He'd starve to death before he'd unbend so much as an inch, that miserable, muley wretch!"

Cristen flung a dish towel down on the counter and stood in the middle of the kitchen tapping her foot, her hands planted on her hips. Her chin rose in determination. "Well, there's more than one way to skin a cat. If I can't tempt you with food, let's see how you like seduction.''

Fiery curls bouncing, Cristen stormed into her room and started pawing through her lingerie drawer. This time she wasn't leaving anything to chance.

Ten minutes later, her temper still simmering, she surveyed her image in the full-length mirror on her closet door, and a small, malicious smile tilted her lips.

Every wisp of intimate apparel that adorned her long, curvaceous body was an unrelenting black, and against it, her fair skin glowed with a soft pearlescence. A daring half bra cupped her breasts, its lacy upper edge barely covering her nipples. The silk bikini panties that hugged her hips had a panel of matching lace at center front. Around her waist she wore a minuscule satin garter belt with long, be-ribboned straps that held up impossibly sheer stockings. Over it all, she wore a floor-length chiffon and lace negligee that was about as substantial as mist.

"You'll do," she said with satisfaction. With her jaw set at a militant angle, she swept from the room in a swirl of black chiffon and intoxicating perfume.

Outside Ryan's door Cristen paused and took a deep breath, then arranged herself carefully. Placing a languid hand against the doorframe, she thrust one hip forward and tilted her head back at a provocative angle. She tapped lightly on the door, then quickly placed her hand on her jutting hip and arranged her features into a sultry, come-hither expression.

"Yes?" Ryan said, the word already forming as he opened the door, but when he saw Cristen his brows shot skyward.

She smiled and blinked slowly, giving him a sizzling look from beneath half-lowered lids. In a throaty voice guaranteed to raise the blood pressure of a saint, she said, "Hi, handsome. Wanna fool around?"

Ryan sucked in his breath as his gaze drifted over her, from her tousled curls to the strappy high heels on her feet. He had obviously just stepped from the shower, for he was naked except for the towel knotted around his hips. His dark curls were wet and falling over his forehead, and droplets of water still glistened in the hair on his chest.

He smelled of soap and shampoo and that wonderful scent that was his alone, and Cristen breathed it all in greedily. His nearness, his scent, the sight of his beautiful strong body made her nipples harden and sent a fiery sensation zinging to the core of her womanhood. It was all she could do not to fling herself against him.

When Ryan's gaze met hers once again he gave her a regretful smile and shook his head. "It's a tempting offer," he said gently. "But no, I don't think so."

Cristen's jaw dropped.

How dare he stand there and say no when she knew darned well he wanted her! He might have that mealy-mouthed bland expression on his face, but she'd seen the feverish look in his eyes. And in that skimpy towel there was no way he could hide his body's reaction. Cristen's temper shot ten notches higher.

"No? *No!*" She stepped forward and stuck out her chin. "What do you mean, no? Why, you jerk! You dimwitted Neanderthal! You sorry excuse for a sow's son! You... you... Oh!" Cristen began to pummel his chest with her fists, too furious to think of anything vile enough to call him.

"Hey! Hey! Watch it!" Ryan grabbed her wrists, but Cristen just struggled harder. She butted her head up under his chin, making his teeth clack. "Ow!" He gave her a shake and roared, "Dammit! Will you calm down!"

Cristen lashed out at him with her feet. For a moment he managed to evade her, but when she tried to hook her foot around his leg, he jerked her close and in one motion tumbled them both down onto the bed, rolling Cristen to her back and pinning her to the mattress with his body.

He held her arms over her head and glared at her, nose to nose. "Now, will you behave, you little wildcat?"

She glared right back. "No. Not until you're honest with me. I know you want me. Why are you doing this to us?"

All the anger left Ryan's face. He closed his eyes, and his body sagged as he expelled a long breath. "All right. Yes, I want you. I love you. I want more than anything to make love to you until neither of us can move. But, sweetheart, a night of passion just isn't enough. I'm not going to settle for an affair, Cristen. I told you, I want a hell of a lot more than that."

"So do I," she flared back, giving him an exasperated look.

Ryan's head snapped back, his eyes wide and incredulous. "What?"

"Just answer me one question, O'Malley," Cristen demanded belligerently. "Do you still want to marry me or not?"

"Of course I do. Are you saying that's what you want, too?"

"Yes, that's what I'm saying," she replied in a singsong, thoroughly disgusted voice. "And if you hadn't been such a horse's rump, you'd have heard me say it over a romantic, candlelit dinner."

Throwing his head back, Ryan gave a burst of happy, exultant laughter, a rich, full-bodied, masculine sound that rumbled up from deep inside him. Cristen felt it vibrate against her belly and breasts, and the sensation raised goose bumps of awareness all over her.

As his laughter faded, Ryan released Cristen's hands and his fingers found the warm hollows behind her ears. "Oh, Cris, Cris. I do love you so," he murmured, and the look of adoration on his face as he gazed down at her pierced Cristen's heart with a sweet, sweet pain. Her anger dissolved like smoke, and her body grew soft and pliant beneath his.

"I love you, too."

A smile of wonder curved her mouth, and Cristen reached up and touched his cheeks, then ran her fingertips over his sable mustache. Their eyes delved, blue into green, soft with love, seeking solace for the misery they had endured, promising a future filled with joy immeasurable. Sighing, Cristen looped her arms around his neck and winnowed her fingers through the damp hair on his nape.

"Then you meant it when you said you'd marry me?" Ryan asked, and Cristen was touched by the lingering note of uncertainty in his voice.

"Yes, I'll marry you," she said in a voice that quavered with emotion. "Whenever you say."

"Good. How about next week?"

Cristen laughed shakily and blinked hard at the tears of happiness that were gathering in her eyes. "Oh, my darling, I would love to marry you next week, but don't you think that's rushing it just a bit? I mean, there are so many things we have to consider. So many decisions we have to work out."

"Such as?"

"Well, for one, where would we live? Most of your business is in California, and mine is here."

"That's no problem. I'll relocate the main offices here."

Cristen was so touched by his generosity that she just stared at him, feeling the hot rush of tears overflow and streak down her face, wetting the hair at her temples. "Really? You'd do that?"

"Sure."

"But... but what about your life in California? Your friends? Your family?"

"I'll make new friends. And the only family I have is Jennifer."

"Jennifer! Oh, dear. I didn't think about her. What if she doesn't approve? What if—"

Ryan placed three fingers over her mouth, halting the frantic flow of words. "Cristen, will you stop? I guarantee that Jennifer will be overjoyed."

"Are you sure?"

"Yes, I'm sure. But if you want, we'll call her later and you can find out for yourself." He gazed down at her with fond exasperation and shook his head. "Now is there anything else you're worried about?"

The look of love and tenderness brimming in Ryan's blue eyes made Cristen go weak and warm all over. She touched the hair at his temples, then ran her fingertips over the rim of his ear, her gaze a soft, liquid green. "No," she whispered, giving him a melting smile. "Not a single thing."

"Good."

Ryan's head dipped, and their mouths met, tenderly at first, then open and hungry, as each sought to make up for the barren loneliness of the past weeks. Wet tongues dueled in a rough caress, twisting and twining, speaking of need that had grown to near desperation since last they loved. The kiss went on and on, their lips rocking together in greedy passion, as hearts thudded and their blood rushed hotly through their veins. Ryan nipped Cristen's lower lip, then drew it into his mouth and sucked gently. She made a low, throaty sound and stroked the back of his neck, telling him without words of the depth of her feelings.

In their tumble to the bed, her negligee had fallen open and now lay spread out on either side of them like gossamer wings. Ryan ran his hands down her sides, outlining the enticing curves of breasts, waist and hips, boldly fingering each tiny scrap of cloth that covered them. "Now, about this outfit you're wearing," he murmured against her lips.

"You don't like it?"

"Mmm, on the contrary." He shifted to his side and ran a fingertip along the top edge of the tiny bra, smiling with wicked delight as her nipples peaked against the flimsy lace. "I think it has great possibilities."

With maddening leisure, he continued his delicate exploration, running his fingers over the satin garter belt, testing its smooth texture, tracing the lace pattern on the minuscule panties, playfully snapping the beribboned garter straps and running his finger beneath the tops of her stockings.

Cristen lay still, quivering with anticipation, watching the sensual fire flame in his eyes as his gaze followed the path of his roaming hands. He pressed his face against the strip of white flesh between her panties and garter belt and inhaled deeply. While his lips nibbled and caressed the silky skin, his hand slid downward and released the fasteners at the tops of her stockings. A hand beneath her knees lifted her legs, and the ones in back were dealt with.

His hand stroked up the inside of her thigh, and Cristen moaned and closed her eyes, her fingers digging into the broad muscles of Ryan's back. He raised his head and smiled, watching her eyelids tremble with pleasure as he pressed the heel of his hand against her throbbing womanhood.

"Have I ever told you how much I like your sexy undies?" His hand moved upward and deftly released the three hooks at the side of the garter belt. Obeying his silent urging, Cristen lifted her hips, and he pulled it free. "And the nicest thing is, they're so easy to take off," he added as he tossed the strip of black satin over his shoulder.

"I . . . I'm glad you like them."

"Oh, I do. I do." Leaning down, he touched his tongue to her lace-covered nipple, then placed his open mouth over it. The feel of his warm breath filtering through the fragile lace was incredibly erotic, and Cristen moaned, shivering as her breasts burgeoned and throbbed. With his mouth and tongue, Ryan nuzzled aside the flimsy bra. He took the yearning bud into his mouth and drew on her sweetly, and as Cristen arched upward he released the clasp at the front of her bra.

"Oh, Ryan, love me. Love me," she urged in a husky whisper. "It's been so long."

"I will, darling. Soon," he murmured.

Cristen thought she would surely die as Ryan took his time reacquainting himself with every inch of her body, his big hands smoothing over her, his mouth and tongue and teeth driving her wild. But finally bra and panties were discarded, and with slow, sensual movements he peeled down her stockings and tossed them aside.

His towel had long ago fallen away, and when he drew her back into his arms and their fevered flesh melded together they both sighed with pleasure. For a heady, torturous moment they simply held each other, savoring the warmth, the closeness, the triumph of their love, letting the sweet anticipation build. They were pressed together from shoulder to knee, male to female, soft feminine flesh to sinewed strength, pale silk to dark bronze.

But after a moment touching was not enough. Cristen's hands roamed Ryan's back restlessly, finally sliding down to clutch his buttocks. Ryan slipped his hand between their bodies, his fingers threading through the feminine nest of curls and probing intimately.

"I need you so, my love," he rasped as he caressed her.

"Oh, yes, darling. Yes!"

After weeks of heartache and loneliness their desire for each other had become an urgent need that demanded fulfillment. Ryan rolled her to her back and rose above her. He gazed lovingly into her shining eyes and whispered, "My love, my life," as he made them one.

A sigh. A kiss. A moment of quivering anticipation. Eyes closed in ecstasy. Breathing quickened.

And then the movement began.

Together they soared. Each seeking and giving pleasure, sharing that special rapture that only true love brings. The sweet tension stretched tighter and tighter. Ryan's face was flushed and contorted with fierce gladness as he watched Cristen's eyes go smoky with pleasure.

Cristen threw her head back on the pillow and clutched Ryan's back. And then his name ripped from her throat as again they shared that shattering explosion of joy that rocked them to the depths of their being.

As thundering hearts calmed, as breathing returned to normal, they drifted back to reality with a sigh of satisfaction. Ryan pressed a soft kiss on her mouth, then shifted his weight and rolled to his back, tucking her firmly against his side. With her cheek nestled against his chest, his hand sifting absently through her hair, in blissful lassitude they lay in each other's arms.

"Ryan?" Cristen said a long while later.

"Hmm?"

"Thank you for helping with the loan."

"So you found out about that, did you? Donaldson wasn't supposed to tell you."

"Why not?"

"I wanted you to accept me, but not because you felt obligated. Or out of gratitude."

Cristen wrapped a curl of his chest hair around her finger and gave it a sharp tug. "Foolish man. I love you, you dope."

"Ow! Watch it, woman."

Cristen laughed and snuggled closer, hooking her legs over his thighs. "Ryan?"

"Hmm?"

"I've been so miserable these past weeks. After I refused to marry you I was terrified that you were going to move out, but I wouldn't have blamed you if you had. Why... why did you stay?"

"I was waiting for you to come to your senses," he answered with sleepy unconcern.

"What!" Cristen jerked up and braced herself on one palm, glaring down at him.

Ryan opened his eyes and grinned. "Worked, didn't it?"

This time she grabbed a handful of hair. "You wretch!"

Laughing, Ryan pried her hand loose before she could do serious injury. "I figured if I put some distance between us—not much, but some—you'd see just how rotten life would be if we parted."

"I see," she said haughtily. "And just how long did you intend to keep it up?"

"As long as it took. I told you, I'm a very patient man."

Cristen tried to keep her face stern, but her heart was warmed by the knowledge that Ryan would not have given up on her—ever. His steadfastness was yet another facet to this tough, tender, funny, complex man, and it made her love him just that much more.

Still, she wasn't going to let him off that easily. Affecting an indignant pout, she said, "I'm not so sure I want to marry such a devious, scheming man."

"Sure you do."

Ryan startled her by bounding up off the bed. "Come on, let's go." He grabbed her hand to pull her with him, but Cristen held back.

"Go where?" she questioned warily. "Ryan! Stop!" she squealed a second later as she was jerked from the bed and slung over his shoulder.

With her anchored firmly in place by a strong arm across the backs of her knees, he stalked out the door. Cristen bounced with every jarring step, her mane of Gypsy curls dangling down and swaying against his bare posterior.

"Put me down, O'Malley!"

"No way." Chuckling, he marched determinedly down the hall.

"Beast!" she squawked.

"Quiet, woman." He nipped her enticing bare backside, then brushed it with his sable mustache. "Can't you tell when your man is starving?"

"Well, why didn't you just say so? There's a scrumptious meal waiting in the kitchen. If you'll just put me down, I'll—"

Cristen screamed as Ryan tipped her off his shoulder and she fell through space. A second later her back hit something soft, and she bounced once before Ryan pinned her down with his body. She blinked and looked around, bewildered. "This isn't the kitchen."

"No, it's our bedroom, and we're back in our bed where we belong."

"I thought you said you were hungry."

He smiled, his eyes glinting with wicked intent as he moved his hips against hers. "Oh, I am, I am. But not for food."

Cristen's lips twitched. "Ryan, you're awf—" she began, but her halfhearted scolding was cut off by Ryan's warm lips, and a moment later she discovered that her appetite equaled his.

COMING NEXT MONTH

VOYAGE OF THE NIGHTINGALE—Billie Green
Braving exotic poisons and native sacrifices, cultured Bostonian
Rachel McNaught scoured the tropics for her missing brother. But
what she found was ruffian sailor Flynn, who scorned her money...and
stole her heart.

SHADOW OF DOUBT—Caitlin Cross
Who *was* widow Julia Velasco? A decadent gold digger who'd kidnapped
her own son for profit? Or a desperate mother in need of protection?
Mesmerized by her, attorney Anson Wolfe sought the elusive truth.

THE STAR SEEKER—Maggi Charles
"Your lover will be tall, dark and handsome," the palm-reader told
her. But shopkeeper Hilary Forsythe was avoiding men—particularly
banker J.A. Mahoney, who handled her business loan...and mismanaged
her emotions!

IN THE NAME OF LOVE—Paula Hamilton
Madcap Samantha Graham was determined to join the CIA. Agent
Jim Collins was bedazzled but skeptical. To "protect" her from her
impulsive self, would he ruin her chances—in the name of love?

COME PRIDE, COME PASSION—Jennifer West
When Cade Delaney returned to Dixie, he had bitter revenge on his
mind. The object: proud Elizabeth Hart. The obstacle: his burning
passion for her.

A TIME TO KEEP—Curtiss Ann Matlock
Jason Kenyon was old enough to be Lauren Howard's father, but that
didn't stop them from falling in love. Could their precious time together
last...or would the odds against them tear them apart?

AVAILABLE THIS MONTH:

ATTRACTIVE, SPACE SAVING BOOK RACK

Display your most prized novels on this handsome and sturdy book rack. The hand-rubbed walnut finish will blend into your library decor with quiet elegance, providing a practical organizer for your favorite hard-or soft-covered books.

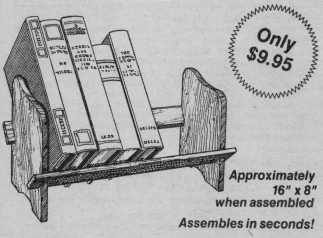

Only $9.95

Approximately 16" x 8"
when assembled

Assembles in seconds!

To order, rush your name, address and zip code, along with a check or money order for $10.70* ($9.95 plus 75¢ postage and handling) payable to *Silhouette Books*.

Silhouette Books
Book Rack Offer
901 Fuhrmann Blvd.
P.O. Box 1325
Buffalo, NY 14269-1325

Offer not available in Canada.

*New York residents add appropriate sales tax.

BKR-2R

FOUR UNIQUE SERIES
FOR EVERY WOMAN YOU ARE...

Silhouette Romance

Heartwarming romances that will make you
laugh and cry as they bring you all the wonder
and magic of falling in love.

6 titles per month

Silhouette Special Edition

Expanded romances written with emotion and
heightened romantic tension to ensure
powerful stories. A rare blend of passion and
dramatic realism.

6 titles per month

Silhouette Desire

Believable, sensuous, compelling—and
above all, romantic—these stories deliver
the promise of love, the guarantee
of satisfaction.

6 titles per month

Silhouette Intimate Moments

Love stories that entice; longer, more
sensuous romances filled with adventure,
suspense, glamour and melodrama.

4 titles per month

Silhouette Romances
not available in retail outlets in Canada

SIL-GEN-1A